OUT OF THE FRYING PAN . . .

They were skimming along just above cloud level. Mandel and Amaranth were almost straight ahead, giant, blinding orbs in a near-black sky.

The perspiration ran in rivulets down Darya's face and soaked her clothing. In its rapid descent, the car was thrown around the sky like a cork in a sea storm. And in less than a minute they plunged through the bottom of the cloud layers.

Everyone craned forward. Was there a solid surface down there? Or had they escaped Mandel and Amaranth's searing beams only to die in Quake's pools of molten lava?

By Charles Sheffield
Published by Ballantine Books:

The Heritage Universe:
    Book One: SUMMERTIDE
    Book Two: DIVERGENCE

PROTEUS UNBOUND
SIGHT OF PROTEUS
TRADER'S WORLD
THE WEB BETWEEN THE WORLDS

SUMMERTIDE

Book One of
The Heritage Universe

Charles Sheffield

A Del Rey Book
BALLANTINE BOOKS • NEW YORK

For Ann, Kit, Rose, and Toria, and everyone else whose (average) age is sixteen.

Expansion
1086 (3170 A.D.).

A NINETY-SEVEN-YEAR SILENCE was ending.

For close to a century the ship's interior had heard no human voice and felt no human footstep. The vessel whispered its way between the stars, passengers close to absolute zero in dreamless paradeath. Once a year their bodies warmed to liquid-nitrogen temperatures while shared experiences were fed to them from the ship's central data bank: memories of a hundred years of interstellar travel, for bodies that would age less than one day.

As the final weeks of deceleration began it was time to start the awakening. When the destination was reached, decisions might be needed that went beyond machine judgment—a notion that to the ship's main computer, the first of its kind to be equipped with the Karlan emotional circuits, was both insulting and implausible.

First warming was initiated. Interior sensors picked up the reassuring flutter of returning heartbeats, the initial sigh and murmur of working lungs. The emergency crew would be awakened first, two by two, on a last-in, first-out basis; only with their approval would others begin emergence.

The first pair drifted up to consciousness with one question burning in their minds: Was it arrival—or was it override?

The computer had been programmed to rouse them for only three reasons. They would be disturbed if the ship were closing at last on their destination, Lacoste-32B, a minor G-2 dwarf star that lay three light-years beyond the rose-red stellar beacon of Aldebaran. They would wake if an onboard problem had arisen within the ship's half-kilometer ellipsoid, a disaster too big for the computer to handle without human interaction.

Or, the final possibility, they would be pulled from hibernation if one of spacefaring humanity's oldest dreams had become reality:

I/T—Immediate Transfer; Interstellar Transition; Instantaneous Travel; the superluminal transportation system that would end Crawlspace exploration.

For more than a thousand years the exploration and colony ships had crept outward, widening the sphere of Earth's influence. The millennium had yielded forty colonies, scattered through a Sol-centered globe seventy light-years in diameter. But every inch within that sphere had been traveled at less than a fifth of light-speed. And every colony, no matter how small and isolated, had a research program that sought the superluminal . . .

The first two wakened were one man and one woman. They fought a century-long lassitude, queried the ship's internal status panels, and shared their relief. No on-board disaster had occurred. The message center held no urgent incoming file, no news of a great breakthrough. There would be no party of superluminal travelers waiting to welcome late-arrival colonists at Lacoste.

Ahead of the ship the target star already showed a visible naked-eye disk. Gravitational perturbations of the star had long predicted the presence of at least two orbiting giant planets. Now their existence could be confirmed by direct observation, together with five smaller bodies closer to the primary.

The woman was recovering faster than the man. It was she who first left the Schindler hibernation unit, stood up shakily in the one-tenth-gee field, and moved to stare at the external displays. She uttered a low sound, a grunt of satisfaction from sluggish vocal cords, followed by an experimental clearing of her throat.

"We made it! There it is."

And there it was. The molten-gold disk of Lacoste lay at the exact center of the forward screen. Two minutes later the man had eased his way to her side, still wiping protective gel from his face. He touched her arm in congratulations, relief, and love. They were life-partners.

"Time to waken the others."

"In a few minutes," she said. "Remember Kapteyn. Make sure we've got something."

The example of Kapteyn's Star was written in every explorer's memory: eight planets, all apparently with wonderful potential; and all, on close inspection, useless for human habitation or for supplies. The early colony ship that had arrived at Kapteyn had been too depleted to reach any second target.

"We're only two light-days out," she went on. "We can start scanning. Let's take a look for oxygen atmospheres before we wake anyone else."

The on-board computer picked up her command and responded to it. *One oxygen world,* said its soft voice. *Life probability 0.92.* The field of view zoomed and swung so that Lacoste first grew rapidly in size and then disappeared from the top of the screen, while a new pinpoint of light appeared at the screen center and swelled to fill it.

Fourth planet, the computer said. *Overall figure of merit for Earth isomorphism, 0.86. Mean distance, 1.22; mean temperature range, 0.89 to 1.04; axial tilt—*

"What the devil is *that?*"

The computer paused. The man's question had no meaning.

The screen held a planet at its center, a blue-gray sphere

already seen in enough detail to reveal the broad bands and swirls of atmospheric circulation patterns. But it also showed a web of hazy lines and bright spirals surrounding the planet and cradling it in multiple strands of light.

"Somebody got here ahead of us . . ." The woman's voice faded before the sentence was completed. The information network among inhabited planets was in continuous operation. It was limited to light-speed, but even so she could not believe that some exploring ship had also been sent to Lacoste, unknown to them. And if another ship *had* arrived here, the scale of what they were seeing went beyond anything that an exploring colony might accomplish in a few years.

Or in a few centuries.

"Pan view."

The computer heard her words and adjusted the image. The planet shrank to pea size, a bright bead of light at the middle of the screen. The surrounding nimbus of intensive in-space construction was revealed, a gleaming nacreous setting within which the planet nestled like a pearl in an oyster. Slender tendrils of construction stretched out endlessly, thinner and thinner, until they fell below the resolution of the observing sensors.

"Not our kind, Tamara," the man said softly. "That's not us."

No human works, not even the ring cities that surrounded Earth itself, came close in size and complexity. Some of the spiraling filaments around the planet had to be over four hundred thousand kilometers long and many kilometers across. They should have been unstable to gravitational forces from the planet, to tidal perturbations, and to their own interactions. And yet clearly they were not.

"Time to wake the others," Tamara said.

"And then?"

"And then . . ." She sighed. "And then, I don't know what. We finally did it, Damon. We found another intelligent species. A technologically advanced one, too. But if they could build *that*"—she gestured at the dazzling structure on the screen, and her voice became husky—"why didn't *they* find *us*? Well, I guess we'll know the answer to that in a few more days."

Three weeks later the ship's pinnaces were roving the veins and arteries of the space artifact. For fifteen days the main vessel had hovered five million kilometers away, waiting for and expecting contact from the planet in response to radio and laser signals. They had been met with total silence. Finally they had approached and begun direct exploration.

The misty filaments on the screen resolved themselves to the interlocking network of a colossal artifact. They stretched down to the surface of the planet, an uninhabited world apparently well suited to human colonization; but the tendrils also reached far out into space, for purposes that could not even be guessed at.

And those purposes could not be found out from their creators. Like the planet, the artifact was uninhabited.

Tamara and Damon Savalle found themselves cruising in their pinnace along one of the filaments, a metal-and-polymer tube three kilometers wide and fifty thousand long. Maintenance machines crept along the inner surface, moving so slowly that their motion was hardly perceptible. The machines ignored the little pinnace completely.

Tamara was at the communications panel, in contact with the main ship. "They confirm our analyses of meteorite pitting," she said. "At least ten million years old, uninhabited for more than three. And I don't see anything to grin at."

"Sorry." Damon did not look it. "I was thinking of the old paradox from before Expansion. If there are aliens, *where are they*? Twenty days ago we thought we had the answer: no aliens. Now we're asking it all over again. Where are they, Tammy? Who built all this stuff? And where are the builders?"

She shrugged. Damon's question would remain unanswered for more than three thousand years.

But while they stared and marveled, a weak incoming signal was reaching the main ship from a small and struggling colony on Eta Cassiopeiae A. It told of an intriguing new physical theory involving Bose-Einstein statistics, along with a suggestion for a subtle and complex deep-space experiment far beyond the limited resources of the little colony.

With everyone at Lacoste focused on the Builders, the new message received no attention at all.

But the Builders were long gone; and superluminal travel was on the way.

ARTIFACT: COCOON.
UAC#: 1
Galactic Coordinates:
26,223.489/14,599.029/+112.58
Name: Cocoon
Star/planet association: Lacoste/Savalle
Bose Access Node: 99
Estimated age: 10.464 $\pm$ 0.41 Megayears

Exploration History: Cocoon holds a special place in human history, as the first artifact to be discovered by human explorers, just as Cusp (see Entry 300) was the first to be discovered by the Cecropian clade. Cocoon was found in E. 1086 by a Crawlspace colony ship seeking habitable planets in the Lacoste system.

Physical Description: The form of Cocoon is a three-dimensional development of the familiar ring cities in place around many inhabited worlds. However, it goes far beyond the standard equatorial-plane assemblies, in both extent and presumed function. This artifact employs forty-eight Basal Stalks connecting Cocoon to the equatorial planetary surface and reaching up to the continuous ring structure at stationary altitude. Four hundred and thirty-two thousand exterior filaments stretch five hundred thousand kilometers from the planet. No two filaments are identical, but typical dimensions of the hollow cylindrical tubes are from two to four kilometers, exterior radius. Viewed from many locations, the surface of Savalle is completely obscured by Cocoon.

The corridors of Cocoon's interior are extensively patrolled by Phages (see Entry 1067). Explorers must monitor continuously for their presence.

Physical Nature: Construction of Cocoon employs the standard superstrength polymers used in most Builder artifacts. The absence of a second natural satellite for Savalle, even though the fossil record clearly shows that double-satellite tides occurred until twelve million years ago, suggests a now-vanished moon as the main source of Cocoon's construction materials.

Cocoon's filaments are held in stable position by a balance of gravity, rotating reference frames, and stellar radiation pressure. No unfamiliar science is needed to explain that stability, although the system design calls for the solution of large, discrete optimization problems beyond the best computers available within the Clades. Elephant (see Entry 859) was applied to the problem and reached a constrained solution (the so-called Cocoon Restricted Problem) in four standard years of computation time.

Intended Purpose: There are few secrets to Cocoon, if we except the *need* for such a massive system. The Basal Stalks permit materials to pass to and from the planetary surface of Savalle at negligible cost; the Exterior Filaments allow economical payload transfer to any point of the Lacoste stellar system, using the momentum-bank principle. The capacity of Cocoon is enormous: one fifty-thousandth of the mass of Savalle could in principle be transferred to space each year, enough to slow the planetary rotation rate appreciably and change Savalle's day by two seconds.

—From the *Lang Universal Artifact Catalog,*
Fourth Edition.

CHAPTER 1

Expansion
4135 (6219 A.D.).

WHERE AM I?

A man who had seen fifty planets and succeeded in a hundred difficult jobs ought to be like a cat, turning instinctively to land on his feet in any situation. But recently he seemed to be just the opposite, more disoriented with every new task.

Hans Rebka came fully awake and lay with eyes closed, waiting for memory of place and function to seep into his brain. As that came, confusion was replaced by anger.

A week earlier he had been in orbit around Paradox, preparing for one of the most challenging assignments of his life. He and three companions were to enter the Paradox sphere, carrying with them new shielding and a completely new type of recording sensor. If they succeeded they would bring back for the first time information from the Paradox interior—perhaps new information about the Builders themselves.

To Rebka, Paradox was the most enigmatic and intriguing of all Builder structures. The dark, spherical bubble, fifty kilometers across, permitted ready entry but on exit removed all memories, organic or inorganic. Computers emerged with no recording on any storage medium. Humans who had reached the interior returned with the minds of newborn infants.

Exploration efforts had finally been abandoned; but lately visitors to the region of Paradox had been reporting changes. The bubble was different in external appearance, and possibly in internal status. A new effort might succeed.

It was a dangerous mission, but Hans Rebka had been looking forward to it. He had volunteered, and he had been accepted as team leader.

And then the call had come, just one day before the descent into Paradox.

"An alternative assignment . . ." The voice was thin and whispering, reduced in frequency spectrum by its passage through the Bose communications network. ". . . to the double-planet system of Dobelle. You must leave without delay . . ."

The space-thinned voice sounded in no way imperious, but the command emanated from the highest government level of the Phemus Circle. And it was an assignment for Rebka alone; his companions would proceed to explore Paradox. At first it sounded like an honor, a privilege that he should be singled out in that way. But as the assignment was explained to him, Rebka's confusion began.

He knew his talents. He was a doer and a fixer, and a damned good one. He could think on his feet and improvise solutions in real-time to tough problems; he was a typical product of his home world, Teufel.

"What sins must a man commit, in how many past lives, to be born on Teufel?" Half the spiral arm knew that saying. Like all the planets of the Phemus Circle, Teufel was resource-poor and metal-poor. Settled in despair and dire necessity as the life-support systems of an early colony ship faltered and failed, it was also an outcast planet, too hot, too small, and with a barely breathable atmosphere. The life expectancy of a human who grew to maturity on Teufel—most did not—was less than half the average for the Phemus Circle, and less than a third of that for an inhabitant of any

world of the Fourth Alliance. All those born and raised on Teufel found an instinct for self-preservation before they could talk—or they never lasted long enough to talk.

Rebka was a slight, large-headed man with hands and feet too big for his body. He had the wan, slightly deformed look of someone who had suffered persistent childhood malnutrition and trace-element deficiency. But that early privation had affected his brains not at all. He had learned the odds early, when at eight years old he had seen a set of images from the wealthy worlds of the Alliance bordering the Phemus Circle. Strong anger was born within him. He learned to use it, to channel and control it to fuel his progress, at the same time that he learned to hide his feelings with a smile. By the time he was twelve years old he had worked his way off Teufel and was in a Phemus Circle government training program.

Rebka was proud of his record. Starting with less than nothing, he had risen steadily for twenty-five years. He had run massive terraforming projects, taking the harshest and most inhospitable planetary bodies and converting them to human paradises (someday he would do as much for Teufel); he had led dangerous expeditions to the heart of the mirror-matter comet region, far from any chance of help if things went wrong; he had flown so close to stellar surfaces that communications were impossible in the roar of ambient radiation, and his returning ship was ablated and melted past hope of further use. And he had led a crew on a near-legendary trip through the *Zirkelloch,* the toroidal space-time singularity that lay in the disputed no-man's-land between the worlds of the Fourth Alliance and those of the Cecropia Federation.

All that. And suddenly—at the thought, confusion was replaced by anger; anger was still his friend—he was demoted. Stripped, without a word of explanation, of all real responsibilities and sent to a distant, unimportant world to act as nursemaid or father-confessor for someone ten years his junior.

"Just who *is* Max Perry? Why is he important?"

He had asked that question during his first briefing, as soon as the planetary doublet of Dobelle became more than a name to him. For Dobelle was an insignificant place. Its twin planetary components, Opal and Quake, orbiting a second-class star far from the main centers of the local spiral arm, were almost as poor as Teufel.

Scaldworld, Desolation, Teufel, Styx, Cauldron—sometimes it seemed to Rebka that poverty was their only bond, the single link that held the Phemus Circle worlds together and separated them from their richer neighbors. And from the records, Dobelle was a worthy member of the club.

The records on Perry were transmitted to him, too, to be scanned at his leisure. Typically, Hans Rebka reviewed them at once. They made little sense. Max Perry had come from origins as humble as Rebka's own. He was a refugee from Scaldworld, and like Rebka he had made his way rapidly upward, apparently bound for a job at the very top of Circle government. As part of the general grooming process for future leaders, he had been sent for a one-year tour of duty on Dobelle.

Seven years later he had still not returned. When promotions were offered, he refused them. When pressures were exerted to encourage him to leave the Dobelle system, he ignored them.

"A large investment," whispered the distant voice beyond the stars. "We have trained him for many years. We want to see that investment in him repaid . . . as you repaid it. Determine the cause of his difficulties. Persuade him to return, or at least to tell us why he refuses to do so. He ignores a direct order. Opal and Quake desperately need people, and Dobelle law prohibits extradition."

"He won't tell me anything. Why should he?"

"You will go to Dobelle as his supervisor. We have arranged for a senior position to be created within the ruling oligarchy. You will occupy it. We agree that Perry will not reveal his motives as the result of a simple inquiry. That has been tried. Use your own strengths. Use your subtlety. Use your initiative." The voice paused. "Use your anger."

"I am not angry with Perry." Rebka asked more questions, but the answers offered no enlightenment. The assignment still made no sense. The central committee of the Phemus Circle could waste its resources if it so chose, but it was a stupid mistake to waste Rebka's talents—he lacked false modesty—where a psychiatrist seemed more likely to succeed. Or had that already been tried, and failed?

Hans Rebka swung his legs off the bunk and walked over to the window. He stared up. After a three-day trip through five Bose Network nodes and a subluminal final stage, he had finally landed on the Starside hemisphere of Opal. But Starside was a bad joke—even before dawn there was not a star to be seen. At that time of year, close to Summertide, cloud breaks on Opal were rare. Approaching the planet, he had seen nothing but a uniform, shining globe. The whole world was water, and when Dobelle swung in at its closest to its stellar primary, Mandel, the summer tides reached their peak and the oceans of Opal never saw the sun. Safety lay only on the Slings, natural floating rafts of earth and tangled vegetation that moved across Opal's surface at the prompting of winds and tides.

The biggest Slings were hundreds of kilometers across. The Starside spaceport was situated on one of the largest. Even so, Rebka wondered how it would fare at Summertide. Where would it go, and would it survive when the main tides came?

If his birthworld of Teufel had been Fire, then Opal was surely Water.

And Quake, the other half of the Dobelle planetary doublet?

Hell, from what he had heard of it. Nothing that Rebka had read or been told in his briefings had had one good word to say about Quake. Events on Opal at Summertide were said to be spectacular and hair-raising—but survivable. On Quake they were deadly.

He looked up at the sky again and was startled to see that it was light. Opal and Quake were tidally locked to each other, and they spun around their common center of mass at a furious rate. One day in the Dobelle system was only eight standard hours. His morning musings had taken him well past dawn. He would just have time for a quick breakfast; then an aircar would carry him around the planet to Quakeside—and to the most stupid and least productive job of his life.

Rebka swore, cursing the name of Max Perry, and walked across to the door. He had not yet met the man, but he was ready to dislike him.

ARTIFACT: PARADOX.

UAC#: 35

Galactic Coordinates: 27,312.443 / 15,917.902 / +135.66

Name: Paradox

Star/planet association: Darien/Kleindienst

Bose Access Node: 139

Estimated age: 9.112 $\pm$ 0.11 Megayears

Exploration History: It is not known how many times Paradox was discovered, and all knowledge of it then lost. What is known is that in E. 1379 Ruttledge, Kaminski, Parzen, and Lu-lan organized a two-ship expedition to investigate the light-refraction anomaly now known as Paradox.

Arriving first, Ruttledge and Kaminski recorded on their ship's main computer the intention of entering the Paradox sphere using the exploration pinnace, while the main ship remained well clear. Five days later, Parzen and Lu-lan arrived and found the other ship and its pinnace, both in perfect working condition. Ruttledge and Kaminski were in the pinnace, alive but suffering from dehydration and malnutrition. They were incapable of speech or simple motor movement, and subsequent tests showed that their memories held no more information than the mind of a newborn baby. The data banks and computer memory on the pinnace were wiped clean.

Following a review of the other ship's records, Parzen and Lu-lan drew lots to decide who would make a second trip inside the Paradox sphere. Lu-lan won and made the descent. No signals were received from him by Parzen, although there had been prior agreement to send a message every four hours. Lu-lan returned, physically unharmed, after three days. His memory was empty of all learned information, though somatic (instinctive) knowledge was unchanged.

Paradox was declared off-limits to all but specially trained investigators in E. 1557.

Physical Description: Paradox is a spherical region, fifty kilometers in diameter. Its outer boundary displays "soap bubble" color shifts across the surface, reflecting or transmitting different wavelength radiation apparently randomly.

The sphere is opaque in certain spectral regions (1.2–223 meters) and perfectly transparent in others (5.6–366 micrometers). Nothing is known of the appearance of Paradox's interior.

Paradox's size and appearance are not invariant. Changes in size and color have been reported nine times during its history.

Physical Nature: Based on transmissions through it, Paradox is believed to have a complex interior structure. However, no firsthand information has ever been obtained, because of Paradox's information-destroying nature. Most analysts believe that Paradox is the four-dimensional extrusion in space and time of a body of much higher dimension, perhaps the twenty/three/seven knotted manifold of Ikro and H'miran.

Intended Purpose: Unknown. However, Scorpesi has conjectured that Paradox is a "cleansing vat" for large Builder intelligent artifacts, such as Elephant (see Entry 859), prior to reuse. Note, however, that this suggestion is inconsistent with the physical dimensions (4,000 x 900 kilometers) of Elephant itself, unless such objects were subjected to multiple passes through the Paradox sphere.

> —From the *Lang Universal Artifact Catalog,*
> Fourth Edition.

CHAPTER 2

Summertide
minus thirty-six.

THE SECOND SHIFT of the working day was just beginning, and already it was clear to Birdie Kelly that it was going to be a bad one. The new supervisor might still be half a world away on Starside, but already the boss was brooding over the man's impending arrival.

"How can someone who has never even *visited* this system be competent to control travel between Opal and Quake?" Max Perry stared at Birdie with pale, unhappy eyes. Birdie looked back, saw the starved jut of Perry's jaw, and thought how much good it would do if the other man could just eat a square meal and relax for a day or two.

"Quake traffic is *our* job," Perry went on. "We've been doing it for six years. How much does this Rebka, a total stranger, know about that? Not a thing. Do they think at Circle headquarters that there's nothing to it, and any idiot can understand Quake? *We* know the importance of forbidding access to Quake. Especially now, with Summertide almost here. But do they know it?"

Birdie listened to Max Perry's stream of complaints and nodded sympathetically. One thing was sure: Perry was a good man and a conscientious boss, but he had his obsessions. And Captain Hans Rebka, whoever he might be, was sure going to make Birdie's own life more difficult.

Birdie sighed and leaned back in his wicker chair. Perry's office stood on the top floor of Opal's highest Quakeside building, a four-story experimental structure that had been built to Perry's own specifications. Birdie Kelly still felt uncomfortable inside it. The foundation extended down through layers of mud and a tangle of dead and living roots, right on past the lower basement of the Sling to the brackish waters of Opal's ocean. It was buoyed by a hollow chamber just below the surface, and the hydrostatic lift from there carried most of the load.

Even such a low building did not feel safe to Birdie. The Slings were delicate; without firm foundations, most buildings on Opal were held to one or two stories. For the past six months this Sling had been tethered in one spot, but as Summertide approached that would be too dangerous. Perry had ordered that in eight more days the Sling should be released to move at the mercy of the tides—but was that soon enough?

The communicator sounded. Max Perry ignored it. He was leaning back in his reclining chair, staring up at the ceiling. Birdie rubbed at his threadbare white jacket, leaned forward, and read the crude display.

He sniffed. It was not a message likely to put Max Perry in a better mood.

"Captain Rebka is closer than we thought, sir," he said. "In fact, he left Starside hours ago. His aircar should be ready to land in a few minutes."

"Thanks, Birdie." Perry did not move. "Ask the Slingline to keep us posted."

"I'll do that, Commander." Kelly knew he had been dismissed, but he ignored it. "Before Captain Rebka gets here you should take a look at these, sir. As soon as you can."

Kelly laid a folder on the plaited-reed tabletop that lay between them, sat back, and waited. Max Perry could not be rushed in his current mood.

The ceiling of the room was transparent, looking directly up into Opal's normally cloudy skies. The location had been carefully chosen. It was close to the center of Quakeside, in a region where atmospheric circulation patterns increased the chance of clear patches. At the moment there was a brief predusk break in the overcast, and Quake was visible. With its surface only twelve thousand kilometers from the closest point of Opal, the parched sphere filled more than thirty-five degrees of the sky like a great, mottled fruit, purple-gray and overripe, poised ready to fall. From that distance it appeared peaceful, but already the dusky limb of the planet showed the softening of edges that spoke of rising dust storms.

Summertide was just thirty-six days away, less than two standard weeks. In ten days' time Perry would order the evacuation from Quake's surface, then monitor that evacuation personally. In every exodus for the past six years he had been the last man or woman to leave Quake, and the first to return after Summertide.

It was a compulsion with Perry. And regardless of what Rebka might want, Birdie Kelly knew that Max Perry would try to keep it that way.

Already night was advancing on the surface of Opal. Its dark shadow would soon create the brief false-night of Mandel eclipse on Quake. But Perry and Kelly would not be able to see that. The break in the overcast was closing, eaten away by swirls of rapidly moving cloud. There was a final flash of silver from far above, light reflected from the glittering knot of Midway Station and the lower part of the Umbilical; then Quake faded rapidly from view. Minutes later the roof above their heads showed the starred patterns of the first raindrops.

Perry sighed, leaned forward, and picked up the folders. Kelly knew that the other man had registered his earlier words without really hearing them. But Perry knew that if his right-hand man said he ought to look at the folder at once, there was a good reason for it.

The green covering held three long message summaries, each one a request for a visit to the surface of Quake. There was nothing very unusual in that. Birdie had been ready to give routine approval pending examination of travel plans—until he saw the source of the requests. Then he knew that Perry had to see them and would want to study them in detail.

The communicator buzzed again as Perry began to concentrate on the contents of the folder. Birdie Kelly took one look at the new message and quietly left the room. Rebka was arriving, but Perry did not need to be on the airstrip to welcome him. Birdie could do that. Perry had quite enough to worry about with the visit requests. Every one had come from outside the Dobelle system—outside, in fact, the worlds of the Phemus Circle. One was from the Fourth Alliance, one from a remote region of the Zardalu Communion, so far away that Birdie Kelly had never heard of it; and one, oddest of all, had been sent by the Cecropia Federation. That was unprecedented. So far as Birdie knew, no Cecropian had ever come within light-years of Dobelle.

Stranger yet, every visitor wanted to be on the surface of Quake at Summertide.

When Birdie Kelly returned he did something that he reserved for emergencies. He knocked on the door before he came in. The action guaranteed Perry's instant attention.

Kelly was holding yet another folder, and he was not alone. Behind him stood a thin, poorly dressed man who stared about with bright dark-brown eyes and was apparently more interested in the room's meager and tattered furnishings than in Perry himself.

His first words seemed to bear out that idea. "Commander Perry, I am pleased to meet you. I am Hans Rebka. I know that Opal is not a rich planet. But your position here would surely justify something better than this."

Perry put down the folder and followed the other man's inquisitive eyes as they surveyed the room. It was a sleeping chamber as well as an office. It held no more than a bed, three chairs, a table, and a desk, all battered and well used.

Perry shrugged. "I have simple needs. This is more than enough."

The newcomer smiled. "I agree. All men and women would not."

Regardless of whatever other feelings his smile might hide, part of Rebka's approval was quite genuine. In the first ten seconds with Max Perry he was able to dispose of one idea that had come to him after reading the other's history. Even the poorest planet could provide great luxury for one person, and some men and women would stay on a planet because they had found wealth and high living there, with no way to export it. But whatever Perry's secret, that could not be it. He lived as simply as Rebka himself.

Power, then?

Hardly. Perry controlled access to Quake, and little else. Permits for offworld visitors went through him, but anyone with real clout could appeal to a higher authority in the Dobelle system council.

So what was the driving force? There had to be one; there always was. But what was it?

During the official introductions and the exchange of meaningless courtesies on behalf of the government of Opal and the General Coordinators' office for the Phemus Circle, Rebka turned his attention to Perry himself.

He did it with real interest. He would rather be exploring Paradox, but despite his contempt for the new assignment he could not turn off his curiosity. The contrast between Perry's early history and his present position was just too striking. By the time Perry was twenty years old he had been a section coordinator in one of the roughest environments the Circle could offer. He had been subtle in handling problems, and yet he had been tough. The final assignment for one year to Opal was almost a formality, the last tempering of the metal before Perry was judged ready for work in the Coordinators' office.

He had come. And he had stuck. In one dead-end job for

all those years, unwilling to leave, lacking all his old drive. Why?

The man himself gave no clue as to the source of the problem. He was pale-faced and intense, but Rebka could see as much pallor and intensity just by looking in the mirror. They had both spent their early years on planets where survival was an achievement and thriving was impossible. The prominent goiter in Perry's neck spoke of a world where iodine was in short supply, and the thin, slightly crooked legs suggested an early case of rickets. Scaldworld's tolerance of plant life was grudging. At the same time Perry appeared in excellent health—something that Rebka could and would check in due course. But physical well-being only made it clearer that there must be mental problems. They would be harder to examine.

The inspection was not one-sided. While the formal exchanges of government greetings were taking place, Rebka knew that Perry was making his own assessment.

Did he hope that the new supervisor would be a man burned out from previous service or excesses, or perhaps some lazy pensioner? The Circle government had its share of people looking for sinecures, idlers willing to let Perry and others like him run the operation any way they wanted to, provided that the boss was not asked to do any work.

Apparently Perry wanted to find out whom he was dealing with and would waste no time in doing so, for as soon as the final courtesies had been exchanged he asked Kelly to leave and gestured Rebka to one of the chairs. "I assume that you will take up your duties here very soon, Captain?"

"More than soon, Commander. My duties on Opal and Quake have begun. I was told that they commenced at the moment the ship touched down on Starside Port."

"Good." Perry held out the green folder plus the fourth and latest document that Kelly had handed to him. "I was in the middle of reviewing these. I would appreciate it if you would take a look and give me your opinion."

In other words, let me see how smart you are. Rebka took

the documents and skimmed them in silence for a minute or two. He was not sure what the test was, but he did not want to fail it. "These all appear to be in the correct official format," he said at last.

"You see nothing unusual in them at all?"

"Well, perhaps in the diversity of the applicants. Do you often have visit requests from outside the Dobelle system?"

"Very seldom." Perry was nodding in grudging respect. "Now we get four requests, Captain, in one day. All want to visit Opal and Quake. Individuals from the three major groups, *plus* a member of an Alliance council. Do you know how many visitors a year we usually get to Dobelle? Maybe fifty—and they all come from *our* people, worlds in the Phemus Circle. And nobody ever wants to go to Quake."

Max Perry picked up the folder again. Apparently Rebka had met some initial acceptance criterion, because Perry's manner had lost a little of its stiffness. "Look at this one. It's from a *Cecropian,* for God's sake. No one on Dobelle has ever *seen* a live Cecropian. I haven't seen one myself. No one here knows how to communicate with one."

"Don't worry about that." Rebka focused again on the sheets in front of him. "She'll have her own interpreter. But you're right. If you get only fifty a year, four in a day is way outside statistical limits." And you haven't said it to me, he thought, but as far as you're concerned it's *five* in a day, isn't it? These requests arrived at the same time I did. So far as you are concerned, I'm just another outsider. "So what do they all want, Commander? I didn't read their reasons."

"Different things. This one"—Perry poked at the page with an emaciated finger—"just came in. Did you ever hear of a man called Julius Graves? He represents the Fourth Alliance Ethical Council, and according to this he wants to come to Opal to investigate a case of *multiple murder,* somehow involving twins from Shasta."

"Rich world, Shasta. A long way from Dobelle, in more ways than one."

"But if he wants to, according to the way I read the regulations, he can overrule anything that we say locally."

"Overrule us, or anyone else on Dobelle." Rebka took the document from Perry. "I never heard of Julius Graves, but the ethical councils carry the weight of all the groups. He'll be a hard man to argue with."

"And he doesn't say why he's coming here!"

"He doesn't have to." Rebka looked again at the application. "In his case, this request is a formality. If he wants to come, no one can stop him. What about the others, though? Why do they want to go to Quake?"

"Atvar H'sial—that's the Cecropian—says her specialty is the evolution of organisms under extreme environmental stress. Quake certainly qualifies. She says she wants to go there and see how the native life-forms adapt during Summertide."

"She's traveling alone?"

"No. With someone or something called J'merlia. A Lo'tfian."

"Okay, that'll be her interpreter. The Lo'tfians are another life-form from the Cecropia Federation. Who else?"

"Another female, Darya Lang from the Fourth Alliance."

"Human?"

"I assume so. She claims to be interested in seeing Builder artifacts."

"I thought there was only one in the Dobelle system."

"There is. The Umbilical. Darya Lang wants to take a look at it."

"She doesn't have to go down to Quake to do that."

"She says she wants to see how the Umbilical is tethered at the Quake end. She has a point there. No one has ever understood how the Builders arranged for its retraction to space at Summertide. Her story is plausible. Believe it if you want to."

Perry's tone of voice made it clear that he did not. It occurred to Rebka that they had at least one thing in common—their cynicism.

"And then there's Louis Nenda," Perry went on. "From the Zardalu Communion. When did you last hear from *them*?"

"When they had their last skirmish with the Alliance. What's he say he wants?"

"He doesn't bother to tell us in detail, but it's something about being interested in studying new physical forces. He wants to investigate the land tides on Quake during Summertide. And then there's a footnote, talking about the theory of the stability of biospheres, as it applies to Quake and Opal. Oh, and Nenda has a Hymenopt along with him, as a pet. That's *another* first. The only Hymenopts anyone has ever seen on Opal are stuffed ones in the Species Museum. Add them all up, Captain, and what do you get?"

Rebka did not answer that. Unless all the records on Perry were false, there was a subtle, flexible intelligence hiding behind those pale, mournful eyes. Rebka did not believe for a moment that Perry was asking advice because he thought he needed it. He was feeling out Rebka himself, probing the other man's intuition and sense of balance.

"When do they request arrival?"

"According to this, Darya Lang cleared the last Bose Node three days ago. That means she's on final subluminal approach to Starside Port. Landing request could come anytime. The rest of them are maybe a few days away."

"What do you recommend we do?"

"I'll tell you what I recommend we *don't* do." For the first time, emotion appeared on Max Perry's thin face. "We can let them visit Opal—though that's going to be no joke this Summertide—but we don't, under any circumstances, let them set foot on Quake."

Which means, Rebka thought, that my instinct back on Starside was spot on. If I'm going to find out what keeps Max Perry on Dobelle, I'll probably have to do exactly that: visit Quake, at Summertide. Well, what the hell. It can't be any more dangerous than the descent into Paradox. But let's test things here a little bit more before we jump too far.

"I'm not convinced of what you say," he replied, and watched apprehension flicker in Perry's pale eyes. "People are coming a long way to see Quake. They'll be willing to pay Dobelle a lot for the privilege, and this system needs all the credit it can get. Before we deny access, I want to talk at least to Darya Lang. And I think I may need to see the surface of Quake close to Summertide for myself—soon."

Quake close to Summertide. At those words another expression appeared on Max Perry's face. Sorrow. Guilt. Even longing? It could be any of them. Rebka wished he knew the other man better. Perry's countenance surely revealed the answers to a hundred questions—to someone who knew how to read it.

CHAPTER 3

Summertide
minus thirty-three.

HANS REBKA HAD arrived on Dobelle disoriented and angry. Darya Lang, following his subliminal path just three days later on her run from the final Bose Transition Point to the Opal spaceport, did not have room for anger.

She was nervous; more than nervous, she was *scared.*

For more than half her life she had been a research scientist, an archeologist whose mind was most comfortable seven million years in the past. She had performed the most complete survey of Builder artifacts, locating, listing, comparing, and cataloguing every one so far discovered in Fourth Alliance territory, and noting the precise times of any changes in their historical appearance or apparent function. But she had done all that *passively*, from the tranquil harbor of her research office on Sentinel Gate. She might know by heart the coordinates of the twelve hundred-odd artifacts scattered through the whole spiral arm, and she could reel off the current state of knowledge concerning each one. But other than the Sentinel, whose shining bulk was visible from the surface of her home planet, she had never seen one.

And now she was approaching Dobelle—when no one else had even *wanted* her to go.

27

"Why shouldn't I go?" she had asked when the Committee of the Fourth Alliance on Miranda sent their representative to her. She was trembling with tension and annoyance. "The anomaly is mine, if it's anyone's. I discovered it."

"That is true." Legate Pereira was a small, patient woman with nut-brown skin and golden eyes. She did not appear intimidating, but Darya Lang found it hard to face her. "And since you reported it, we have confirmed it for every Artifact. No one is trying to deny you full credit for your discovery. And we all admit that you are our expert on the Builders, and are most knowledgeable about their technology—"

"No one understands Builder technology!" Even in her irritation, Darya could not let that pass.

"*Most* is a comparative term. No one in the Alliance knows more. Since, I repeat, you are most knowledgeable about the technology of the Builders, you are clearly the best-qualified individual to pursue the anomaly's significance." The woman's voice became more gentle. "But at the same time, Professor Lang, you must admit that you have little experience of interstellar travel."

"I have none, and you know it. But everyone, from you to my House-uncle Matra, tells me that interstellar travel offers negligible risk."

The legate sighed. "Professor, it is not the travel that we question. Look around you. What do you see?"

Darya raised her head and surveyed the garden. Flowers, vines, trees, the cooing birds, the last rays of evening sunlight throwing dusty shafts of light through the trellis of the bower . . . It was all normal. What was she *supposed* to see?

"Everything looks fine."

"It *is* fine. That is my point. You have lived all your life on Sentinel Gate, and this is a garden world. One of the finest, richest, most beautiful planets that we know—far nicer than Miranda, where I live. But you are proposing to go to Quake. To nowhere. To a dingy, dirty, dismal, dangerous world, in the wild hope that you will find there new evidence of the Builders. Can you give me one reason for thinking that Quake has such potential?"

"You know the answer. My discovery provides that reason."

"A statistical anomaly. Do you want to endure misery and discomfort for the sake of *statistics*?"

"Of course I don't." Darya felt that the other woman was talking down to her, and that was the one thing she could not stand. "No one *wants* discomfort. Legate Pereira, you admit that no one in the Fourth Alliance has more knowledge of the Builders than I do. Suppose I do not go, and someone else does, and whoever goes in my place fails for lack of knowledge where I might have succeeded. Do you think that I could ever forgive myself?"

Instead of replying, Pereira went to the window and beckoned Darya Lang to her side. She pointed into the slowly darkening sky. The Sentinel gleamed close to the horizon, a shining and striated sphere two hundred million kilometers away and a million kilometers across.

"Suppose I told you that I knew a way to break in through the Sentinel's protective shield and to explore the Pyramid at the center. Would you want to go with me?"

"Of course. I've studied the Sentinel since I was a child. If I'm right, the Pyramid could contain a library for the Builder sciences—maybe their history, too. But no one knows how to break the shield. We have been trying for a thousand years."

"But *suppose* we could crack it."

"Then I would want to go."

"And suppose it involved danger and discomfort?"

"I would still want to go."

The legate nodded and sat in silence for a few seconds as the darkness deepened. "Very well," she said at last. "Professor Lang, you are said to be a logical person, and I like to think that I am, too. If you are willing to run the risks of the Sentinel's shield, and those are *unknown* risks, then you have a right to endure the lesser risks of Quake.

As for travel to the Dobelle system, we humans built the Bose Drive, and we understand exactly how it works. We know how to employ the Bose Network. The experience is frightening at first, but the danger is small. And perhaps if you can use that Network to explore the statistical anomaly that you alone discovered, it will finally provide the tool you need to crack the secret of the Sentinel. I cannot deny that chain of logic. You have the right to make the journey. I will approve your travel request."

"Thank you, Legate Pereira." With the victory, Darya felt a chill that was not caused by the night air. She was passing from pleasant theory to commitment.

"But there is one other thing." Pereira's voice sharpened. "I trust that you have not told anyone outside the Alliance about your discovery of the anomaly?"

"No. Not a person. I sent it only through regular reporting channels. There is no one else here who would care to hear about it, and I wanted—"

"Good. Be sure you keep it that way. For your information, the anomaly is now to be treated as an official secret of the Fourth Alliance."

"Secret! But anyone could perform the same analysis that I did. Why . . ." Lang subsided. If she said that anyone could do the work, she might lose her claim to the anomaly—and the trip to Quake.

The legate stared at her soberly and finally nodded. "Remember, you are about to embark on a journey of more than seven hundred light-years, beyond the borders of the Alliance. In some ways I envy you. It is a journey more than I have ever made. I have nothing more to say, except to give you my good wishes for a safe trip and a successful mission."

Darya could hardly believe that she had won, after weeks of red tape and dithering from the authorities of the Fourth Alliance. And the perils of the Bose Drive had indeed faded, once she was on her way and made her initial step through the Network. The first Transition was disconcerting, not for the feelings that it introduced but for their *absence*. The Transition was instantaneous and imperceptible, and that did not seem right. The human brain required some *notice* that it and the ship that carried it had been transported across a hundred light-years or more. Perhaps a slight shock, Darya thought; a little nausea, maybe, or some feeling of disorientation.

Then at the second and third Transitions that concern vanished, just as Legate Pereira had promised. Darya could take the mysteries of the Bose Drive for granted.

But what did not decrease was her own feeling of inadequacy. She was a bad liar; she always had been. The Dobelle system contained just one structure that dated back to the Builders: the Umbilical. And that was a minor artifact, one whose operations were self-evident even if the controls that governed it remained mysterious. She would never have made so long a journey merely to look at the Umbilical. No one would. And yet that was the Alliance's official rationale for her visit.

Someone was going to ask her why she had done so odd a thing; she just knew it. And nothing in half a lifetime of research work had taught her how to fake things. Her face would give her away.

The sight of Dobelle eased her uneasiness a little. In a universe that she saw as populated by the miracles of the Builders, here was a natural wonder to rival them. Forty or fifty million years earlier the planetary doublet of Quake and Opal had orbited the star Mandel in a near-circular path. That orbit had been stable for billions of years, resisting the gravitational tugs of Mandel's small and remote binary-system partner, Amaranth, and of its two great gas-giant planets, moving in their eccentric orbits five and seven hundred million kilometers farther out. The environment had been tranquil on both members of the Dobelle planetary pair, until a close encounter of the two gas-giants had thrown one of them into a grazing swing-by of Mandel. That unnamed stranger had emerged from its sun-skimming trajectory with a modified path that took it clear out of the stellar system and into the void.

That would have been the end of the story—except that Dobelle lay in the stranger's exit route. The gas-giant had done a complex dance about the doublet planet, moving Quake and Opal closer together while changing their combined orbit to one with a periastron that skimmed much closer to Mandel. Then the stranger had vanished into history. Only Dobelle and the gas-giant called Gargantua remained, their still-changing orbital elements allowing an accurate reconstruction of past events.

Summertide, Dobelle's time of closest approach to Mandel, was just a couple of weeks away. It would be a time, if Darya Lang's analysis was correct, of great significance in the spiral arm. And also in her own life. Her theories would at last be proved true.

Or false.

She went to the port and watched as the ship approached Dobelle. Opal and Quake whirled dizzily around each other in a mad dance, spinning three full turns in a standard day. She could actually see their motion. However, speed was all relative. The ship's rendezvous with the landing field on Opal's Starside sounded difficult, but it was a trivial problem for the navigation computers that would make the rendezvous.

The problems would come not from there, but from the humans who waited to greet her. The tone of the message permitting her entry to Opal sounded ominous. "Provide the full identification of your sponsor. State in full the proposed length of stay. Give details of expected findings. Explain why the time of your requested visit is critical. Say just why you wish to visit Quake. Provide credit information or nonrefundable advance payment. Signed, Maxwell Perry, Commander."

Were the immigration officials on Opal so hostile to every offworld visitor? Or was her paranoia not paranoia at all, but a well-merited uneasiness?

She was still standing by the port as the ship began its final approach. They were coming in from the direction of Mandel, and she had a fine sunlit view of the doublet. She knew that Opal was only slightly larger than Quake—5,600 kilometers mean radius, compared with Quake's 5,100—but the human eye insisted otherwise. The cloud-covered irides-cent ball of Opal, slightly egg-shaped and with its long axis pointing always to its sister world, loomed large. The darker, smaller ovoid of Quake brooded next to it, a smooth-polished heliotrope against the brighter gemstone of its part-ner. Opal was featureless, but the surface of Quake was full of texture, stippled with patches of deep purple and darkest green. She tried to make out the thread of the Umbilical, but from that distance it was invisible.

Entry to the Dobelle system offered no options. There was only one spaceport, set close to the middle of Opal's Starside hemisphere. There was no spaceport of any kind on Quake. According to her reference texts, safe access to Quake came only via Opal.

Safe access to Quake?

A nice idea, but Darya recalled what she had read of Quake and of Summertide. Maybe the reference texts needed to find different words . . . at least at this time of the year.

The reference files of the Fourth Alliance had even fewer good things to say than Legate Pereira about the worlds controlled by the Phemus Circle. "Remote . . . impov-erished . . . backward . . . thinly populated . . . barbaric."

The stars of the Circle lay in a region overlapped by all three major clades of the spiral arm. But in their outward expansions the Fourth Alliance, the Zardalu Communion, and the Cecropia Federation had shown negligible interest in the Phemus Circle. There was nothing there worth buy-ing, bargaining for, or stealing—hardly enough to justify a visit.

Unless one was looking for trouble. Trouble was supposed to be easy to find on any world controlled by the Circle.

Darya Lang stepped out of the ship onto the spongy ground of Opal's Starside spaceport and looked around her with misgiving. The buildings were low and ground-hugging, built of what looked like plaited reeds and dried mud. No one was waiting to greet the ship. Opal was described as metal-poor, wood-poor, and people-poor. All it had was water, and lots of it.

As her shoe sank an inch or two into the soft surface she felt even more uneasy. She had never visited a waterworld, and she knew that instead of hard rock and solid ground beneath her feet, there was only the weak and insubstantial crust of the Sling. Below that was nothing but brackish water, a couple of kilometers deep. The buildings hugged the ground for good reason. If they were too tall and heavy, they would break through it.

An irrelevant thought came to her: she could not even swim.

The crew of the ship that had brought her were still involved with the final stages of landing procedure. She began to walk toward the nearest building. Two men were finally emerging from it to greet her.

It was not a promising introduction to Opal. Both men were short and thin—Darya Lang was ten centimeters taller than either of them. They were dressed in identical dingy uniforms, with clothes that shared a patched and well-worn look, and from a distance the two might have been taken for brothers, one ten years or so older than the other. Only as she came closer were their differences revealed.

The older man had a friendly, matter-of-fact air to him and a self-confident walk. The faded captain's insignia on his shoulder indicated that he was the senior of the two in rank as well as age. "Darya Lang?" he said as soon as they were within easy speaking distance. He smiled and held out his hand, but not to shake hers. "I'll take your entry forms. I'm Captain Rebka."

Add "brusque" to the list of words describing the inhabitants of the Phemus Circle, she thought. And add "unkempt" and "battered" to Rebka's physical description. The man's face had a dozen scars on it, the most noticeable running in a double line from his left temple to the point of his jaw. And yet the overall effect was not unpleasant—rather the opposite. To her surprise, Darya sensed the indefinable tingle of mutual attraction.

She handed over her papers and made internal excuses for the scars and the grimy uniform. Dirt was only superficial, and maybe Rebka had been through some exceptional misfortune.

Except that the younger man looked just as dirty, and he had his own scars. At some time his neck and one side of his face had been badly burned, with a bungled attempt at reconstructive surgery that would never have been accepted back on Sentinel Gate.

Maybe the burn scars had also left the skin of his face lacking in flexibility. Certainly he had a very different expression from Rebka. Where the captain was breezy in manner and likeable despite his grubbiness and lack of finesse, the other man seemed withdrawn and distant. His face was stiff and expressionless, and he hardly seemed aware of Darya, although she was standing less than two meters from him. And whereas Rebka was clearly in top physical shape, the other had a run-down and unhealthy look, the air of a man who did not eat regular meals or care at all about his own health.

His eyes were at variance with his young face. Dead and disinterested, they were the pale orbs of a man who had withdrawn from the whole universe. He was unlikely to cause Darya any trouble.

Just as she reached that comforting conclusion the face before her came alive and the man snapped out, "My name is Perry. Commander Maxwell Perry. Why do you want to visit Quake?"

The question destroyed her composure completely. Coming without the preliminary and traditional courtesies of Alliance introductions, it convinced Darya Lang that these people *knew*—knew about the anomaly, knew about her role in discovering it, and knew what she was there to seek. She felt her face turning red.

"The—the Umbilical." She had to struggle to find words. "I—I have made a special study of Builder artifacts; it has been my life's work." She paused and cleared her throat. "I have read all that I could find about the Umbilical. But I want to see it for myself and learn how the tethers work on Opal and Quake. And discover how Midway Station controls the Umbilical for the move to space at Summertide." She ran out of breath.

Perry remained expressionless, but Captain Rebka had a little smile on his face. She was sure that he saw right through her every word.

"Professor Lang." He was reading from her entry papers. "We do not discourage visitors. Dobelle needs all the revenue it can get. But this is a dangerous time of year on Opal and Quake."

"I know. I have read about the sea tides on Opal, and the land tides on Quake." She cleared her throat again. "It is not my nature to seek danger." That at least was true, she thought wryly. "I propose to be very careful and take all precautions."

"So you have *read* about Summertide." Perry turned to Rebka, and Darya Lang detected a tension between the two men. "As have you, Captain Rebka. But reading and experiencing something are not the same. And neither of you seems to realize that Summertide this time will be different from all others in our experience."

"Every time must be different," Rebka said calmly. He was smiling, but Darya Lang could feel the conflict. Rebka was the older and more senior, but on the issue of Summertide Commander Perry did not accept the other's authority.

"This is exceptional," Perry replied. "We will be taking

extraordinary precautions, even on Opal. And as for what may happen on Quake, I cannot begin to guess."

"Even though you have experienced half a dozen Summertides?"

Rebka had lost his smile. The two men faced each other in silence, while Darya looked on. She sensed that the fate of her own mission hung on the argument that they were having.

"The Grand Conjunction," Perry said after a few seconds. And finally Darya had a statement that made sense to her as a scientist.

She had studied the orbital geometry of the Mandel system in detail while working on the Lang catalog of artifacts. She knew that Amaranth, the dwarf companion of Mandel, normally moved so far from the primary that the illumination it provided to Dobelle was little more than starlight. However, once every few thousand years its motion brought it much closer, to less than a billion kilometers of Mandel. Gargantua, the remaining gas-giant planet of the system, moved in the same orbital plane, and it, too, had its own point of close approach to Mandel.

Dobelle's critical time of Summertide usually occurred when Gargantua and Amaranth were both far from Mandel. But all three orbits were in resonance lock. On rare occasions, Amaranth and Gargantua swung in together to Mandel, at a time that coincided with Summertide for Opal and Quake. And then . . .

"The Grand Conjunction," Perry repeated. "When everything lines up at periastron, and the sea tides and land tides on Opal and Quake are as big as they can possibly be. We have no idea how big. The Grand Conjunction happens only once every three hundred and fifty thousand years. The last time was long before humans settled Dobelle. But the next time will happen just thirty-three days from now—less than two standard weeks. No one knows what Summertide will do to Opal and Quake then, but I do know that the tidal forces will be devastating."

Darya looked at the soft ground beneath their feet. She had the terrible feeling that the flimsy mud-raft of living and dead plants was already crumbling under the assault of monstrous tides. No matter what the dangers might be on Quake, surely they were preferable to staying on Opal.

"So wouldn't you all be *safer* on Quake?" she asked.

Perry shook his head. "The permanent population of Opal is more than a million people. That may seem like nothing for someone like you, from an Alliance world. But it is a lot for a Circle world. My birth planet had less than a quarter of that."

"And mine less than an eighth of it," Rebka said mildly. No one stayed on Teufel who had any way to get off it.

"But do you know the permanent population of Quake?" Perry glared at both of them while Lang wondered how she had ever thought him calm and passionless.

"It is *zero,*" he said after a pause. "Zero! What does that tell you about life on Quake?"

"But there *is* life on Quake." She had studied the planetary index. "*Permanent* life."

"There is. But it is not human life, and it could not be. It is *native* life. No human could survive Quake during Summertide—even a normal Summertide."

Perry was becoming increasingly assertive. Darya knew that her case for visiting Quake was lost. He would deny her access, and she would get no closer to Quake than the Starside spaceport. As she decided that, help came from an unexpected direction.

Rebka turned to Max Perry and pointed a thin finger up to Opal's cloudy skies. "You are probably right, Commander Perry," he said quietly. "But suppose strangers are coming to Dobelle *because* it will be the Grand Conjunction? We did not consider that possibility when we were examining their applications." He turned to stare at Darya Lang. "Is that your *real* reason for being here?"

"No. Definitely not." She felt relief at being able to give

an honest answer. "I never thought about the Conjunction until Commander Perry mentioned it."

"I believe you." Rebka smiled, and she was suddenly convinced that he did. But she recalled Legate Pereira's words: "Don't trust anyone from the Phemus Circle. They practice survival skills that we in the Alliance have never been forced to learn."

"People's reasons for coming here are not too relevant, of course," he went on. "They don't make Quake any safer." He turned to Perry. "And I feel sure you are right about the dangers of Quake at Summertide. On the other hand, I have a responsibility to maximize the revenues of Dobelle. That's my job. We have no responsibility to protect visitors, beyond a duty to warn them. If they choose to proceed, knowing the risks, that is their option. They are not children."

"They have no notion of what Quake is like at Summertide." Perry's face had turned blotchy white and red. He was overwhelmed by strong emotion. "*You* have no idea."

"Not yet. But I will have." Rebka's manner changed again. He became a boss who was clearly giving orders. "I agree with you, Commander. It would be irresponsible for Professor Lang to visit Quake—until we are sure of the hazards. But once we do understand them—and can explain them—we have no duty to be overprotective. So you and I will go to Quake, while Professor Lang remains here on Opal."

He turned to Darya. "And when we return . . . well, then, Professor Lang, I will make my decision."

ARTIFACT: SENTINEL.
UAC#: 863
Galactic Coordinates: 27,712.863/16,311.031/761.157
Name: Sentinel
Star/planet association: Ryders-M/Sentinel Gate
Bose Access Node: G-232
Estimated age: 5.64 + 0.07 Megayears

Exploration History: Sentinel was discovered in Expansion Year 2649 by human colonists of the trans-Orionic region. First entry attempt, E. 2674, by Bernardo Gullemas and the crew of exploration vessel D-33 of Cyclops class. No survivors. Subsequent approaches attempted E. 2682, E. 2695, E. 2755, E. 2803, E. 2991. No survivors.

Sentinel warning beacon set in place, E. 2739; monitoring station established on nearest planet (Sentinel Gate), E. 2762.

Physical Description: Sentinel is a near-spherical inaccessible region, a little less than one million kilometers across. No visible internal energy sources, but Sentinel glows faintly with its own light (absolute magnitude +25) and is visible from every point of the Ryders-M system. The impassable surface of Sentinel readily permits two-way passage of light and radiation of any wavelength, but it reflects all material objects including atomic and subatomic particles. There is photon flux only from the interior, with no particle emission. Laser illumination of the interior is possible, and reveals a variety of structures at the center of the sphere. The most prominent such feature is "The Pyramid," a regular tetrahedral structure which absorbs all light falling onto it. If interior distances within Sentinel have meaning (there is evidence that they do not—see below) then the Pyramid would be approximately ninety kilometers on a side. No increase in temperature of the Pyramid is detectible, even when incident absorbed radiation is at the gigawatt level.

Path-length measurements using lasers show that the interior of Sentinel is not simply-connected; minimal light travel time across Sentinel is 4.221 minutes, compared with a geodesic travel time of 3.274 seconds for equivalent distance across empty space remote from matter. For light incident normally on the Sentinel "equator" travel times across Sentinel are infinite, or certainly in excess of a thousand years. Red shift and grazing incidence laser beams indicate that no mass is present within Sentinel, a result that is inconsistent with the observed interior structure.

Sentinel holds a precise distance of 22.34 a.u. from the Ryders-M primary star, but is not in orbit about it. Gravitational forces and radiation pressure forces either are exactly compensated by some unknown mechanism in Sentinel, or do not act on the structure at all.

Physical Nature of Sentinel: According to Wollaski'i and Drews, Sentinel takes advantage of and is built around a natural anomaly of space-time and possesses only weak physical coupling to the rest of the universe. If so, this is one of only thirty-two Builder artifacts that were created with the use of preexisting and natural features.

Sentinel topology appears to be that of a Ricci-Cartan-Penrose knot in 7-space.

Intended Purpose: Unknown. However, it is conjectured (by analogy with other Builder artifacts, see Entry 311, 465, and 1223) that the Pyramid may possess near-infinite information storage capacity and lifetime. It has therefore been suggested (Lang, E. 4130) that the Pyramid and possibly the whole of Sentinel form a Builder library.

—From the *Lang Universal Artifact Catalog,*
Fourth Edition.

CHAPTER 4

Summertide
minus thirty-one.

THE FIRST PART of the flight to Quake was conducted in total silence. Once it was clear that Hans Rebka was insistent on going and could not be dissuaded, all Perry's energy had vanished. He sank into a strange lethargy, sitting at Rebka's side in the aircar and staring straight ahead. He roused briefly when they came to the foot of the Umbilical, but only long enough to lead the way to a passenger capsule and initiate the command sequence for ascent.

Seen from sea level the Umbilical was impressive but not overwhelming. It appeared to Rebka as a tall slender tower of uniform thickness, maybe forty meters across, stretching from the surface of Opal's ocean at the lower end up into the thick and uniform cloud layer. The main trunk of the structure was a silvery alloy, up and down which passengers and cargo could move in huge cars. The attachments were electromagnetic, held and driven by linear synchronous motors. The detailed design might be unfamiliar, but Rebka had seen the concept used on a dozen worlds, carrying people and materials up and down multikilometer buildings, or high into orbit. The knowledge that there were over two kilometers more of the Umbilical below sea level, reaching down to a tether on the ocean floor, was more surprising, but the mind could accept it.

What the mind—or Rebka's mind at least—could not so readily accept was the twelve *thousand* kilometers of the Umbilical above the clouds, reaching all the way from Opal to Quake's parched and turbulent surface. The observer who climbed into a capsule was seeing less than one ten-thousandth of the whole structure. With a maximum free-space car speed of a thousand kilometers an hour, travelers would expect to see two sunrises on Quake before they got there.

And now they were on their way.

The capsule was as tall and broad as Opal's biggest buildings. As the Builders had left it, the inside was one large empty space. Humans had added interior floors, from a massive cargo hold at the bottom to the control-and-observation chamber at the top.

The car's motors were silent. All that could be heard as they rose smoothly through the cloud layer was a whistle of air and the mutter of atmospheric turbulence. Five seconds more, and Hans Rebka had his first view of Quake as seen from Opal. He heard Max Perry grunt at his side.

Maybe Rebka grunted, too. For Opal's permanent cloud layer suddenly seemed like a blessing. He was glad that the other planet had been hidden when he had been down on Opal's surface.

Quake stood huge in the sky, a sunlit, mottled ball that was poised and ready to crash down onto him. His hindbrain told him that no force in the universe could hold such a weight, that one would never become used to the sight. At the same time his forebrain did a calculation of orbital rates and the matching of centrifugal and gravitational forces, and assured him that everything was in perfect dynamic balance. People might be uncomfortable with the threat of Quake overhead for a day or two; then they would get used to it and ignore it.

From this distance no details were visible, but it was clear that he was looking at a world without major seas and oceans. Rebka thought at once of terraforming; not just

Quake or Opal, but of the doublet together. It was the perfect application. Quake had the metals and minerals; Opal
had the water. It would be a substantial task, but no bigger
than others he had undertaken. And the beginning of the
necessary transportation system was already in position.

He looked along the thread of the Umbilical. The line upward was visible for perhaps a hundred kilometers before
he lost it. Midway Station, four thousand kilometers above
them at the center of mass of the Opal-Quake system, could
be seen as a tiny golden knot on an invisible thread. They
would be there for changeover in half a day. Plenty of time
to think.

And plenty to think about.

Rebka closed his eyes and sorted through his worries.

Begin with Max Perry. After only a couple of days of exposure to the man it was clear that there were two Max Per-
rys. One was a quiet, dull bureaucrat, someone whom
Rebka would expect to find in a dead-end job on any rat-
hole world in the Phemus Circle. But somewhere under that
there was a second personality, an energetic and subtle person with strong ideas of his own. The second Max Perry
seemed to wake only on random occasions.

No, that was wrong. The other Max awoke when Quake
was the issue, and only then. And Max II must be the clever
and determined man that Perry had been, all of the time,
seven years before—when he was assigned to Dobelle.

Rebka leaned back in his seat, physically relaxed and
mentally active. So. Accept that there was a mystery in Max
Perry. But ask if that mystery justified pulling a senior,
action-oriented man like Hans Rebka away from a key project involving exploration of Paradox to become an amateur
psychologist on the minor world of Opal.

It did not add up. If the men and women who ran the
Phemus Circle were good at anything, it was at conserving
resources; and human resources were the most precious
of all.

Look for another motive, another reason for his being assigned there.

Rebka was not naive enough to believe that his superiors would tell him the whole story behind his assignments. They might not even *know* the whole story. He had found that out the hard way, on Pelican's Wake. A troubleshooter was expected to be able to operate without a full deck, and Rebka functioned best when he was forced to work things out for himself.

Terraforming of Quake and Opal?

His superiors must know that as soon as he saw the planetary doublet of Dobelle he would evaluate both worlds as possible subjects for terraforming. Was that the real reason he had been assigned there? To set in motion that project?

Still it did not feel right.

So add in some of the other variables. Four groups were requesting a visit to Quake at Summertide. He might believe that one was a genuine coincidence—the Alliance Council had no reputation for deceit—but four at once was not plausible.

And the upcoming Summertide would be the biggest ever. Maybe that was the key. They were there for that special Summertide.

Again, it did not feel complete. Darya Lang had told him that she did not know it was to be a specially big Summertide until Perry had told her.

Rebka believed her. But that belief itself was suspect. He had left a woman companion behind him on the station orbiting Paradox. No matter what his brain told him, his glands were probably seeking a replacement. In the first two minutes with Lang he had been aware of an attraction between them. And that must make him more cautious in dealing with her, since he *wanted* to believe her.

Lang did not know that Opal and Quake were scheduled for monster Summertides. Fine. Believe that, and still it did not mean that she was what she pretended to be. She could have another and more complex role to play.

Was she what she claimed to be? That could be checked. Before he left Starside, Rebka had already sent an encrypted message through the Bose communications net, asking for confirmation by Circle intelligence that Darya Lang was an expert on Builder artifacts. The reply would be waiting when they returned from Quake. Until then, questions regarding Lang had to be put to one side.

But there were plenty of other questions left. Hans Rebka was interrupted by a light touch on his arm. He opened his eyes.

Max Perry was gesturing upward, along the line of the Umbilical. Quake loomed above them, half again as big as when they had started. But at the moment it reflected only the murky dried-blood light of Amaranth. Mandel was hidden behind the planet, and as Summertide approached, its dwarf companion was swinging in closer. Soon night would disappear completely on Quake and Opal.

Perry was pointing again, and Rebka realized that Quake was not his current interest. They were almost to Midway Station, and amazingly the Umbilical seemed to end there. Rebka could see a break, a region where the cylindrical structure terminated as a point of blazing blue. They moved rapidly toward it, until Quake itself began to be blocked from view by the shining gold of Midway Station.

"What's happening?" Rebka said. "I thought the Umbilical ran all the way between Opal and Quake." He should have been a little nervous, because it was sheer vacuum outside the car; but Perry had a smile on his face, and he certainly did not act like a man facing disaster.

"It does," he said. "We're approaching the Winch. We have to be shunted here, and reconnected on the other side of Midway Station. Travelers can go into the station if they want to—it's well equipped, power and food and shelter—but I see no point in that. If you like we can take a closer look at Midway on the way back."

As Perry spoke, the car they were riding in was swinging away from the main cable and running through a series of gates and connecting rails. Quake had vanished. Midway Station was off to the right. Rebka could see a whole line of ports, any one of them big enough to accept the capsule. He looked back to the place where the main cable of the Umbilical disappeared into bright blue nothingness and then, a few kilometers farther on, reappeared.

"I don't see any winch."

"You won't." The second Max Perry was back, alert and energetic. "That's just a name we give it. You see, Opal and Quake are in a near-circular mutual orbit, but their separation distance varies all the time—anything up to four hundred kilometers. A permanent Umbilical can't work unless you have something to reel in or pay out cable. That's what the Winch does."

"That hole in space?"

"Right. It works fine, and at Summertide it reels in extra so that the coupling is lost at the surface of Quake. And it's smart enough to leave the tether on Opal intact. But it's all Builder technology. We have no idea where the cable goes to or comes from, or how it knows what to do. People on Quake and Opal don't care, so long as they can raise or lower the Umbilical through the special control sequences."

Perry's reluctance to visit Quake had vanished at liftoff from Opal. He was peering forward as they rounded the bulk of Midway Station, seeking Quake again in the sky ahead.

The capsule moved back to attach to the new length of the Umbilical, and they began to pick up speed. Soon they passed the mass center of the Dobelle system, and there was a clear sense of falling toward Quake, their own centrifugal force adding to Quake's gravity. The dark planet grew visibly, minute by minute, in the sky ahead of them. They began to see more surface detail.

And Rebka could see another change in Perry. The younger man's breathing was faster. He was staring at Quake's approaching surface with rapt attention, his eyes bright and staring. Rebka was willing to bet that his pulse rate had increased.

But what was down there? Rebka would have given a lot to see Quake through Max Perry's eyes.

Quake had no sea-sized water bodies, but it did have plenty of rivers and small lakes. All around them grew the characteristic dark-green and rust-colored vegetation. Most of it was tough and prickly, but in certain places there flourished a cover of lush ferns, soft and resilient. One of those areas was on the biggest lake's shore, not far from the foot of the Umbilical. It was a natural place for a person to sink down and rest. Or for two people to find other pleasures.

Amy was talking, her voice breathless in his ear. "You're the expert, aren't you?"

"I don't know about that." He sounded lazy, relaxed. "But I probably know as much about this place as anyone."

"Same thing. So why won't you bring me here again? You could, Max, if you wanted to. You control the access."

"I shouldn't have brought you here at all."

The feeling of power. He had done it originally to show off his new authority, but once on the planet there were other and better reasons. Quake was still safe, still far from Summertide, yet already there was volcanic dust high in the atmosphere. The evenings, flaming in every eight hours, were an unspeakable beauty of red, purple, and gold. He knew of nothing like it in the rest of the universe—nothing he had read, nothing he had heard rumored. Even with his eyes closed, he would still see those glorious colors.

He had wanted to show it off to Amy—and he did not want to stop looking himself, not just yet. He lay on his back, gazing up past the shattering sunset to the brightening disk of Opal. By his side, Amy had broken off one of the soft fronds of fern and was tickling his bare chest. After a few moments she moved over him, blocking his view of Opal and gazing down at him with wide, serious eyes.

"*You will, won't you? You will, you definitely will. Say you will.*"

"*Will what?*" He was feigning incomprehension.

"*Will bring me here again. Closer to Summertide.*"

"*I definitely won't.*" He rolled his head from side to side on the soft ferns, too lazy to lift it fully. He felt like the king of the world. "*It wouldn't be safe, Amy. Not then.*"

"*But you come here then.*"

"*Not at Summertide. I get out well before that, while it's still safe. Nobody stays here then.*"

"*So I could leave with you, when it's still safe. Couldn't I?*"

"*No. Not near Summertide.*"

Amy was moving her body down toward him, as the last light bled from the air of Quake. He could no longer see her face. It had faded with the dying light.

"*I could.*" Her lips were an inch away from his. "*Say I could. Say yes.*"

"*No,*" he repeated. "*Not close to Summertide.*"

But Amy did not reply. She was busy with other arguments.

CHAPTER 5

Summertide minus thirty.

DARYA LANG HAD a terrible sense of anti-climax. To come so far, to steel herself for confrontation and danger and exciting new experiences . . . and then to be left to cool her heels for days on end, while others decided when—and if—she would be allowed to undertake the final and most crucial part of her journey!

No one in the Alliance had suggested that her task on Quake would be easy. But also no one had suggested that she might have trouble *reaching* Opal's sister world once she got to the Dobelle system. So far she had not even *seen* Quake, except from a distance. She was stuck on Opal's Starside for an indefinite period, with nothing to do, only short-range transportation available to her, and no say in what happened next.

Perry had given her a whole building to herself, just outside the spaceport. He had assured her that she had complete freedom to wander as she chose, talk to anyone she liked, and do anything that she wanted to.

Very kind of him. Except that there was no one else in the building, and nothing there but living quarters—and he had told her to be available to meet as soon as he returned. He and Rebka were sure to be away for days. Where was she supposed to go? What was she supposed to do?

She called maps of Opal onto the display screens. To anyone accustomed to the fixed continents and well-defined land-water boundaries of Sentinel Gate, the maps were curiously unsatisfying. The ocean floor contours of Opal were shown as permanent planetary features, but they seemed to be the only geographic constants. For the Slings themselves she could find no more than the present positions and drift rates of a couple of hundred of the largest of them; plus— an unsettling set of data—the approximate thickness and estimated lifetime of each Sling. At the moment she was standing on a layer of material less than forty meters deep, with a thickness that changed unpredictably every year.

She turned off the display and sat rubbing her forehead. She did not feel good. Part of it might be the reduced gravity, only four-fifths of standard here on Opal's Starside. But maybe part of it was disorientation produced by rapid interstellar travel. Every test insisted that the Bose Drive produced no physical effects on humans. But she recalled the inhabitants of the old Arks, who permitted themselves only subluminal travel and claimed that the human soul could travel no faster than light-speed.

If the Ark dwellers were correct, her soul would be a long time catching up with her.

Darya went to the window and stared up at Opal's cloudy sky. She felt lonely and very far from home. She wished that she could catch a glimpse of Rigel, the nearest supergiant to Sentinel Gate, but the cloud layer was continuous. She was lonely, and she was also annoyed. Hans Rebka might be an interesting character, and interested in her—she had seen the spark in his eyes—but she had not come so far to have all her plans thwarted by the whim of some back-world bureaucrat.

The way she was feeling, it would be better to walk around the Sling than to remain cooped up inside the low, claustrophobic building. She went outside, to find that a steady drizzle was beginning to fall. Exploration of the Sling on foot in those conditions might be difficult—the surface was uneven clumps of sedges and ferns, on a light and friable soil bound by a tight-rooted and slippery tangle of ground vines.

But she went barefoot all the time at home, and her naked toes could catch a good purchase on the tough vines. She bent down and slipped off her shoes.

The ground became more uneven outside the controlled area of the spaceport, and it was tough going. But she needed the exercise. She had traveled a good kilometer and was all set to walk for a long time when a dense clump of ferns a few meters in front of her produced an angry hiss. The tops of the plants bowed down and flattened under the weight of some large, low-slung, and invisible body.

Darya gasped and jumped backward, sitting down hard on the wet soil. Barefoot walking—or walking of any kind— suddenly seemed like a very bad idea. She scurried back to the spaceport and requisitioned a car. It had a limited flying range, but it could take her past the edge of the Sling and permit her a look at Opal's ocean.

"You didn't have to worry," said the engineer who gave her the car. He was insisting on showing her how to use the simple controls, though she was quite sure she could have worked them out for herself. "Nothing bad ever makes it shoreside here, an' people didn't bring in nothing dangerous when she was first settled. Nothin' poisonous here, neither. You was all right."

"What was it?"

"Big ole tortoise." He was a tall, pale-skinned man with a filthy coverall, a gap-toothed smile, and a very casual manner. "Weighs mebbe half a ton, eats all the time. But only ferns an' grasses an' stuff. You could ride on his back and he'd never notice you."

"A native form?"

"Naw." The short lesson on aircar use was over, but he was in no hurry to leave. "No vertebrates native to Opal. Biggest thing ashore is a kind o' four-legged crab."

"Is there anything dangerous out in the ocean?"

"Not to you 'n' me. Least, not dangerous by design. When you get a ways offshore, watch for a big, green hump coming up to the surface, 'bout a kilometer across. That'll be a Dowser. It'll damage boats now an' agin, but only 'cause it don't know they're there."

"Suppose one came up underneath a Sling?"

"Now why'd she be dumb enough to do that?" His voice was teasing. "She come up for air and sunlight, an' there's none of them under a Sling. Go find yourself a Dowser— seein' one's a real experience. They come up a lot at this time of year. An' you were lucky to meet that ole tortoise, you know. 'Nother few days and he'll be off. They're leaving extra early."

"Where are they going to?"

"Ocean. Where else? They know Summertide is on the way, and they want to be nice an' cozy when it comes. Must know it's going to be extra big this year."

"Will they be safe there?"

"Sure. Worst thing that can happen to one of 'em is he gets to sit high and dry for a while at real low tide. Couple of hours later, he's back swimmin'."

He stepped down from the running board on the left side of the car. "If you want to find the quickest way to the edge of the Sling, fly low an' see where the turtles' heads are pointing. That'll get you straight there." He wiped his hands on a dirty rag, leaving them as black as when he started, and gave Darya the warmest, most admiring smile. "Anyone ever tell you you walk an' move real nice? You do. If you want company when you get back, I'll be here. I live right near. Name's Cap."

Darya Lang took off wondering about the worlds of the Phemus Circle. Or was it was just in the air of Opal, the thing that led men to look at her differently? In twelve adult years on Sentinel Gate she had had one love affair, received maybe four compliments, and noticed half a dozen admiring looks. Here it was two in two days.

Well, Legate Pereira had told her not to be surprised by

anything that happened outside Alliance territory. And House-uncle Matra had been a lot more explicit when he learned where she was going: "Everyone on the Circle worlds is sex-mad. They have to be, or they'd die out."

The big turtles were not visible at the flying height she chose, but a path to the edge of the Sling was easy to find. She flew out over the ocean for a while and was gratified to see the monstrous green back of a Dowser rising from the deep. From a distance it could have been a smaller, perfectly round Sling, until the moment when the whole back opened to ten thousand mouths, and each released a hissing spout of white vapor. After ten minutes the vents slowly closed, but the Dowser remained basking in the warm surface water.

Darya realized for the first time what perfect ecological sense the Slings made on a tidal waterworld like Opal. The tides were a destructive force on worlds like Sentinel Gate, where the rising and falling ocean waters were impeded in their movement by fixed land boundaries. But here everything could move freely, with the Slings riding buoyantly on the changing water surface. In fact, although the Sling that bore Starside's spaceport must even at that very moment be moving up or down in response to the gravitational pull of Mandel and Amaranth, it was completely at rest relative to the ocean's surface. Any disruptive force came from third-order effects produced by its large area.

The life-forms should be equally safe. Unless a Dowser were unlucky enough to be caught in an area where extra-low tides left the ocean bed exposed, the animal should be totally unaware of Summertide.

Darya flew to a point near the edge of the Sling, far enough inland to feel comfortable, and set the car down. It was not raining there, and there was even a suggestion that the disk of Mandel might show its face through the clouds. She climbed out and looked around. It was strange to be on a world so empty of people that there was no one to be seen from horizon to horizon. But it was not an unpleasant experience. She walked closer to the edge of the Sling. The soft-stemmed, long-leaved plants that fringed the ocean were bowed down with yellow fruit, each one as big as her fist. If Cap could be believed, they were safe to eat, but that seemed like an unnecessary risk. Although her intestinal flora and fauna had been boosted on arrival by forms suited to Opal, the microorganisms inside her were probably still deciding who did what. She walked closer to the ragged boundary of the Sling, took off her shoes, and leaned forward to scoop up a handful of seawater. That much she was willing to chance.

She sipped a few drops from her palm. It was brackish, not quite sea-salt. Rather like the taste of her own blood.

The complicated chemical balance of a planet like Opal made her sit back on her haunches and think. In a world without continents, streams and rivers could not perform their steady leaching of salts and bases from upthrust deep structures. Microseepage of primordial methane and the higher hydrocarbons must occur on the seabed, with absorption taking place through the water column. The whole land-water balance had to be radically different from the world that she knew. Was it truly a stable situation? Or were Opal and Quake still evolving from their condition before that traumatic hour, forty-odd million years ago, when they had been cast into their wild new orbit around Mandel?

She walked a hundred meters inland and squatted cross-legged on a hummock of dark green.

The parent star showed as a bright patch, high in the cloud-covered sky. There would be at least another two hours of daylight. Now that she had taken a closer look at Opal, she saw it as a warm and friendly world, not at all the raging fury of her imagination. Surely humans could thrive there, even at Summertide. And if Opal was so pleasant, could its twin, Quake, be all so different?

But it would have to be very different, if her own conclusions had any validity. She stared at the gray horizon, unmarked by boats or other land, and reviewed for the thousandth time the train of analysis that had brought her to Dobelle. How persuasive were those results, of minimal least-square residuals? To her, there was no way that such a precise data fit could occur by coincidence. But if the results were so persuasive and indisputable to her, why had others not drawn the same conclusions?

She came up with only one answer. She had been helped in her thinking because she was a stay-at-home, a person who had never traveled between the stars. Humanity and its alien neighbors had become conditioned to think of space and distances in terms of the Bose Drive. Interstellar travel employed a precise network of Bose Nodes. The old measure of geodesic distance between two points no longer had much significance; it was the number of Bose Transitions that counted. Only the Ark dwellers, or perhaps the old colonists creeping along through Crawlspace, would see a change in a Builder artifact as generating a signal wavefront, expanding out from its point of origin and moving across the galaxy at the speed of light. And only someone like Lang, fascinated by everything to do with the Builders, might ask if there were single places and times where all those spherical wavefronts intersected.

Each piece of the argument felt weak, but taken together they left Darya fully persuaded. She felt a new anger. She *was* in the right place—or would be, if she could just leave Opal and get herself over to Quake! But instead she was stuck in a sleepy dreamland.

Sleepy dreamland. Even as those words formed in her mind there came a grating whirr from behind. A figure from a nightmare flew through the air and landed right in front of her, its six jointed legs fully extended.

If Darya did not cry out, it was only because her throat refused to function.

The creature standing in front of her lifted two of its dark-brown legs off the ground and reared up to tower over her. She saw a dark-red, segmented underside, and a short neck surrounded by bands of bright scarlet-and-white ruffles. That was topped by a white, eyeless head, twice the size of her own. There was no mouth, but a thin proboscis grew from the middle of the face and curled down to tuck into a pouch on the bottom of the pleated chin.

Darya heard a high-pitched series of chittering squeaks. Yellow open horns in the middle of the broad head turned to scan her body. Above them a pair of light-brown antennas, disproportionately long even for that great head, unfurled to form two meter-long fans that quivered delicately in the moist air.

She screamed and jumped backward, stumbling over the grassy tussock that she had been sitting on. As she did so a second figure came in a long, gliding leap to crouch down before the carapace of the first. It was another arthropod, almost as tall but with a sticklike body no thicker than Darya's arm. The creature's thin head was dominated by lemon-colored compound eyes, without eyelids. They swiveled on short eyestalks to examine her.

Darya became aware of a musky smell, complex and unfamiliar but not unpleasant, and a moment later the second being's small mouth opened. "Atvar H'sial gives greetings," a soft voice said in distorted but recognizable human speech.

The other creature said nothing. As the first shock faded Darya was able to think rationally again.

She had seen pictures. Nothing in them had suggested such a size and menacing presence, but the first arrival was a Cecropian, a member of the dominant species of the eight-hundred-world Cecropia Federation. The second animal must be an interpreter, the lower species that every Cecropian was said to need for interaction with humankind.

"I am Darya Lang," she said slowly. The other two were so alien that her facial expressions probably had little meaning to them. She smiled anyway.

There was a pause, and again she was aware of the unfamiliar odor. The Cecropian's twin yellow horns turned to-

ward her. She could see that their insides were a delicate
array of slender spiral tubes.

"Atvar H'sial offers apologies through the other." One
of the jointed arms of the silent Cecropian waved down to
indicate the smaller beast by its feet. "We think perhaps we
startled you."

Which had to be the understatement of the year. It was
disconcerting to hear words that had originated in the mind
of one being issuing from the mouth of another. But Darya
knew that the seed world for the Cecropian clade—their
mother-planet as Earth had been the mother-planet for all
humans—was a cloudy globe circling the glimmer of a red
dwarf star. In that stygian environment the Cecropians had
never developed sight. Instead they "saw" through echolocation, using high-frequency sonic pulses emitted from the
pleated resonator in the chin. The return signal was sensed
by the yellow open horns. As one side benefit, a Cecropian
knew not only the size, shape, and distance of each object
in the field of view, it could also use Doppler shift of the
sonic return to tell the speed with which targets were moving.

But there were disadvantages. With hearing usurped for
vision, communication between Cecropians had to be performed in some other way. They did it chemically, "speaking" to each other via the transmission of pheromones,
chemical messengers whose varying composition permitted
them a full and rich language. A Cecropian not only knew
what her fellows were saying; the pheromones also allowed
her to *feel* it, to know their emotions directly. The unfurled
antennas could detect and identify a single molecule of
many thousands of different airborne odors.

And to a Cecropian, any being that did not give off the
right pheromones did not exist as a communicating being.
They could "see" them all right, but they did not feel them.
Those nonentities included all humans. Darya knew that
early contacts between Cecropians and humans had been
totally unproductive until the Cecropians had produced

from within their federation a species with both the capability for speech and the power to produce and sense pheromones.

She pointed to the other creature, which had disconcertingly swiveled its yellow eyes so that one was looking at her and one at the Cecropian, Atvar H'sial. "And who are you?"

There was a long, puzzling silence. Finally the small mouth with its long whiskers of sensing antennas opened again.

"The name of the interpreter is J'merlia. He is of low intelligence and plays no part in this meeting. Please ignore his presence. It is Atvar H'sial who wishes to speak with you, Darya Lang. I seek discussion concerning the planet of Quake."

Apparently Atvar H'sial used the other in the same way as the richer worlds of the Alliance employed service robots. But it would require a very complex robot to perform the translation trick that J'merlia was doing—more sophisticated than any robot that Darya had heard of, except for those on Earth itself.

"What about Quake?"

The Cecropian crouched lower, placing its two forelegs on the ground so that the blind head was no more than four feet from Darya. Thank God it doesn't have fangs or mandibles, Darya thought, or I couldn't take this.

"Atvar H'sial is a specialist in two fields," J'merlia said. "In life-forms adapting to live with extreme environmental stress, and also in the Artificers—the vanished race whom humans choose to call the Builders. We arrived on Opal only a few short time units ago. Long since we sent request for permission to visit Quake near to Summertide. That permission had not yet been granted, but at Opal Spaceport we spoke to a human person who told that you plan to go to Quake also. Is this true?"

"Well, it's not quite true. I *want* to go to Quake." Darya

hesitated. "And I want to be there close to Summertide. But how did you find me?"

"It was simple. We followed the emergency locator on your car."

Not that, Darya thought. I mean, how did you know that I even *existed*?

But the Cecropian was continuing. "Tell us, Darya Lang. Can you arrange permission for Atvar H'sial's visit to Quake also?"

Was Darya's meaning being lost in translation? "You don't understand. I certainly *want* to visit Quake. But I don't have any control of the permits to go there. That's in the hands of two men who are on Quake at the moment, assessing conditions."

There was a brief glint of Mandel through the cloud layers. Atvar H'sial reflexively spread wide her black wing cases, revealing four delicate vestigial wings marked by red and white elongated eyespots. It was those markings, the ruffled neck, and the phenomenal sensitivity to airborne chemicals that had led the zoologist examining the first specimens to dub them fancifully "Cecropians"—though they had no more in common with Earth's cecropia moth than with any other Terran species. Darya knew that they were not even insects, though they did share with them an external skeleton, an arthropod structure, and a metamorphosis from early to adult life-stage.

The dark wings vibrated slowly. Atvar H'sial seemed lost in the sensual pleasure of warmth. There were a few seconds of silence, until the cloud gap closed and J'merlia said, "But men are males. You control them, do you not?"

"I do not control them. Not at all."

Darya wondered again about the accuracy with which she and Atvar H'sial were receiving each other's messages. The conversion process sounded as though it could never work, moving from sounds to chemical messengers and back through an alien intermediary who probably lacked a common cultural data base with either party. And she and

Atvar H'sial also lacked common cultural reference points. Atvar H'sial was a female, she knew that, but what in Cecropian culture was the role played by males? Drones? Slaves?

J'merlia produced a loud buzzing sound, but no words.

"I have no control over the men who will make the decision," Darya repeated, speaking as slowly and clearly as she could. "If they deny me access to Quake, there is nothing that I can do about it."

The buzzing sound grew louder. "Most unsatisfactory," J'merlia said at last. "Atvar H'sial must visit Quake during Summertide. We have traveled far and long to be here. It is not thinkable to stop now. If you cannot obtain permission for us and for yourself, then other methods must be sought."

The great blind head swung close, so that Darya could see every bristle and pore on it. The proboscis reached out to touch her hand. It felt warm and slightly sticky. She forced herself not to move.

"Darya Lang," J'merlia said. "When beings possess a common interest, they should work together to achieve that interest. No matter what obstacles others attempt to put in their way, they should not be deterred. If you could guarantee us your cooperation, there is a way that Darya Lang and Atvar H'sial might visit Quake. Together. With or without official permission."

Was J'merlia misinterpreting Atvar H'sial's thoughts, or was Darya herself misunderstanding the Cecropian's intention? If not, then Darya was being recruited by this improbable alien to join a secret project.

She felt wary, but caution was mixed with a thrill of anticipation. The Cecropian could almost have been reading Darya's own earlier thoughts. If Rebka and Perry agreed to let her go to Quake, all well and good. But if not . . . there might be another project in the making.

And not just any project; an enterprise designed to take her to her objective—at Summertide.

Darya could hear the whistle of air as it was pumped continuously through the Cecropian's spiracles. The proboscis of Atvar H'sial was oozing a dark-brown fluid, and the eyeless face was a demon taken from a bad childhood dream. By Darya's side, the black, eight-legged stick figure of J'merlia was drawn from the same nightmare.

But humans had to learn to ignore appearance. No two beings who shared common thinking processes and common goals should be truly alien to each other.

Darya leaned forward. "Very well, Atvar H'sial. I am interested to hear what you have to say. Tell me more."

She was certainly not ready to *agree* to anything; but surely there could be no harm in *listening*?

CHAPTER 6

Summertide
minus twenty-nine.

THE UMBILICAL AND the capsules that rode along it had been in position for at least four million years when humans colonized Dobelle. Like anything of Builder construction, it had been made to last. The system worked perfectly. It had been studied extensively, but although the analyses told a good deal about Builder fabrication methods, they revealed nothing about Builder physiology or habits.

Did the Builders breathe? The cars were open, built of transparent materials, and lacking any type of airlock.

Did the Builders sleep and exercise? There was nothing that could be identified as a bed, or a place to rest, or a means of recreation.

Then surely the Builders at least had to eat and to excrete. Except that although the journey from Opal to Quake took many hours, there were no facilities for food storage or preparation, and no facilities for the evacuation of waste products.

The only tentative conclusion that human engineers could reach was that the Builders were *big*. Each capsule was a monster, a cylinder over twenty meters long and almost that much across, and inside it was all empty space. On the other hand, there was no evidence that the cars had been used by the Builders themselves—maybe they had been intended *only* as carriers of cargo. But if that were true, why were they also equipped with internal controls that permitted changes to be made in speed along the Umbilical?

While students of history argued about the nature and character of the Builders, and theoreticians worried about inexplicable elements of Builder science, more practical minds went to work to make the Umbilical of use to the colonists. Quake had minerals and fuels. Opal had neither, but it possessed living space and a decent climate. The transportation system between the two was much too valuable to be wasted.

They began with the amenities necessary to make a comfortable journey between the components of the planetary doublet. They could not change the basic size and shape of the capsules; like most Builder products, the cars were integrated modules, near-indestructible and incapable of structural modification. But the cars were easily made airtight and fitted with airlocks and pressure adjustment equipment. Simple kitchens were installed, along with toilets, medical facilities, and rest areas. Finally, in recognition of the discomfort of planet-based humans with great heights, the transparent exteriors were fitted with panels that could be polarized to an opaque gray. The main observation port lay only at the upper end of the capsule.

Rebka was cursing that last modification as their car came closer to Quake. While they were ascending to Midway Station and beyond he had enjoyed an intriguing view of the planet ahead of them—enough to be willing to leave for a later occasion an exploration of the Builder artifact of Midway Station itself. He had assumed that he would continue to see more and more details of Quake until they finally landed. Instead, the car inexplicably swung end-over-end when they were still a few hundred kilometers above the surface. In place of Quake he was suddenly provided with an uninformative and annoying view of Opal's shifting cloud patterns.

He turned to Max Perry. "Can you swing us back? I can't see a thing."

"Not unless you want us to crawl the rest of the way." Perry was already jumpy in anticipation of their arrival. "We'll be entering Quake's atmosphere any minute now. The car has to be bottom-down for aerodynamic stability, or we have to crawl. In fact . . ." He paused, and his face became taut with concentration. "Listen."

It took a moment for Rebka to catch it; then his ears picked up the faintest high-pitched whistle, sounding through the capsule's walls. It was the first evidence of contact with Quake, of rarefied air resisting the passage of the plunging capsule. Their rate of descent must already be slowing.

Five minutes later another sensory signal was added. They were low enough for pressure equalization to begin, and air from Quake was being bled in. A faintly sulfurous odor filled the interior. At the same time the capsule began to shake and shiver with the buffeting of winds. Rebka felt an increased force pushing him down into the padded seat.

"Three minutes," Perry said. "We're on final deceleration."

Rebka looked across at him. They were about to land on the planet that Perry described as too dangerous for visitors, but there was no sign of fear in Perry's voice or on his face. He showed nervousness, but it could just as well be the excitement and anticipation of a man returning home after too long a time away.

How was that possible, if Quake was so dangerous a death trap?

The car slowed and stopped, and the door silently opened. Rebka, following Perry outside, felt that his suspicions were confirmed. They were stepping out onto a level surface, a blue-gray dusty plain sparsely covered with dark-green shrubs and a low-profile ochre lichen. It was certainly dry and hot, and the smell of sulfur in the midafternoon air was stronger; but less than a kilometer away Rebka could see the gleam of water, with taller plants on its boundary, and near them stood a herd of low, slow-moving animals. They looked like herbivores, quietly grazing.

There were no erupting volcanoes, no earth tremors, and no monstrous subterranean violence. Quake was a peaceful, sleepy planet, drowsy in the heat, its inhabitants preparing to endure the higher temperatures that went with Summertide.

Before Rebka could say anything, Perry was staring all around and shaking his head.

"I don't know what's going on here." His face was puzzled. "I said we'd find trouble, and I wasn't joking. It's too damned quiet. And we're less than thirty days from Summertide, the biggest one ever."

Rebka shrugged. If Perry were playing some deep game, Rebka could not see through it. "Everything looks fine to me."

"It does. And that's what's wrong." Perry waved an arm, to take in all the scene around them. "It shouldn't be like this. I've been here before at this time of year, many times. We should be seeing quakes and eruptions by now—big ones. We should *feel* them, under our feet. There should be ten times as much dust in the air." He sounded genuinely confused.

Rebka nodded, then turned slowly through a full three hundred and sixty degrees, taking plenty of time for a thorough inspection of their surroundings.

Right in front of them stood the broad foot of the Umbilical. It touched the surface, but it was not held by a mechanical tether. The coupling was performed electromagnetically, field-bound to Quake's metal-rich mantle. Perry had told him that it was necessary because of the instability of the planetary surface near Summertide. That was plausible, and consistent with Perry's claim about the violence of the event. Why else would the Builders have avoided a real tether? But mere plausibility did not make the statement *true*.

Beyond the Umbilical, in the direction of Mandel's setting disk, stood a brooding range of low mountains, purple-gray in the dusty air. The peaks were uniform in size and strangely regular in their spacing. From their harsh profile and the steep angle of their ascent, they had to be volcanic. But he could see no pall of smoke standing above them, nor any evidence of recent lava flows. He looked closer. The ground beneath his feet was smooth and fissure-free, with no gaps in plant growth to testify to recent fracturing of the surface.

So this was Quake, the great and terrible? Rebka had slept easy in environments ten times as threatening. Without a word he began walking toward the lake.

Perry hurried after him. "Where are you going?" He was nervous, and it was not simulated tension.

"I want to have a look at those animals. If it's safe to do it."

"It should be. But let me go first." Perry's voice was agitated as he moved on in front. "I know the terrain."

Nice and thoughtful of you, Rebka thought. Except that I don't see a thing in the terrain that *needs* knowing. The ground was marked here and there by patches of igneous outcrops and broken basaltic rubble, a sure sign of old volcanic activity, and the footing was sometimes difficult and uneven. But Rebka would have no more trouble traveling across it than Perry.

As they moved toward the water the going actually became easier. Closer to the lake lay a sward of springy dark-green ground cover that had managed to find purchase on the dry rocks. Small animals, all invertebrates, scuttled to hide away in it from the approaching strangers. The herbivores held their ground until the two men were a few meters away, then unhurriedly sidled off toward the lake. They were round-backed creatures with radial symmetry, multilegged and with cropping mouths set all around their periphery.

"You know what's bugging me, don't you?" Rebka asked suddenly.

Perry shook his head.

"All this." Rebka gestured at the plant and animal life around them. "You insist that humans mustn't come to Quake too near to Summertide. You say we can't survive here, and I'm supposed to tell Julius Graves and the others that they are not allowed to visit, and we'll lose the revenue they'd generate for Dobelle. But *they* stay here." He pointed to the animals making their slow way to the water's edge. "They survive, apparently with no trouble. What can they do that we can't do?"

"Two things." They had reached the lakeside, and Perry had for some reason lost his nervousness. "First of all, they avoid the surface of Quake during Summertide. Each one of the animals that you'll find on Quake either dies before Summertide, and its eggs hatch after summer is all over, or else it estivates—hides away for the summer. Those herbivores are all amphibians. In a few more days they'll go down into the lakes, dig deep into the mud at the bottom, and sleep until it's safe to come out again. We can't do that. At least, you and I can't. Maybe the Cecropians can."

"We could do something like that. We could make habitats, domes under the lakes."

"All right. We could, but I doubt if Darya Lang and the others would agree to it. Anyway, that's only half the story. I said they do two things. The other thing they do is, they breed *fast*. A big new litter every season. We can mate all we want to, every day, but we won't match that." Perry's grin had no humor in it. "They have to do it here. The death rate for animals and plants on Quake is over ninety percent per year. Evolution really pushes, so they've adapted as far as they can adapt. Even so, nine out of every ten will die at Summertide. Are you willing to try odds like that? Would you let Darya Lang and Julius Graves risk them?"

It was a powerful argument—*if* Rebka were willing to accept Perry's claim of Summertide violence. And so far he was not. A close approach to Mandel, consistent with Perry's claim about the violence of Summertide, would exert great tidal forces on Quake. No one could doubt that. But it was not clear how much those land tides would damage the surface. Quake's flora and fauna had survived for over forty million years. And that included dozens of Grand Conjunctions, even if there had been no humans to observe them. Why would it not easily survive another?

"Let's go." Hans Rebka had made up his mind. Mandel was close to setting, and he wanted to be off the planet before they were reduced to depending on Amaranth's dimmer glow. He was convinced that Perry was not telling him everything; that the man had his own reasons for trying to keep people away from Quake. But even if Max Perry were right, Rebka could not justify closing Quake. The evidence that the world was dangerous was just not there to send back to the government of the Phemus Circle.

The arguments all seemed to be the other way round. The native animals might have trouble making it through Summertide, but they did not have human knowledge and resources. Based on what Rebka could see, he would be quite willing to spend Summertide here himself.

"We have a duty to tell people the odds," he went on. "But we are not their guardians. If they choose to come here, knowing the dangers, we shouldn't stop them."

Perry hardly seemed to be listening. He was staring all around, frowning up at the sky and down at the ground and over to the distant line of hills.

"There's no way this can happen, you know," he said. His voice was perplexed. "Where's it all going?"

"Where's what all going?" Rebka was ready to leave.

"The energy. The tidal forces are pumping energy in— from Mandel and Amaranth and Gargantua. And none of it is coming out. That means there has to be some monstrous internal storage—"

He was interrupted by a flash of ruddy light from the west. Both men looked that way and saw that between them and the setting sphere of Mandel a line of dark, spreading fountains had appeared, shot with fire and rising from the distant mountains.

Seconds later the sound wave arrived; the ground shock came later yet, but the animals did not wait. At the first bright flash they were heading for the water, moving much faster than Rebka had realized they could ever manage.

"Blow out! We'll get flying rocks!" Perry was shouting, through a rumble like thunder. He pointed to the multiple plumes. "Molten, some of 'em, and we're within easy range. Come on."

He started running back toward the Umbilical, while Rebka hesitated. The line of eruptions was curiously orderly, their spreading darkness bursting precisely from every third peak. He gave one quick look the other way—would water be a safer haven?—and then followed Perry. The ground began to shake, to seesaw back and forth so that he was close to losing his balance. He felt he had to slow down, until a mass of glowing ejecta, a semimolten rock the size of an aircar, plummeted in and lay sizzling within twenty meters of him.

Perry was already in the capsule at the foot of the Umbilical, holding the lower entry port wide open.

Rebka hurled himself through it headfirst, sacrificing dignity for speed. "All right. I'm in. Move it!"

Perry ran madly up the stairs to the control-and-observation chamber, and the car was starting into upward motion before Rebka had picked himself up and checked for injuries. Instead of securing the hatch and following Perry, he turned to the entry port and left it open a foot or so. He peered out.

Whistling lumps of rock and lava continued to pelt the area they had left. He could see fires as the ejecta seared the brush and the dry ground, and hear occasional fragments smacking into the Umbilical above and below them. They would do no damage, unless one entered the open port. He would have time enough to see it coming and to slam the door closed.

The most vulnerable items were the imported aircars. They sat in a neat line at the foot of the Umbilical, built by humans and brought from Opal for local exploration and use. As Rebka watched, a smoking chunk of rock hurtled toward the top of one of them. When it bounced away without making contact, he realized that the cars were sitting beneath a protective sheet of transparent Builder material—cannibalized, probably, from part of Midway Station.

He looked to the horizon. From their present height of two or three hundred meters he could see a long way through Quake's murky air. The surface was aflame with small flash fires, all the way to the distant peaks. Rising smoke brought a pungent aroma to his nostrils, resinous and aromatic, and the ground below was shimmering with heat and blurred by dust.

It was clear that the source of the disturbance was restricted to the single line of volcanoes that lay between them and Mandel's glowing face, low to the west. Every third peak carried a dusky plume and a pall of smoke above it. But already the force of the eruption was dwindling. The smoke clouds were no longer shot through with crimson and orange, and fewer rocks came sailing through the air toward the car. The herbivores had disappeared long ago, presumably hiding in the protective depths of the lake. They would know when to come out again.

Perry had left the controls and was crouched at Rebka's side. The car's movement up the Umbilical had ceased.

"All right." Rebka prepared to close the port. "I'm persuaded. I wouldn't want to take the responsibility for allowing people here at Summertide. Let's get out of here and head back to Opal."

But Perry was holding the door open and shaking his head. "I'd like to go back down."

"Why? Do you want to get killed?"

"Of course not. I want to take a good look at what's happening, and really understand it."

"Quake is approaching Summertide, Commander. That's what's happening. The volcanoes and earthquakes are starting, just the way you said they would."

"No. They're not." Perry was more contemplative than alarmed. "There's a mystery here. Remember, I've been on Quake before at this time of year, many times. What we just saw is nothing, just a little local fireworks. We should have found *more* activity than we did, one hell of a lot more. The surface was quiet when we arrived; it should have been shaking all the time. And the eruptions looked impressive, but the ground tremors were nothing. You saw how quickly they died away." He gestured out of the port. "Look at it now, everything becoming quiet again."

"I'm no planetary geologist, but that's just what you would expect." Rebka could not understand what was going on in Perry's head. Did the man want people there at Summertide, or did he not? Now that there was a good argument against it, Perry seemed to be changing his mind. "You expect stress buildup and stress release. The internal forces build up for a while, until they reach a critical value, and then they let go. Quiet spells, and violent ones."

"Not here." Perry finally closed the port. "Not at Summertide. Think of it, Captain. This isn't normal planetary vulcanism. Opal and Quake revolve around each other every eight hours. Tidal forces from Mandel and Amaranth squeeze and pull their interiors every revolution. At normal Summertide those forces are huge, and the Grand Conjunction makes them even bigger—hundreds of times stronger than they are during the rest of the year."

He sat down in the lower cargo hold and stared at the wall. After a few moments, Rebka went up to the control chamber and restarted their ascent himself. When he came down again, Perry had not moved.

"Come on, snap out of it. I believe you; the tidal forces are strong. But that's true for Opal as well as Quake."

"It is." Perry finally roused himself and stood up. "But the effects are damped on Opal. The ocean surface deforms freely and reaches new high and low tides every four hours. Any seabed changes—seaquakes and eruptions—are damped by the depth of water above them. But the land tides on Quake have no oceans to reduce their effects. At this time of year Quake should be active *all the time.* It isn't. So. Where is all that energy going?"

Perry dropped back into his seat and sat there frowning at nothing.

Rebka felt oddly dissatisfied as the upward speed of the car increased and the soft whistle of rapid travel through Quake's atmosphere began. He had been to Quake and seen evidence for himself. The place seemed fully as dangerous as Perry had warned. And yet Perry himself was not *afraid* of Quake. Not at all. He wanted to go back there—while an eruption was still in progress!

Rebka reached a conclusion. If he were to understand Perry, he had to have more data. He sat down facing the younger man.

"All right, Commander Perry. So it doesn't look the way you expected. I can't judge that. Tell me, then, what does Quake *usually* look like at this time of year?"

But that was exactly the wrong question. Perry's look of concentrated thought vanished. An expression of indefinable sadness crept onto his face. Rebka sat waiting for an answer, until he realized after a couple of minutes that he was not going to receive one. Instead of pulling Max Perry out of his reverie, that question had driven him deeper into it. The man was far gone, off in some strange fugue of unhappy memories.

Memories of what? Surely of Quake at Summertide.

Rebka did not speak again. Instead he swore an internal oath, stared up the Umbilical at the distant knot of Midway Station, and admitted an unpleasant truth. He had not wanted this job, a nursemaid task that had interrupted the most challenging project of his career. He had resented being taken away from Paradox, he resented being assigned to Dobelle, he resented Max Perry, and he resented having to worry about the interrupted career of a minor bureaucrat.

But his own pride would not allow him to abandon the job until he knew for certain what had destroyed the man. For Perry *was* destroyed, even if it did not show on the surface.

One other thing was clear. Whatever had destroyed Perry lived on Quake, close to Summertide.

Which meant that Rebka himself would surely be returning, to a place and to a time where all the evidence proved that humans could not survive.

ARTIFACT: UMBILICAL.
UAC#: 269
Galactic Coordinates: 26,837.186/17,428.947/363.554
Name: Umbilical
Star/planet association: Mandel/Dobelle (doublet)
Bose Access Node: 513
Estimated age: 4.037 $\pm$ 0.15 Megayears

Exploration History: Discovered by remote sensor observation during the unmanned stellar flyby of Mandel in E. 1446. First close inspection performed in manned flyby of E. 1513 (Dobelle and Hinchcliffe), first visit by colony ship in E. 1668 (Skyscan class, Wu and Tanaka). First used by Dobelle settlers, E. 1742. Employed routinely as working system since E. 1778.

Physical Description: The Umbilical forms a transportation system that joins the twin planets of the Dobelle system, Opal (originally Ehrenknechter) and Quake (originally Castelnuovo). Twelve thousand kilometers long and forty to sixty meters wide, the Umbilical forms a cylinder which is permanently tethered on Opal (seabed tether) and electromagnetically coupled to Quake. Quake coupling is broken at the closest approach of the Dobelle system's highly eccentric orbit to the stellar primary of Mandel. This closest approach occurs every 1.43 standard years.

Variation in Umbilical length is achieved via "the Winch," employing a local space-time singularity (presumed an artifact), which enables the Umbilical to adapt automatically to variations in Opal/Quake separation. The Winch also performs automatic withdrawal of the Umbilical from the surface of Quake at times of Mandel tidal maximum ("Summertide"). Control technique is understood operationally, but the trigger signal has not been determined (i.e., as time signal, force signal, or some other). Midway Station (9,781 kilometers from Opal center of mass, 12,918 kilometers from Quake center of mass) permits the addition to or removal from the Umbilical of payloads intended for free space launch or capture.

Note: The Umbilical is one of the simplest and most comprehensible of all Builder artifacts, and it is for that reason of less interest to most serious students of Builder technology. And yet it is also something of a mystery in its own right, since although simple it is one of the most recent feats of Builder construction (less than five million years). Some archeo-analysts have conjectured that this fact indicates the beginning of a decline in Builder society, culminating in the collapse of their civilization and their disappearance from the Galactic scene more than three million years ago.

Physical Nature: Defect-free solid hydrogen support cables with stabilized muonium splicing. Cable tensions rival those of human and Cecropian skyhooks but do not exceed them.

Transportation car propulsion is by linear synchronous motors with conventional power trains. The technique for cable-and-car attachments is unclear, but related to the Cocoon system free-space nets (see Cocoon, Entry 1).

The nature of the Winch is also debated, but it is probably a Builder artifact, rather than a natural feature of the Dobelle system.

Intended Purpose: Transportation system. Until the arrival of humans, this system had been unused for at least three million years. Currently it is reported in regular operation. There is no indication of other and earlier uses.

> —From the *Lang Universal Artifact Catalog,*
> Fourth Edition.

CHAPTER 7

Summertide
minus twenty-seven.

QUAKE WAS CHANGING. Not in the way that Max Perry had warned, moving as Summertide approached from a parched but peaceful world of high seismic activity to a trembling inferno of molten lava flows and fissured ground. Instead, Quake in this year of the Grand Conjunction had become—unpredictable.

And in its own way, Opal might be changing just as much. More than anyone on the planet realized.

That thought had come to Rebka as they were flying back around Opal, from the foot of the Umbilical to the Starside spaceport where Darya Lang would be waiting for them.

Six days earlier the journey around the clouded planet to the Umbilical had been dull, with no turbulence and little to see but uniform gray above and below. Now, with Summertide still twenty-seven Days away, the car was buffeted and beaten by swirling and violent winds. Sudden updrafts ripped at the lifting surfaces and jolted the fuselage. Max Perry was forced to take the aircar higher and higher to escape the driving rain, black thunderheads, and whirling vortices of air and water.

So the inhabitants of Opal were convinced that they would be safe, were they, even with tides far greater than normal?

Hans Rebka was not so sure.

"You're making a big assumption," he told Perry, as they began a descent through choppier air for their approach to Starside port. "You think Opal's tides this year will be just the same as at other Summertides, but bigger."

"That's overstating things." Once all sight of Quake had been lost under Opal's ubiquitous cloud layer, Perry's other personality had surfaced again: cool, stiff, and indifferent to most events. He did not want to discuss their experiences on the surface of Quake, nor his mystification at what was happening there. "I do not say that nothing different will occur on Opal," he went on. "Yet I believe that is not far from the truth. We may get forces too great for some of the bigger Slings, and one or two of them may break up. But I see no danger to people. If necessary, everyone on Opal can take to the water and ride out Summertide at sea."

Rebka was silent, holding on to the arms of his seat as they dropped through an air pocket that left both men floating free for a second or two. "It may not be like that," he said, as soon as his heart was no longer rising to stick in his throat.

Again and again he had the urge to poke and probe at Max Perry and watch his reactions. It was like control theory, feeding a black box with a defined set of inputs and monitoring the output. Do that often enough, and the theory said one could learn precisely all of the box's functions, though not, perhaps, *why* it performed them. But in Perry's case, there seemed to be two different boxes. One of them was inhabited by a capable, thoughtful, and likable human. The other was a mollusc, retreating into its protective and impervious shell whenever certain stimuli presented themselves.

"This situation reminds me of Pelican's Wake," Rebka went on. "Did you hear what happened there, Commander?"

"If I did, I forgot it." That was not the sort of reaction that Rebka was seeking, but Max Perry had an excuse. His attention was on the automatic stabilization system as it fought to bring them down to a smooth landing.

"They had a situation not too different from Opal," Rebka continued. "Except that it involved a plant-to-animal mass ratio, not sea tides.

"When the colonists first landed there, everything was fine. But every forty years Pelican's Wake passes through part of a cometary cloud. Little bodies of volatiles, mostly small enough to vaporize in the atmosphere and never make it to the ground. The humidity and temperature take a quick jump, a few percent and a few degrees. The plant-animal ratio swings down, oxygen drops a bit, then in less than a year it all creeps back to normal. No big deal.

"Everyone thought so. They went on thinking it, even when their astronomers predicted that on the next passage through the cloud, Pelican's Wake would pick up thirty percent more material than usual."

"I think I remember it now." Perry was showing a distant and polite interest. "It's a case we studied before I came to Dobelle. Something went wrong, and they came close to losing the whole colony, right?"

"Depends who you talk to." Rebka hesitated. How much should he say? "Nothing could be proved, but I happen to think you're correct. They came close. But my point is this: Nothing went wrong that could have been *predicted* with anybody's physical models. The higher level of comet material influx changed the Pelican's Wake biosphere to a new stable state. Oxygen went from fourteen to three percent in three weeks. It stayed there, too, until a terraforming gang could get in and start to change it back. That sudden switch would have killed almost everybody, because in the time available they wouldn't have had a hope of shuttling everyone out."

Max Perry nodded. "I know. Except that one man down on Pelican's Wake decided to move people offworld anyway, long before they got near the comet shower. He'd seen fossil evidence for changes, right? It's a classic case—the man on the spot knew more than anyone light-years away *could* know. He overrode instructions from his own headquarters, and he was a hero for doing it."

"Not quite. He got *chewed out* for doing it." The car had touched down and was taxiing toward the edge of the port, and Rebka was ready to let the subject drop. It was not the right time to tell Max Perry the identity of the man involved. And although he had been reprimanded in public, he had been congratulated in private for his presumption in countermanding a Sector Coordinator's written instructions. The fact that his immediate supervisors had *deliberately* left him ignorant of those written instructions was never mentioned. It seemed to be part of the Phemus Circle's government philosophy: Troubleshooters work better when they do not know too much. More and more, he was convinced that he had not been given all the facts before he was sent to Dobelle.

"All I'm saying is that you could face a similar situation on Opal," he went on. "When a system is disturbed by a periodic force, increasing the force may *not* simply lead to a bigger disturbance of the same kind. You may hit a bifurcation and change to a totally different final state. Suppose the tides on Opal become big enough to interact chaotically? You'll have turbulence everywhere—whirlpools and waterspouts. Monstrous solitons, maybe, isolated waves a mile or two high.

"Boats wouldn't live through that, nor would the Slings. Could you evacuate everyone if you had to, during Summertide? I don't mean to sea—I mean right off-planet?"

"I doubt it." Perry was switching off the engine and shaking his head. "I can be more definite than that. No, we couldn't. Anyway, where would we take them *to*? Gargantua has four satellites nearly as big as Opal, and a couple of them have their own atmospheres. But they're methane and nitrogen, not oxygen—and they're far too cold. The only other place is Quake." He stared at Rebka. "I assume we've given up on the idea that anyone should go *there*?"

The torrential rain that had plagued their approach to Starside had eased, and the car had come to a halt close to the building that Perry had assigned to Darya Lang as living quarters.

Hans Rebka stood up stiffly from his seat and rubbed at his knees. Darya Lang was supposed to be waiting to meet them, and she must surely have heard the aircar's approach. But there was no sign of her at the building. Instead, a tall, skeletal man with a bald and bulging head was standing half-clear of the overhanging eaves, staring at the arriving car. He was holding a garish umbrella above his head. The shimmering white of his suit, with its gold epaulets and light-blue trim, could have come only from the spun-fiber cocoon of a Ditron.

From a distance he appeared elegant and commanding, even though his face and scalp had been burned purple-red by hard radiation. Close up, Rebka could see that his lips and eyebrows jerked and twitched uncontrollably.

"Did you know he'd be here?" Rebka jerked a thumb below the window level of the car, so that the newcomer could not see it. He did not need to mention the stranger's identity. Members of the Alliance councils were seldom seen, but the uniform was familiar to every clade on every world in the spiral arm.

"No. But I'm not surprised." Max Perry held the car door so that Rebka could step down. "We've been gone for six days, and his schedule fitted that time slot."

The man did not move as Perry and Rebka stepped out of the car and hurried to shelter under the broad eaves. He folded his umbrella and stood for half a minute, ignoring the raindrops that spattered his bald head. Finally he turned to meet them.

"Good day. But not good weather. And I gather that it is getting worse." The voice matched the man, big and hollow, with an edge of roughness overlaid on the sophisticated accent of a native of Miranda. He held out his left wrist, where identification was permanently imprinted. "I am Julius Graves. I assume that you received notice of our arrival."

"We did," Perry said.

He sounded ill at ease. The presence of a council member from any clade was enough to make most people ponder their past sins, or realize the limits of their authority. Rebka wondered if Graves might have a second agenda for his visit to Opal. One thing he did know: Council members were kept desperately busy, and they did not like to waste time on incidentals.

"The information sheets did not provide details as to the reason for your visit," he said, and held out his hand. "I am Captain Rebka, at your service, and this is Commander Perry. Why are you visiting the Dobelle system?"

Graves did not move. He stood silent and motionless for another five seconds. At last he inclined his bulging head to the two men, nodded, and sneezed violently. "Perhaps your question is better answered inside. I am chilled. I have been waiting here since sunrise, expecting the return of the others."

Perry and Rebka exchanged glances. The others? And a return from where?

"They left eight hours ago," Graves continued, "at the time of my own arrival. Your weather prediction indicates that a—" The deep-set eyes clouded, and there was a moment's silence. "That a Level Five storm is heading for Starside Port. For strangers to Circle environments, such storms must be dangerous. I am worried, and I wish to talk to them."

Rebka nodded. One question was answered. Darya Lang had been joined on Opal by more visitors from outside the Phemus Circle. But who were they?

"Better check the arrival manifests," he said softly to Perry. "See what we've got."

"Do that if you wish." Graves stared at him; the pale-blue eyes seemed to see right into Rebka's head. The councilor flopped onto a chair of yellow cane and plaited reeds, sniffed, and went on. "But you do not need to check. I can assure you that Darya Lang of the Fourth Alliance has been joined on Opal by Atvar H'sial and J'merlia of the Cecropia Federation. After I met them I examined the backgrounds of all three. They are what they claim to be."

Rebka did the calculation and started to open his mouth, but Perry was well ahead of him.

"That's impossible!"

Graves stared, and the busy eyebrows twitched.

"One day, you said, since your arrival here," Perry said. "If you sent an inquiry through the nearest Bose Network point as soon as you got here, and it was forwarded through the Nodes and answered *instantly,* the total turnaround time can't be less than a full standard day—three Opal days. I know, I've tried it often enough."

Perry's quite right, Rebka thought. And he's quicker than I realized. But he's making a tactical error. Council members don't lie, and it's asking for trouble to accuse them of it.

But Graves was smiling for the first time since they had met. "Commander Perry, I am grateful to you. You have simplified my next task." He pulled a spotless white cloth from his pocket, wiped the damp top of his hairless head with it, and tapped his massive and bulging brow.

"How can I know that, you ask. I am Julius Graves, as I said. But in a sense I am also Steven Graves." He leaned back in the chair, closed his eyes for a few seconds, blinked, and went on. "When I was invited to join the Council, it was explained to me that I would need to know the history, biology, and psychology of every intelligent and potentially intelligent species in the whole spiral arm. That data volume exceeds the capacity of any human memory.

"I was offered a choice: I could accept an inorganic high-density memory implant—cumbersome and heavy enough that my head and neck would need a permanent brace. That is preferred by Council members from the Zardalu Communion. Or I could develop an interior mnemonic twin, a second pair of cerebral hemispheres grown from my own brain tissue and used solely for memory storage and recall. That would fit inside my own skull, posterior to my cerebral cortex, with minimal cranial expansion.

"I chose the second solution. I was warned that because the new hemispheres were an integral part of me, their efficiency for storage and recall would be affected by my own physical condition—how tired I was, or whether I had been taking stimulants of any kind. I tell you this so that you will not think I am antisocial if I refuse a drink, or that I am a valetudinarian, excessively concerned with my own health. I have to be careful about rest and recreational stimulants, or the mnemonic interface is impaired. And Steven does not like that."

He smiled, and conflicting expressions chased themselves across his face, just as a sudden howl of wind hit the low building from outside. The fiber walls shivered. "For what I was *not* told, you see," he went on, "was that my interior mnemonic twin might develop *consciousness*—self-awareness. It happened. As I said, I am Julius Graves, but I am also Steven Graves. He is the source of my information on Darya Lang and on the Cecropian, Atvar H'sial. Now. Can we proceed to other business?"

"Can Steven talk?" Rebka asked. Max Perry seemed to be in shock. One member of the Council poking around in one's affairs was bad enough—now they had *two* of them. And was Julius Graves always in charge? From the changing expressions on his face, a continuous battle could be going on inside.

Graves shook his head. "Steven cannot talk. He also cannot feel, see, touch, or hear, except as I send my own sensory inputs to mnemonic storage through an added corpus callosum. But Steven can *think*—better, he insists, than I can. As he tells me, he has more time for it. And he sends signals back to me, his own thoughts, in the form of returning memories. I can translate those, well enough so that most people would believe Steven to be speaking directly. For instance."

He was silent for a few moments. When he spoke his voice was noticeably younger and more lively. *"Hi. Glad to be here on Opal. No one said that the weather here would be so lousy, but one nice thing about being where I am, you don't get wet when it rains."* The voice returned to its hollow, gravelly tone. "My apologies. Steven has a fondness for weak jokes and an appalling sense of humor. I fail to control both, but I do try to screen them. And I confess that I also allow myself to become too dependent on Steven's knowledge. For instance, he holds most of our local information about conditions on this planet, while my own learning is sadly deficient. I deplore my own laziness.

"But now, may we continue with business? I am here on Dobelle regarding a matter for which humor is not at all appropriate."

"Murder," Perry muttered after a long pause. The height of the storm was almost there, and as the sounds of the wind increased he had become more clearly uncomfortable. Unable to sit still, he was prowling in front of the window, looking out at the threshing ferns and tall grasses, or up at racing clouds ruddy with the rusty light of Amaranth.

"Murder," he repeated. "Multiple murder. That's what your request to visit Opal said."

"It did. But only because I was reluctant to send word of a more serious charge over the Bose Network." Julius Graves was surely not joking now. "A more accurate word is *genocide*. I will moderate that, if you prefer, to *suspected* genocide."

He stared quietly around him, while new rain lashed the walls and roof. The other two men had frozen, Max Perry motionless in front of the window, Hans Rebka on the edge of his seat.

"Genocide. Suspected genocide. Is there a significant difference?" Rebka asked at last.

"Not from some points of view." The full lips twitched and trembled. "There is no statute of limitations, in time or space, for the investigation of either. But we have only circumstantial evidence, without proof and without confession. It is my task to seek those. I intend to find them here on Opal."

Graves reached into the blue-trimmed pocket of his jacket and produced two image cubes. "Improbable as it seems, these are the accused criminals, Elena and Geni Carmel, twenty-one standard years old, born and raised on Shasta. And, as you can see, identical twin sisters."

He held the cubes out to the other two men. Rebka saw only two young women, deeply tanned, big-eyed, and pleasant looking, dressed in matching outfits of russet green and soft brown. But Max Perry apparently saw something else in those pictures. He gave a gasp of recognition, leaned forward, and grabbed the data cubes. He stared into them. It was twenty more seconds before the tension drained from him and he looked up.

Julius Graves was watching both men. Rebka was suddenly convinced that those misty blue eyes missed nothing. The impression of quaintness and eccentricity might be genuine, or it might be a pose—but underneath it lay a strange and powerful intelligence. And fools did not become council members.

"You seem to know these girls, Commander Perry," Graves said. "Do you? If you have ever met them, it is vital that I know when and where."

Perry shook his head. His face was even paler than usual. "No. It's just that for a few moments, when I first saw the cubes, I thought they were . . . someone else. Someone I knew a long time ago."

"Someone?" Graves waited, and then, when it was clear that Perry would say nothing more, he went on. "I propose to keep nothing from you, and I strongly urge you to keep nothing from me. With your permission, I will allow Steven to tell the rest of this. He has the most complete information, and I find it difficult to speak without emotion clouding my statements."

The twitching ceased. Graves's face steadied and took on

the look of a younger and happier man. "Okay, here goes," he said. "The sad story of Elena and Geni Carmel. Shasta's a rich world, and it lets its youth do pretty much what they like. When the Carmel twins hit twenty-one they were given a little space tourer, the *Summer Dreamboat,* as a present. But instead of just hopping around their local system, the way most kids do, they talked their family into sticking a Bose Drive in the ship. Then they set off on a real travel binge: nine worlds of the Fourth Alliance, three of the Zardalu Communion. On their final planet, they decided to see life 'in the rough'—that's how their 'grams home put it. It meant they wanted to live in comfort but observe a backward world.

"They landed on Pavonis Four and set up a luxury tent. Pav Four's a poor, marshy planet of the Communion. Poor now, I should say—rich enough before human developers had a go at it. Along the way, a native amphibian species known as the Bercia were a nuisance. They were almost wiped out, but by that time the planet was picked clean and the developers left. The surviving members of the Bercia— what few there were—were given the probationary status of a potential intelligence. They were protected. At last."

Graves paused. His face became a changing mask of expressions. It was no longer obvious whether it was Julius or Steven who was speaking.

"Were the Bercia intelligent?" he said softly. "The universe will never know. What we do know is that the Bercia are now *extinct.* Their last two lodges were wiped out two months ago . . . by Elena and Geni Carmel."

"But not by design, surely?" Perry was still clutching the data cubes and staring down at them. "It must have been an accident."

"It may well have been." From the serious manner, Julius Graves was again in charge. "We do not know, because when it happened the Carmel twins did not stay to explain. Inexplicably, they fled. They continued to flee, until one week ago we closed the Bose Network to them. And now they can flee no farther."

The storm had arrived in full force. From outside the building a mournful wail sounded, the cry of a siren audible over the scream of wind and the thresh of rain on the roof. Rebka could still listen to Graves, but some other conditioning in Perry took over. At the first note of the siren he headed for the door.

"A landing! That siren means someone's in trouble. They're crazy, if they don't have the right experience, in a Level Five storm . . ."

He was gone. Julius Graves began to rise slowly to his feet. He was restrained by Hans Rebka's grip on his arm.

"They fled," Rebka prompted. Through the rain-streaked window he could see the lights of a descending aircar, dipping and veering drunkenly in treacherous crosswinds. It was only a few meters from the ground, and he had to get out there himself. But first he had to confirm one thing. "They fled. And they came—to Opal?"

Graves shook his scarred and massive head. "That is what I thought, and that is why I requested a landing here. Steven had calculated that the trajectory had its end-point in the Dobelle system. But when I arrived I spoke at once with the Starside Spaceport monitors. They assured me that no one could have landed a ship with a Bose Drive on this world, without them being aware of it."

There was a new wail of alarm equipment from outside, and the lurid glare of orange-red warning flares. Voices were screaming at each other. Watching at the window, Rebka saw the car touch down, bounce back high into the air, and then flip over to hit upside down. He started for the door, but he was held back by Graves's sudden and strong grip on his arm.

"When Commander Perry returns, I will inform him of a new request," Graves said quietly. "We do not want to search Opal. The twins are not here. But they are in the Dobelle system. And that can only mean one thing: they are on Quake."

He cocked his head, as though hearing the scream of sirens and the sounds of tearing metal for the first time. "We must search Quake, and soon. But for the moment, there seem to be more immediate problems."

CHAPTER 8

Summertide minus twenty-six.

THE MOMENT OF death. A whole life flashing before your eyes.

Darya Lang heard the side-wind hit just as the wheels of the aircar touched down for the second time. She saw the right wing strike—felt the machine leave the runway—knew that the car was flipping onto its back. There was a scream of overstressed roof panels.

Suddenly dark earth was whizzing past, a foot above her head. Soggy mud sprayed and choked her. The light vanished, leaving her in total darkness.

As the harness cut savagely into her chest, her mind cleared with the pain. She felt cheated.

That was her whole life, supposedly rushing past her? If so, it had been a miserably poor one. All that she could think of was the Sentinel. How she would never understand it, never penetrate its ancient mystery, never learn what had happened to the Builders. All those light-years of travel, to be squashed like a bug in the dirt of a lousy minor planet!

Like a bug. The thought of bugs made her feel vaguely guilty.

Why?

She remembered then, hanging upside down in her harness. Thinking was hard, but she had to do it. She was alive.

That liquid dripping down her nose and into her eyes stung terribly, but it was too cold to be blood. But what about the other two, Atvar H'sial and J'merlia, in the passenger seats? *Not* bugs, she thought; in fact, less like insects than she was. *Rational beings.* Shame on you, Darya Lang!

Had she killed them, though, with her lousy piloting?

Darya craned her head around and tried to look behind her. There was something wrong with her neck. A shock of pure heat burned its way into her throat and her left shoulder even before she turned. She could see nothing.

"J'merlia?" No good calling for Atvar H'sial. Even if the Cecropian could hear, she could not reply. "J'merlia?"

No answer. But those were human voices outside the ship. Calling to her? No, to each other—hard to hear above the whistling wind.

"Can't do it that way." A man's voice. "The top's cracked open. If that strut goes, the weight will smash their skulls in."

"They're goners anyway." A woman. "Look at the way they hit. They're crushed flat. Want to wait for hoists?"

"No. I heard someone. Hold the light. I'm going inside."

The light! Darya felt a new panic. The darkness before her was total, blacker than any midnight, black as the pyramid in the heart of the Sentinel. At that time of year Opal had continuous daylight, from Mandel or its companion, Amaranth. Why could she not see?

She tried and failed to blink her eyes; reached up her right hand to rub at them. Her left hand had vanished—there was no sensation from it, no response but shoulder pain when she tried to move it.

Rubbing just made her eyes sting worse. Still she could see nothing.

"God, what a mess." The man again. There was the faintest glimmer in front of her, like torchlight seen through closed eyes. "Allie, there's three of 'em in here—I think. Two of 'em are aliens, all wrapped round each other. There's bugjuice everywhere. I don't know what's what, and

I daren't touch 'em. Send a distress call; see if you can find anybody near the port who knows some alien anatomy."

There was a faint and unintelligible reply.

"Hell, I don't know." The voice was closer. "Nothing's moving—they could all be dead. I can't wait. They're covered in black oil, all over. One good flame in here, they'll be crisps."

Distant chatter, diffuse: more than one person.

"Doesn't matter." The voice was right next to her. "Have to pull 'em out. Somebody get in here to help."

The hands that took hold of Darya did not mean to be rough. But when they grabbed her shoulder and neck multiple galaxies of pain pinwheeled across the blackness in her eye sockets. She gave a scream, a full-throated howl that came out like a kitten's miaow.

"Great!" The grip on her shifted and strengthened. "This one's alive. Coming through. Catch hold."

Darya was dragged on her face across a muddy tangle of roots and broken stalks of fern. A clod of slimy and evil-tasting moss crammed into her open mouth. She gagged painfully. As a protruding root dug deep into her broken collarbone it suddenly occurred to her: She did not *need* to stay awake for such indignity!

Darkness enveloped her. It was time to stop fighting; time to rest; time to escape into that soothing blackness.

It had taken Darya a day to learn, but at last she was sure: *dialog* between human and Cecropian was impossible without the aid of J'merlia or another Lo'tfian intermediary; but *communication* was feasible. And it could carry a good deal of meaning.

A Cecropian's rigid exoskeleton made facial expression impossible in any human sense. However, body language was employed by both species. They merely had to discover each other's movement codes.

For instance, when Atvar H'sial was confident that she knew the answer that Darya would give to a question, she would lean away a little. Often she also lifted one or both front legs. When she did *not* know the answer and was anxious to hear it, the delicate proboscis pleated and shortened—just a bit. And when she was truly excited—or worried; it was difficult to know the difference—by a comment or a question, the hairs and bristles on her long fanlike antennas would stand up straighter and a fraction bushier.

As they had done, strikingly, when Julius Graves had come on the scene.

Darya knew about the Council—everyone did—but she had been too preoccupied with her own interests to take much notice of it. And she was still vague about its functions, though she knew it involved ethical questions.

"But everyone is *supposed* to be vague, Professor Lang," Graves had said. He gave her a smile which his enlarged, skeletal head turned into something positively menacing. It was not clear how long ago he had landed at Starside Port, but he had certainly chosen to pay her a visit at an inconvenient time. She and Atvar H'sial had held their preliminary discussions and were all set to get down to the nitty-gritty: who would do what, and why, and when?

"Everyone is vague, that is," Graves went on, "except those whose actions make the Council *necessary.*"

Darya's face was betraying her again, she was sure of it. What she was about to do with the Cecropian ought to be no business of the Council; there was nothing *unethical* about short-circuiting a bureaucracy in a good scientific cause, even if that cause had not been fully revealed to anyone on Opal. What else did council members do?

But Graves was staring at her with those mad and misty blue eyes, and she was sure he must be reading guilt in hers.

If he were not, he surely could detect it in Atvar H'sial! The antennae stood out like long brushes, and even J'merlia was almost gibbering in his eagerness to get out the words.

"Later, esteemed Councilor, we will be most delighted to meet with you later. But at the moment, we have an urgent prior appointment." Atvar H'sial went so far as to take

Darya Lang's hand in one jointed paw. As the Cecropian pulled her toward the door—to the outside, where it was pelting with rain!—Darya noticed for the first time that the paw's lower pad was covered with black hairs, like tiny hooks. Darya could not have pulled away, even if she had been willing to make a scene in front of Julius Graves.

It was another vestigial remnant of a distant flying ancestor of Atvar H'sial, one who had perhaps needed to cling to trees and rocks.

Well, none of us sprang straight from the head of the gods, did we? she reflected. We all have bits and pieces left over by evolution. Darya glanced automatically at her own fingernails. They were filthy. It seemed she was already slipping into the disgusting ways of Opal and Quake.

"Where to?" She spoke in a whisper. Julius Graves would need phenomenal hearing to pick up anything she said over the hissing rain, but she was sure he was staring after them. Wondering, no doubt, where they were going and why, when the weather loomed so foul. She felt a lot better out of his presence.

"We will talk of it in a moment." J'merlia, receiving the direct benefit of Atvar H'sial's nervous pheromones, was hopping up and down as though the sodden apron of the aircar facility were blistering hot. The Lo'tfian's voice quivered with urgency. "Inside the car, Darya Lang. Inside!"

They were both actually reaching out to lift her in!

She pushed the paws away. "Do you *want* Graves to think something illegal is going on?" she hissed at Atvar H'sial. "Calm down!"

Her reaction even made her feel a little superior. The Cecropians had such a reputation for clear, rational thought. Many—including every Cecropian—said that they were far superior to humans in intellectual powers and performance. And yet here was Atvar H'sial, as jittery as if they were planning a major crime.

The two aliens crowded into the car after her, pushing her forward.

"You do not understand, Darya Lang." While Atvar H'sial closed the door, J'merlia was urging her toward the pilot's seat. "This is your first encounter with a member of a major clade council. They cannot be trusted. They are supposed to confine themselves to ethical matters, but they do not! They have no shame. They feel it their right to dabble in everything, no matter how little it concerns them. We could not have discussions with Julius Graves present! He would surely have sensed and sniffed out and interfered with and ruined everything we have planned. We have to get away from him. Quickly."

Even as J'merlia spoke, Atvar H'sial was waving frantically for Darya to take off—into storm clouds that had piled up ominously over half the sky. Darya pointed, then realized that the Cecropian's echolocation would "see" nothing at such a distance. Even with those incredible ears, Atvar H'sial's world must be confined to a sphere no more than a hundred meters across.

"There's bad weather—that way, to the east."

"Then fly west," J'merlia said. "Or north, or south. But *fly.*" The Lo'tfian was crouched on the floor of the aircar, while Atvar H'sial leaned with her head against the side window, her blind face staring off at nothing.

Darya took the car up in a steep climbing turn, fleeing for the lighter clouds far to their left. If once she could get above them, the car could cruise for many hours.

How many? She was not keen to find out. It would be better to keep on ascending, clear the storm completely, and seek a quiet place where she could set them down near the edge of the Sling.

Two hours later she had to abandon that idea. The rough air went on endlessly, and there was no drop in the force of the winds. They had flown to the edge of the Sling and circled far beyond it, seeking another landing spot, and found nothing. Worse than that, the dark mass of major thunderstorms was pursuing them. A solid wall of gray stretched across three quarters of the horizon. Car radio weather reported a "Level Five" storm but did not bother to define it. Mandel had set, and they flew only by the angry light of Amaranth.

She turned to Atvar H'sial. "We can't stay up here forever, and I don't want to leave things to the last minute. I'm going to take us higher, right over the top of the storm. Then we'll stay above it and head back the way we came. The best place to land is the one we started from."

Atvar H'sial nodded complacently as the message was relayed to her by J'merlia. The storm held no fears for the Cecropian—perhaps because she could not see the black and racing clouds that showed its strength. Her worries were still with Julius Graves.

As they flew Atvar H'sial laid out through J'merlia her complete plan. They would learn the official word on the proposed trips to Quake as soon as Captain Rebka came back. If permission were denied, they would then proceed at once to Quakeside, in an aircar whose rental was already paid. It sat waiting for them, on the small takeoff field of another Sling not far from Starside Port. To reach it, they would rent a local car, one whose travel range was so limited that Rebka and Perry would never dream that they intended to go so far.

Atvar H'sial, with J'merlia as interpreter, could make all those arrangements without difficulty. What she could not do, the one task for which Darya Lang was absolutely essential, was to requisition a capsule on the Umbilical.

She stated her reasons, as Darya listened with half an ear and fought the storm. No Cecropian had ever before visited Opal. The appearance of one on Quakeside, trying to board an Umbilical capsule, would produce immediate questions. Permission would not be given without checking entry permits, and that would lead back to Rebka and Perry.

"But you," J'merlia said, "you will be accepted at once. We have the correct documents already prepared for you." The pleated surface of Atvar H'sial's proboscis tightened a fraction. She was leaning over Darya, forelimbs together in a position that looked like earnest prayer. "You are a human . . . and you are a female."

As if *that* helped. Darya sighed. Full interspecies communication might be impossible. She had told them three times, but the Cecropian could not seem to accept the concept that in humans, the females were *not* the unquestioned and dominant ruling gender.

Darya set out to gain altitude. This storm was *something*. They needed to be above and beyond those thundercaps before they started any descent, and despite the stability and strength of the aircar she did not relish the job ahead of her.

"And we know the correct control sequences to employ in ascending the Umbilical," J'merlia went on. "Once you have cleared us for access to the capsule, nothing will stand between us and the surface of Quake."

Those words were intended to encourage Darya and soothe any worries. Curiously, they had the opposite effect. She began to wonder. The Cecropian had arrived on Opal *after* her—and yet she had false documents, already prepared? And she knew all about the Umbilical control sequences. Who had given those to her?

"Tell Atvar H'sial that I'll have to think about all this before I can make a final decision."

Think, and learn a lot more for herself, before she committed to any joint trip to Quake with Atvar H'sial. The alien seemed to know just about everything on Dobelle.

Except, possibly, about the dangers of Opal's storms.

They were descending, and the turbulence was frightening. Darya heard and felt giant wind forces on the car. She prayed that its automatic stabilization and approach system could fly better than she could. She was no superpilot.

Atvar H'sial and J'merlia were quite unperturbed. Maybe beings who were descended, however remotely, from flying ancestors had a more sanguine view of air travel.

Darya would never acquire that, for sure. Her guts were knotting. They were through the clouds and dropping in a rainstorm more violent than any she had ever known on

Sentinel Gate. With visibility less than a hundred meters and no landmarks, she had to rely on the beacons of Starside's automatic landing system.

If it worked at all, in such a downpour.

The view through the forward window was useless, nothing but driving rain. They had been descending for a long time—too long. She steadied herself on the console and peered at the instrument panel. Altitude, three hundred meters. Beacon slant range, two kilometers. They must be just seconds away from landing. But where was the field?

Darya looked up from the panel and saw the approach lights for a couple of seconds. They were right in place, dead ahead. She reduced power, drifting them down along the glowing line. The wheels touched briefly. Then a rolling crosswind grabbed the car, lifted it, and carried them up again and off to the side.

Everything moved to slow motion.

The car dipped. She saw one wing catch on rain-slick earth . . .

. . . watched it dig a furrow, bend and buckle . . .

. . . heard the crack as it broke in two . . .

. . . felt the beginning of the aircar's first cartwheel . . .

. . . and knew, beyond doubt, that the best part of the landing was over.

Darya never once lost consciousness. She was so convinced of that fact that after a while her brain came up with an explanation of what was happening. It was simple: every time she closed her eyes, even for a moment, someone changed the scenery.

First, the agony and indignity of a drag across wet, uneven soil. No scenery there, because her eyes were not working.

(blink)

She was lying face-upward, while someone leaned over her and sponged at her head. "Chin, mouth, nose," a voice said. "Eyes." And terrible pain.

"Transmission fluid, looks like." He was not speaking to her. "It's all right, not toxic. Can you handle it on the others?"

"Yeah," another man said. "But the big one has a crack in its shell. It's dribbling gunk and we can't suture. What should I do?"

"Tape, maybe?" A dark shape moved away from her. Cold raindrops splashed into her stinging eyes.

(blink)

Green walls, a beige ceiling, and the hissing and purring of pumps. A computer-controlled IV dripped into her left arm, cantilevered up over her body by a metal brace. She felt warm and comfortable and just *wonderful.*

Neomorph, said a detached voice in her brain. Fed in by the computer whenever the telemetry shows you need it. Powerful. Rapidly addictive. Controlled use on Sentinel Gate. Employ only under controlled conditions with reverse epinephrine triggers.

Nuts, the rest of her said. Feels great. Phemus Circle really knows how to use drugs. Hooray for them.

(blink)

"Feeling better?"

A stupid question. She did not feel good at all. Her eyes ached, her ears ached, her teeth ached, her toes ached. Her head buzzed, and there were stabs of pain that started near her left ear and ran all the way to her fingertips. But she knew that voice.

Darya opened her eyes. A man had magically appeared at the bedside.

"I know you." She sighed. "But I don't know your first name. You poor man. You don't even have a first name, do you?"

"Yes, I do. It is Hans."

"Captain Hans Rebka. That's all right, then, you do have a name. You're pretty nice, you know, if you'd just smile a bit more. But you're supposed to be away on Quake."

"We got back."

"I want to go to Quake."

The damned drug, she thought. It was the drug, it must be, and now she knew why it was illegal. She had to shut up before she said something really damaging.

"Can I go there, nice Hans Rebka? I have to, you see. I really have to."

He smiled and shook his head.

"See, I knew you'd look a lot better if you smiled. So will you let me go to Quake? What do you say, Hans Rebka?"

She blinked before he could reply. He disappeared.

When she opened her eyes again there was a major addition to the room. Over to her right a lattice of black metal tubes had been erected to form a cubical scaffolding. A harness hung at the center of it, attached by strong cords to the corners. In that harness, pipestem torso swathed in white tape, head drooping low, and thin limbs stretched out vertically and to both sides, hung J'merlia.

The contorted position of the wrapped body suggested the agony of a final death spasm. Darya automatically looked around for Atvar H'sial. There was no sign of the Cecropian. Was it possible that the symbiosis between the two was so complete that the Lo'tfian could not *survive* without the other? Had he died when the two were separated?

"J'merlia?"

She spoke without thinking. Since J'merlia's words were nothing more than a translation of Atvar H'sial's pheromonal speech, it was stupid to expect an independent response.

One lemon eye swiveled in her direction. So at least he knew she was there.

"Can you hear me, J'merlia? You look as though you are in terrible pain. I don't know why you are in that awful harness. If you can understand me, and you need help, tell me."

There was a long silence. Hopeless, Darya thought.

"Thank you for your concern," a dry and familiar voice

said finally. "But I am in no pain. This harness was built at my own request, for my comfort. You were not conscious when it was being done."

Was that really J'merlia speaking? Darya automatically looked around the room again. "Is that you, or Atvar H'sial? Where is Atvar H'sial? Is she alive?"

"She is. But regrettably, her wounds are worse than yours. She required major surgery on her exoskeleton. You have one broken bone and many bruises. You will be fully mobile in three Dobelle days."

"How about you?"

"I am nothing; my situation is unimportant."

J'merlia's self-effacing manner had been acceptable when Darya had thought him no more than a mouthpiece for Cecropian thoughts. But now this was a rational being, with its own thoughts, its own feelings.

"Tell me, J'merlia. I want to know."

"I lost two joints of one hind limb—nothing important; they will grow back—and I leaked a little at my pedicel. Negligible."

It had its own feelings—and its own *rights*?

"J'merlia—" She paused. Was it her business? A member of the Council was here, on this very planet. In fact, running away from him had been the prime cause of their injuries. If anyone should be worrying about the status of the Lo'tfians, it ought to be Julius Graves, not Darya Lang.

"J'merlia." She found herself talking anyway. How long before the drug was out of her system? "When Atvar H'sial is present you never speak any of your own thoughts. You never say anything at all."

"That is true."

"Why not?"

"I have nothing to say. And it would not be appropriate. Even before I reached second shape, when I was no more than postlarval, Atvar H'sial was named my dominatrix. When she is present, I serve only to carry her thoughts to others. I have no other thoughts."

"But you have intelligence, you have knowledge. It's *wrong.* You should have your own rights . . ." Darya paused. The Lo'tfian was wriggling in his harness, so that both compound eyes could be turned toward the human.

He bowed his head to her. "Professor Darya Lang, with permission. You and all humans are far above me, above all Lo'tfians. I would not presume to disagree with you. But will you permit me to tell you of our history, and also of the Cecropians? May I?"

She nodded. That was apparently not enough, for he waited until she finally said, "Very well. Tell me."

"Thank you. I will begin with us, not because we are important, but only for purposes of comparison. Our home-world is Lo'tfi. It is cold and clear-skied. As you might guess from my appearance, we have excellent vision. We saw the stars every night. For thousands of generations we made use of that information only to tell at what time of the year certain foods should be available. That was all. When it was colder or hotter than usual, many of us would starve to death. We could speak to each other, but we were hardly more than primitive animals, knowing nothing of the future and little of the past. We would probably have stayed so forever.

"Think now of Atvar H'sial and her people. They developed on a dark and cloud-covered world—and they were *blind.* Because they see by echolocation, sight for them implies the presence of air to carry the signal. So their senses could never receive information of anything beyond their own atmosphere. They deduced the presence of their own sun, only because they felt its weak radiation as a source of warmth. They had to develop a technology that told them of the very *existence* of light. And then they had to build instruments that were sensitive to light and to other electromagnetic radiation, so that they could detect and measure it.

"That was just the beginning. They had to turn those instruments to look at the sky, and deduce the existence of a universe beyond their homeworld and beyond their sun. And finally they had to acknowledge the importance of the stars, measure their distances, and build ships to travel to and explore them.

"They did this—all this—while we Lo'tfians sat around dreaming. We are the older race, but if they had not found our world and *raised* us to self-awareness and to understanding of the universe, we would be sitting there still, as animals.

"Compared to Cecropians, or to humans, Lo'tfians are nothing. Compared to Atvar H'sial, *I* am nothing. When her light shines, mine should not be seen. When she speaks, it is my honor to be the instrument that gives her thoughts to you.

"Do you hear me, Professor Darya Lang? It is my honor. Darya Lang?"

She had been listening—and listening hard. But she was beginning to hurt, and the computer-controlled IV was not ready to allow that. The pump had started again, a few seconds before.

She forced her eyes to remain open.

I am nothing! What a racial inferiority complex. But the Lo'tfians should not be allowed to be a slave race—even if they wanted it. As soon as she could get to him, she would go and report it.

To him.

To whom?

Mad and misty blue eyes, but she could not recall his name. Was she afraid of him? Surely not.

She would report this to—

(blink).

CHAPTER 9

Summertide
minus twenty.

"SHE'S NOT DEAD, and not dying. She's *healing.* The correct Cecropian response to trauma and physical insult is unconsciousness."

In the middle of Opal's brief night, Julius Graves and Hans Rebka stood by the table that held Atvar H'sial's motionless body. Part of one side of the dark-red carapace had been coated with a thick layer of gypsum and agglutinate, hardening to a gleaming white shell. The proboscis was pleated and secured in its chin pouch, while the antennas lay furled over the broad head. The whistle of air pumping through spiracles was barely audible.

"And it is amazingly effective by human standards," Graves continued. "Recovery from an injury which does not kill a Cecropian outright is fast—two or three days, at most. And Darya Lang and J'merlia consider that Atvar H'sial is already recovered enough to renew a request for access to Quake." He smiled, a death's-head grin. "Not welcome news to Commander Perry, eh? Has he asked you to delay everything until after Summertide?"

Hans Rebka hid his surprise—or tried to. He was becoming used to the feeling that Julius Graves possessed limitless knowledge of every species in the spiral arm. After all, the mnemonic twin had been created for exactly that purpose, and from the moment that they had arrived at the scene of the crash Steven Graves had dictated the treatment for Atvar H'sial's injuries: the shell must be sealed, the legs taped, the broken wing case removed entirely—it would regenerate—and the crushed antenna and yellow auditory horns left to heal themselves.

But it was harder to accept Graves's knowledge and understanding of *humans.*

It occurred to Rebka that he and Julius Graves should switch jobs. If anyone could find out what had changed Max Perry from an up-and-coming leader to a career drop-out and impenetrable mental mystery, Graves could do it. Whereas Rebka was the man who could explore the surface of Quake and find the Carmel twins, no matter where they tried to hide.

"And your own views, Captain," Graves went on. "You have been to Quake. Should Darya Lang and Atvar H'sial be permitted to go there once they have recovered? Or should they be refused access?"

That was exactly what Rebka had been asking himself. It was left unsaid that Graves intended to go to Quake, no matter who opposed him. Perry would accompany him, as his guide. And although Rebka had said nothing, he intended to go, too. His job required it, and anyway Max Perry was biased and unreliable on anything to do with Quake. But what about the others?

He travels fastest who travels alone.

"I'm opposed to the idea. The more people, the more dangerous, no matter what specialized knowledge they bring along. And that applies to Cecropians as well as humans."

Or even more so for Cecropians. He stared down at the unconscious alien, fought off a shiver, and walked away toward the door of the building.

He had no trouble with J'merlia, with his downtrodden look and pleading yellow eyes. But it made him uncomfortable just *looking* at Atvar H'sial. And he considered himself an educated, reasonable man. There was some hidden quality to the aliens that he found hard to tolerate.

"Cecropians still make you uneasy, Captain." It was Graves, following him to the door and reading his mind again—making a statement, not asking a question.

"I guess they do. Don't worry, I'll get used to them."

He would—slowly. But it was hard going. The miracle was that Cecropians and humans had not embarked on total war when the two species had first encountered each other.

And they would have, Rebka's inner voice assured him, if they could have found anything worth fighting about. Cecropians looked like demons. If they had not sought planets around red dwarf stars, while humans were looking for Sol analogs, the two would have encountered each other in the outward crawl. But the unmanned probes and the slow Arks of both species had been targeted for quite different stellar types, and they had missed each other for a thousand years. By the time humans discovered the Bose Drive and found the Cecropians already using the same Network through the spiral arm, both species had had experience with other alien organisms; enough to allow them to coexist with other clades whose needs were for stellar environments so different from their own, even if they could not be viscerally comfortable.

"Vertebrate chauvinism is all too common." Graves fell into step at his side. He was silent for another moment; then he giggled. "Yet according to Steven—who says that he speaks as someone who lacks both a backbone *and* an exoskeleton—we should think of ourselves as the outsiders. Of the four thousand two hundred and nine worlds known to possess life, Steven says that internal skeletons have developed on only nine hundred and eighty-six. Whereas arthropod invertebrates thrive on three thousand three hundred and eleven. In a galactic popularity contest, Atvar H'sial, J'merlia, or any other arthropod would beat you, me, or Commander Perry hands down. And even, if I dare say it, your Professor Lang."

Rebka started to walk faster. It would serve no purpose to point out to Julius Graves that Steven was on the way to becoming a bore. It was all right to *know* everything in the universe—but did he have to *tell* it?

Rebka was not willing to admit the real cause of his irritation. He hated being with someone who knew far more than he did, but worse still he hated to be with a man who saw through him with no effort at all. No one was supposed to know that he had a soft spot for Lang. Damn it, he had only realized it *himself* when he had pulled her out of the crashed aircar. She was something more than a nuisance, more than an unwanted addition to his problems with Quake and Max Perry.

Why had she come, to make life more complicated? It was obvious that she was out of her depth on Opal, a scientist who should have stayed quietly in her lab to do her research. They would have to look after her. *He* would have to look after her. And the best way to do that was to keep her on Opal when he went to Quake.

The Level Five storm was over, and there was a rare break in Opal's night clouds. It was near midnight, but not dark. Amaranth had been swinging in on the final stages of its slow approach to Mandel. It was high in the sky, big enough to show a glowing disk of bright orange. In two more days, the dwarf companion would begin to cast shadows.

Half a sky away from it, lurking near the horizon, lay Gargantua, beginning its own dive toward the furnace of Mandel. It was still no more than a rosy point, but it was brighter than all the stars. In another week the gas-giant would show its own circular disk, barred with stripes of umber and pale yellow.

Rebka headed across the starport to one of the four main buildings. Graves was still tagging along beside him.

"You are heading to meet with Louis Nenda?" the councilor asked.

"I hope so. How much do you know about him?" If

Rebka was stuck with Graves, he might as well try to use his superior knowledge.

"Only what the request told you," Graves said. "Plus our own knowledge of members of the Zardalu Communion—which is less than we would like. The Communion worlds are not noted for their cooperation."

Which might qualify as the best understatement yet, Rebka thought.

Twelve thousand years earlier, long before humans had begun the Expansion, the land-cephalopods of Zardalu had tried to create something that neither humans nor Cecropians had ever been foolish enough to attempt: the Zardalu Communion, a genuine empire, a thousand planets ruled ruthlessly from Genizee, the homeworld of the Zardalu clade. It had failed disastrously. But that failure might have been the object lesson saving humans and Cecropians from the same mistake.

"Louis Nenda is basically human," Graves went on, "but with some Zardalu augmentation."

"Mental or physical?"

"I do not know. But whatever was done, it must be fairly minor. There's no mention of rear-skull or fingertip eyes, no hermaphroditism, no deboning or quadrimanuals or quadripedals. No gigantism or compaction—he's male, and standard size and weight according to the manifest. Of course, there are hundreds of modifications that don't appear on any standard list.

"As for the pet that he brings with him, I can tell you even less. It is a Hymenopt, and needless to say, it is another arthropod—though similar to Earth's Hymenoptera only by analogy. But whether it is a plaything, or a sexual partner, or even a food supply for Nenda—that we will have to wait and see."

And not wait long, Rebka thought. The newly arrived ship sat in the middle of Starside Port, its occupants already in screening for organisms at the arrival building. Since tests for endo- and ecto-parasites took only a few minutes, the newcomers had to be in the final stages of entry.

Rebka and Graves moved to where Max Perry and three officials from Port Entry were already waiting.

"How much longer?" Rebka asked.

Instead of replying, Perry gestured to the sealed double doors of Decontamination. They were beginning to open.

After Graves's suggestions and Rebka's imaginings, Louis Nenda looked surprisingly normal. Short, swarthy, and muscular, he could have passed for an inhabitant of one of the denser worlds of the Phemus Circle. He was a little unsteady on his feet, probably the result of half a dozen changes of gravity in the past few hours, but he had plenty of pep, and his self-confidence showed in his walk. He glared arrogantly around with bloodshot eyes as he strutted out of the exobiology test unit; trotting by his side, mimicking his head movements, came a chubby little alien. It halted when it saw the group of waiting humans.

"Kallik!" Louis Nenda tugged on the harness that passed around the Hymenopt's thorax and encased the abdomen. "Heel."

Then, without a look at anyone except Perry, he said, "Good morning, Commander. I think you'll find I test negative. Kallik also. Here's my access request."

The other men were still staring at the Hymenopt. Julius Graves had seen one in travels through the Zardalu territories, but the rest of them knew only pictures and stuffed specimens.

The alien was hard to match to the Hymenopt's fierce reputation. It was less than half the height of Louis Nenda, with a small, smooth head dominated by powerful traplike mandibles and by multiple pairs of bright black eyes set in a ring around the perimeter. They were in constant motion, independently tracking different objects around it.

The Hymenopt's body was rotund and barrel-shaped and covered with short black fur, a centimeter or two long. That was the prized Hymantel, a tough, water-resistant, and insulating coat.

What was not visible was the gleaming yellow sting, retracted into the end of the blunt abdomen. The hollow needle delivered squirts of neurotoxins, whose strength and composition the Hymenopt could vary at will. No standard serum could be effective as an antidote. Also invisible was the nervous system that provided a Hymenopt with a reaction speed ten times as fast as any human's. Eight wiry legs could carry it a hundred meters in a couple of seconds, or fifteen meters into the air under standard gravity. The Hymantel had been a seldom-seen item of human clothing, even before the Hymenopts had been declared a protected species.

"Welcome to the Dobelle system." Perry's voice said the opposite of his words. He took the access requests from Louis Nenda and glanced through them. "Your original request said little about the reason why you wish to visit Quake. Do you have more details here?"

"Sure do." Nenda's manner was as cocky as his walk. "I want to look at big land tides, and that means Quake. At Summertide. No problem in that, is there?"

"Quake is dangerous at Summertide. More dangerous than ever, with Amaranth coming so close."

"Hell, I don't care about danger." Nenda stuck out his chest. "Me and Kallik, we eat danger. We were down on Jellyroll when they had the hyperflare. Spent nine days in an aircar, chasing round in Jellyroll's shadow to avoid being roasted, got out without even a tan. Before that we were on the next-to-last ship out of Castlemaine." He laughed. "Lucky for us. Last ship out had no supplies and a forty-day crawl to a Bose Node. They had to eat each other. But for a real experience let me tell you what happened on Mousehole—"

"As soon as we've had a chance to review your request." Perry gave Nenda an angry glance. Even on one minute's exposure, it was clear that the newcomer would not take it well if his application were rejected. "We'll show you to temporary accommodation, then some of us need to have a meeting. Is there anything special that he"—he gestured at the Hymenopt—"needs to eat?"

"She. Kallik is female. No, she's an omnivore. Like me." Nenda laughed with no trace of humor. "Hey, I hope I'm not hearing what I think I'm hearing. What's all this 'need to have a meeting' stuff? I've come a damned long way for this. Too far to get the runaround now."

"We'll see what we can do." Perry glanced down at Kallik. At the fury in Louis Nenda's voice a couple of inches of yellow sting had slid from its sheath. "I'm sure we agree on one thing: you don't want to go to Quake and be killed there."

"Don't you worry your head about us. We don't kill easy. Just approve that access request and let me get over there. It'll take more than Quake to do me in."

Maybe it would. Rebka watched as Perry led the new-comer away. Quake was dangerous, no doubt about it; but if self-confidence were any protection, Louis Nenda would be safe anywhere. Maybe it was Quake that needed the protection.

"I would like to hear your recommendation, Com-mander."

But Perry won't look at me, Rebka thought. He thinks he knows my decision. But he's wrong—because I don't know it myself.

"I oppose Summertide access, as you know." Perry's voice was barely audible, and his face was pale.

"Oppose access for anyone?"

"That's right."

"You know that Graves will simply overrule whatever we decide? He has the authority to hunt for the Carmel twins on Quake, anytime he wants to."

"He has that authority, and we both assume that he will

go. But authority won't protect him. Quake at Summertide is a *killer*." Perry's voice rose on the final word.

"Very well. What about the others? They are willing to pay Dobelle very substantial amounts for the privilege of visiting Quake."

"I would approve their visits—well after Summertide. Darya Lang can study the Umbilical without being on the surface; Atvar H'sial has the whole rest of the year to study species under environmental stress."

"They'll never agree. Refuse access at Summertide, and you lose them and the money they would pay to Dobelle. What about Louis Nenda?"

Perry finally met Rebka's eye, and a different tone came into his voice. He even managed a smile. "He's lying, isn't he?"

"I certainly think so."

"And he's not very good at it."

"He doesn't give a damn. He should have picked a more plausible story. He strikes me as the last man in the spiral arm to be interested in land tides—I'm tempted to get Steven Graves to ask him a few technical questions about them. But that wouldn't solve anything. He came a long way to get here, nearly nine hundred light-years—unless he's lying about everything else, as well. But he certainly came from the Zardalu Communion, and that's at least four Bose Nodes. Any suggestions as to what he's really after?"

"I have no idea." Perry went quiet again and looked far off at something invisible. "But I don't think he's the only one who's lying. The inquiry you sent to Circle intelligence about Darya Lang confirmed that she's an expert on Builder artifacts, but there's no reason for her to go down to the surface of Quake. She could do all her work here, or on the Umbilical itself. But whether she's telling the truth or not doesn't make any difference to my opinion. You asked for a recommendation. I'm giving it: no access for Lang, no access for Atvar H'sial, no access for *anyone* until after Summertide. And if Graves chooses to override us, that's up to him."

"You would let him go to Quake alone?"

"God, no." Perry was genuinely shocked. "You might as well kill him here. I'd go with him."

"I thought so." Rebka had made up his mind. "And so will I."

And for all the wrong reasons, he thought. If I *allow* access to Quake, I may find out why everyone is so keen to go there. But if I *refuse* access, I'll find out just how keen they are. And I'll probably force some of them to take action. That, I know how to deal with.

"Commander Perry," he continued. "I have made my decision. I agree with your recommendation." He smiled inwardly at the surprise on Perry's face. "We will refuse access to Quake for all parties until Summertide is over."

"I feel sure that's the right decision." Perry's self-control was excellent, but the expression of relief could not be hidden.

"Which leaves us one more decision to make," Rebka said. "Maybe we should toss a coin for it. Who is going to give the bad news to Darya Lang and to Atvar H'sial? Worst of all, who will tell Louis Nenda?"

ARTIFACT: LENS.
UAC#: 1023
Galactic Coordinates: 29,334.229/18,339.895/
—831.22
Name: Lens
Star/planet association: None, free space entity
Bose Access Node: 108
Estimated age: 9.138 ± 0.56 Megayears

Exploration History: The full history of Lens may never be known. Lying as it does in the clade of the Zardalu Communion, all early records were lost with the collapse of the Zardalu Empire. However, given the preoccupation of the Zardalu with biological science and their relative indifference to physical ones, it is most unlikely that any systematic exploration of Lens was ever attempted by them.

The recorded history of Lens begins with its observation in E. 122, but it was long assumed to be extragalactic. The local nature, as part of the spiral arm, was discovered in E. 388 from parallax effects. The Lens was approached directly in E. 2101 by Kusra (one-way journey), but no physical evidence for material existence could be obtained. Paperl and Ula H'sagta (E. 2377) measured a polarization change of beamed lasers passed through the region of the Lens, confirmed its location, and mapped its extent.

Physical Description: The Lens is a focusing region of space, 0.23 light-years in diameter and of apparently zero thickness · (grazing incidence measurements have been made down to one micrometer). Focusing is performed only for light with wavelength range 0.110 to 2.335 micrometers, approaching within 0.077 radians of normal incidence to the plane surface of the Lens. There is, however, weak evidence of interaction with radiation of wavelength in excess of 0.1 light-years (the low energy of such radiation makes its separation from cosmic background of debatable validity). All other light, all particles or solid objects, and all gravity waves pass through the Lens apparently unaffected. Radiation focusing appears to be perfectly achromatic for all wavelengths in the stated range. In that range, the Lens performs as a diffraction-limited focusing device of 0.22 light-years effective aperture and 427 light-years focal length. With its aid, planetary details have been observed in galaxies more than one hundred million parsecs distant.

Physical Nature: This must unfortunately comprise an eliminative list of what the Lens is *not.* Today's science and technology can provide no tenable suggestion as to what it *is.*

The Lens is not built of any particles known to today's inhabitants of the spiral arm. It is not a form of space-time singularity, since such a singularity cannot affect light of certain wavelengths and leave all other forms of matter and radiation untouched. For the same reason, it cannot be an assembly of bound gravitons. It cannot possess a superstring or superloop structure, since no spontaneous or induced emission is observed.

Intended Purpose: Unknown. The Lens represents macroengineering by the Builders at its largest and most mysterious. The specific wavelength range has, however, induced some students of the artifact to speculate that this range corresponds to the spectral sensitivity range of Builder eyes. Since there is no evidence that the Builders possessed anything equivalent to eyes in human or Hymenopt terms, the conjecture is of passing interest only.

It has also been conjectured that the Lens performs modulation of the light passing through it, in a way not understood. If so, its function as a focusing lens would be no more than an accidental by-product of the structure's true purpose.

—From the *Lang Universal Artifact Catalog,*
Fourth Edition.

CHAPTER 10

Summertide
minus eighteen.

"COME IN," DARYA Lang called out automatically when she heard a tentative knock on the door. She saw it swing open.

"Come in," she repeated. Then she saw that the visitor was already in, or partially so. Just a foot above the ground, a round black head with a ring of bright eyes was peering past the edge of the open door.

"She don't understand you worth a damn," a gruff voice said. "Only knows a few command words in human talk. Get in there."

A frowning, squat, and swarthy man came striding through the door, pushing a diminutive alien ahead of him. A stiff halter around the Hymenopt's plump thorax was connected to a black whipping cane in the man's hand.

"I'm Louis Nenda. This here"—a downward jerk of the cane—"is Kallik. Belongs to me."

"Hello. I'm Darya Lang."

"I know. We need to talk."

He was the worst yet. Darya was becoming impatient with the level of manners in the Phemus Circle. But it was catching. "You may need to talk. I certainly don't. So why don't you leave now?"

Unexpectedly, he grinned. "Wait and see. Where can we talk?"

"Right here. But I don't see why we should."

He shook his head and jerked his thumb toward J'merlia. The Lo'tfian had recovered enough to be released from the support harness, but he still preferred to remain where he could raise himself aloft for sleep periods. "What about the stick insect?"

"He's all right." She bent to look at the ocular membrane. "He's just resting. He'll be no trouble."

"I don't care what he's doing. What I have to say can't be said in front of that bug."

"Then I don't think I want to hear it, either. J'merlia isn't a bug. He's a Lo'tfian, and he's as rational as you are."

"Which don't impress me too much." Nenda grinned again. "There's people say I'm crazy as a Varnian. Come on, let's go talk."

"Can you give me one reason why I should want to?"

"Sure. I can give you twelve hundred and thirty-seven of 'em."

Darya stared at him. "Are you talking about the Builder artifacts? Only twelve hundred and thirty-six of those have been discovered."

"I said *reasons*. And I bet we can both think of one very good reason for talking that's *not* an artifact."

"I don't know what you mean." But Darya could feel her traitorous face, as usual, betraying her.

"Kallik, stay." Louis Nenda added a set of whistles and grunts to the words. He turned to Darya. "Speak any Hymenopt? Thought not. I told her to go over there and keep an eye on the bug. Come on outside. She'll come get us if it wakes up and needs you."

He loosed the cane from Kallik's halter and headed out of the door and out of the building, not even looking back to see if she was following.

What did he know? What *could* he know? Logic said, not

a thing. But Darya found herself following him out onto the sodden surface of the Sling.

Starside Weather Central was predicting another major storm in a day, but for the moment the winds had died away to warm and humid gusts. Mandel and Amaranth were together in the sky, fuzzy bright patches on the cloud layer. Amaranth was growing rapidly in apparent brightness. Green plants had become edged with copper, and there was a rusty tinge to the eastward sky. Louis Nenda walked confidently into the brush—no worries for *him* about giant tortoises, Darya thought. But by now they should all be safely out at sea, anyway, ready to ride out Summertide.

"That's far enough," she called after him. "Tell me what you want."

He turned around and came back toward her. "All right, this'll do. I just don't want an extra audience, that's all. And I assume you don't."

"I don't mind. I have nothing to hide."

"Yeah?" He was smiling up at her, half a head shorter. "Funny, I'd have thought you might. You're Darya Lang, the Fourth Alliance's expert on Builder technology and Builder history."

"I'm not an expert, but I am very interested in the Builders. That's no secret."

"It's not. And you're famous enough so that the Builder specialists in the Zardalu Communion know all about your work and the Lang Catalog. You get invited to conferences and meetings, don't you, all the time? But you've never traveled, they all say, not for a dozen years. Anyone who wants to see Darya Lang, they make that trek to Sentinel Gate. Except that a couple of months ago, you can't be reached there. All of a sudden you take off. For Dobelle."

"I want to explore the Umbilical."

"Sure. Except according to the Lang Catalog, UAC 279—"

"UAC 269," said Darya automatically.

"Sorry, UAC 269. Anyway, it says—mind if I quote

you?—the Umbilical is 'one of the simplest and most comprehensible of all Builder artifacts, and is for that reason of less interest to most serious students of Builder technology.' Remember writing that?"

"Of course I do. What of it? I'm a free agent; I can change my mind. And I can go where I like."

"You can. Except that your bosses back on Miranda made a big mistake. They should have told people who asked that you'd gone off to Tantalus, or Cocoon, or Flambeau, or one of the other really big Builder draws. Or maybe just say you'd gone off for a holiday."

"What *did* they say?" She should not have been asking, but she had to know. What had those dummies back in central government done to her?

"They didn't say nuthin'. They clammed up and told anyone who asked to go away and stop bothering them and come back in a couple of months. You don't tell people that if you want them to stop sniffing around."

"But you found me with no trouble." Darya was feeling very relieved. He was a pest, but he did not know anything, and it was not her fault that he was there.

"Sure did. We found you. It wasn't hard, once we got going; there's transfer information for every Bose Transition."

"So you followed me here. Now what do you want with me?"

"Did I say we followed you, *Professor*?" He turned the title into an insult. "We didn't. You see, we were already on the way. But when we found you were here, too, I knew we really had to get together. Come on, dearie."

Louis Nenda took Darya by the arm and led her through the undergrowth. They came to a tangled ridge of vines and horizontal woody stems, bulging up to form a long and lumpy bench. At pressure from him she sank down to a sitting position. Her legs were wobbly.

"We had to get together," he repeated. "And you know why, don't you? You pretend you don't, Darya Lang, but you sure as hell do." He sat down next to her and patted her familiarly on the knee. "Come on, it's confessional time. You and me have things to tell each other, sweetheart. Real intimate things. Want me to go first?"

If the results are so obvious to *me,* why haven't others drawn the same conclusions?

Darya remembered thinking that, long before she ever set out for Dobelle. And finally she could answer the question. Others *had* drawn the same conclusions. The mystery was only that someone as crude, direct, and unintellectual as Louis Nenda could have done it.

He had not beaten about the bush.

"Builder artifacts, all over the spiral arm. Some in your territory, back in the Alliance, some in the Cecropia Federation, some back where I live in Zardalu-land. Yeah, and one here, too, the Umbilical.

"Your Lang Catalog lists every one of 'em. And you use a universal galactic ephemeris to show every time there's been a *change* in any artifact. In appearance, size, function, anything."

"As best I could." Darya was admitting nothing that was not written in the catalog itself. "Some times weren't recorded to enough significant figures. I'm sure other events were missed entirely. And I suspect some were logged that weren't real changes."

"But you showed an average of thirty-seven changes per artifact, over an observation span of three thousand years—nine thousand years for artifacts in Cecropian territory, 'cause they've been watching longer than anyone else. And no correlation of the times."

"That's right." Darya did not like his grin. She nodded and glanced away.

Nenda squeezed her knee with powerful fingers. His hand was thick and hairy. "Getting too close to the crucial point, am I? Don't feel bad, sweetie. Hang in—we'll be there in a minute. The event *times* didn't correlate, did they? But in one of your papers you made a throwaway suggestion. Remember it?"

How long should she go on stalling? Except that Legate Pereira's instructions had been quite specific. She was not to tell anyone outside the Alliance what she had found—even if they seemed to know it already.

She pushed his hand away from her leg. "I've made a lot of throwaway suggestions in my work."

"So I hear. And I hear you don't forget things. But I'll refresh your memory, anyway. You said that the right way to examine possible time correlation of artifact changes was not through the examination of universal galactic event times. It was to think of the effects of a change as propagating outward from their point of origin, traveling like a radio signal, at the speed of light. So ten light-years after something happened at an artifact, information about that change would be available everywhere on the surface of a sphere, ten years in radius and with center at the artifact. Remember writing that?"

Darya shrugged.

"And any two spheres expand until they meet," Louis Nenda went on. "First they'll touch at one point, then as they grow they'll intersect in a circle that just gets bigger and bigger and bigger. But it gets trickier with three spheres. When they grow and meet, they'll do it at just two points. Four or more spheres don't usually have any points in common. And when you get to twelve hundred and thirty-six artifacts, with an average of thirty-seven changes for each one, you have nearly fifty thousand spheres—each one spreading out at the speed of light with an artifact as the sphere center. What's the chances that twelve hundred and thirty-six of those spheres, one from each Builder artifact, will all meet at one place? It should be negligible, too small to measure. But if they *did* meet, against all the odds, *when* would that happen?

"Sounds like an impossible question, doesn't it? But it's

not hard to program and test for intersections. And do you know the answer that program gives, Professor Lang?"

"Why should I?" It was too late, but she stalled anyway.

"Because you're *here*. Damn it, let's stop pretending. Do you want me to spell it out for you?"

His hand was on her thigh again, but it was his tone of voice that finally made her angry enough to hit back.

"You don't need to spell *anything* out for me, you—you lecherous little dwarf. And you may have followed up on it, but that's *all* you did—follow up! It was my original idea. And get your filthy hand off my leg!"

He was grinning in triumph. "I never said it wasn't your idea. And if you don't want to be friendly, I won't push it. The spheres all coincide, don't they—to as many significant figures as the data permit? One place, and one time, and we both know where. The surface of Quake, at Summertide. That's why you're here, and that's why I'm here, and Atvar H'sial, and everybody but your Uncle Jack."

He stood up. "And now the local bozos say we can't go! Any of us."

"What?!" Darya jerked to her feet.

"You didn't hear it yet? Old stone-head Perry came and told me an hour ago. No Quake for you, no Quake for me, no Quake for the bugs. We come a thousand light-years to sit here on our asses and miss the whole show."

He slashed the black cane from Kallik's harness at the bole of a huge bamboo. "They say, no go. I say, then screw 'em! See now why we have to do something, Darya Lang? We have to pool our knowledge—unless you *want* to sit here on your ass and take orders from pipsqueaks."

Mathematics is universal. But very little else is.

Darya reached that conclusion after another half hour's talk with Louis Nenda. He was a horrible man, someone she would go out of her way to avoid. But when they had traded statistical analyses—grudgingly, carefully, each unwilling to offer more than was received—the agreement was uncanny. It was also in a sense inevitable. Starting from the same set of events and the same set of artifact locations, there was just one point in space and time that fitted all the data. Any small differences in the computed time and place of the final result arose from alternative criteria for minimizing the residuals of the fit, or from different tolerances in convergence of the nonlinear computations.

They had followed near-identical approaches, and used similar tolerances and convergence factors. She and Louis Nenda agreed on results to fifteen significant figures.

Or rather, Darya concluded after another fifteen minutes, she and whoever had done the calculations for Nenda were in agreement. It could not be his own work. He had no more than a rough grasp of the procedures. He was in charge, but someone else had done the actual analysis.

"So we agree on the time, and it's within seconds of Summertide," he said. He was scowling again. "And all we know is that it's somewhere on Quake? Why can't you pin it closer? That's what I was hoping we could do when we compared notes."

"You want miracles? We're dealing with distances of thousands of light-years, thousands of trillions of kilometers, and time spans of thousands of years. And we have a final uncertainty of less than two hundred kilometers in location, and less than thirty seconds in time. I think that's pretty damned good. In fact, it *is* a miracle, right there."

"Maybe close enough." He slapped the cane against his own leg. "And it's definitely on Quake, not here on Opal. I guess that answers another question I had."

"About the Builders?"

"Nuts to the Builders. About the bugs. Why they want to get to Quake."

"Atvar H'sial says she wants to study the behavior of life-forms under extreme environmental stress."

"Yeah. Environmental stress, my ass." He started to walk back toward the cluster of buildings. "Believe that, and you'll believe in the Lost Ark. She's after the same thing as we are. She's chasing the Builders. Don't forget she's a Builder specialist, too."

Louis Nenda was coarse, barbaric, and disgusting. But once he said it, it became obvious. Atvar H'sial had come to Dobelle too well prepared with contingency plans, just as though she had known that the requests for access to Quake would all be refused.

"What about Julius Graves? Him too?"

But Nenda only shook his head. "Old numb-nuts? Nah. He's a mystery. I'd normally have said, sure, he's here for the same reason as we are. But he's Council, an' even if you don't believe half of what you hear about them—I don't— I've never heard of one lying. Have you?"

"Never. And he didn't expect to go to Quake when he came, only to Opal. He thought those twins he's after would be here."

"So maybe he's for real. Either way, we can forget him. If he wants to go to Quake, he'll do it. The bozos can't stop him." They were back at the building, and Nenda paused just outside the door. "All right, we had our little chat. Now for the best question of all. Just *what* is going to happen on Quake at Summertide?"

Darya stared at him. Did he expect her to answer that? "I don't know."

"Come on, you're stalling again. You *must* know—or you wouldn't have dragged all this way."

"You have it exactly backward. If I *did* know what will happen, or if I even had a halfway plausible idea of it, I'd never have left Sentinel Gate. I like it there. You dragged all this way, too. What do *you* think will happen?"

He was glaring at her in frustration. "Lord knows. Hey, you're the genius. If *you* don't know you can be damned sure I don't. You really have no idea?"

"Not really. It will be something significant, I believe that. It will happen on Quake. And it will tell us more about the Builders. Beyond that I can't even guess."

"Hell." He slashed at the damp ground with the cane.

Darya had the feeling that if Kallik had been there, the Hymenopt would have been the recipient of that blow. "So what now, Professor?"

Darya Lang had been worrying the same question. Nenda seemed to want to cooperate, and she had been drawn along by her thirst for any facts and theories relevant to the Builders. But he seemed to have nothing—or at least, nothing he was willing to give. And she was already talking of working with Atvar H'sial and J'merlia. She could not work with both. And even though she had agreed to nothing definite, she could not mention her other conversations to Louis Nenda.

"Are you proposing that we cooperate? Because if you are—"

She did not have to finish. He had thrown his head back and was hooting with laughter. "Lady, now why would I do a thing like that? When you've just told me you don't know a damned thing!"

"Well, we have been swapping information."

"Sure. That's what you're good at, that's what you're famous for. Information and theories. So how are you at lying and cheating? How are you at *action*? Not so good, I'll bet. But that's what you'll need to get yourself over to Quake. And from what I hear, Quake won't be any picnic. I'll have my work cut out there. Think I want to baby you, sweetheart, and tell you when to run and when to hide? No thanks, dear. You arrange your own parade."

Before she could respond he strode ahead of her, into the building and through to the interior room where they had started. Kallik and J'merlia were still there, crouched low on the floor with their multiple legs spread flat and intertwined. They were exchanging ominous whistles and grunts.

Louis Nenda grabbed the Hymenopt roughly by the halter, attached the black cane, and pulled. "Come on, you. I told you, no fighting. We've got work to do." He turned back to Darya. "Nice to meet you, Professor. See you on Quake?"

"You will, Louis Nenda." Darya's voice was shaking with anger. "You can count on it."

He gave a scoffing laugh. "Fine. I'll save a drink for you there. If Perry's right, we may both need one."

He pulled hard on the cane and dragged Kallik out.

Seething, Darya went across to where J'merlia was slowly standing up. "How is Atvar H'sial?"

"Much better. She will be fully ready to resume work in one more Dobelle day."

"Good. Tell her that I have made up my mind and agree to cooperate fully with her. I will do everything we discussed. I am ready to take off for Quakeside and the Umbilical as soon as she is recovered."

"I will tell her this at once. It is good news." J'merlia moved closer, studying Darya's face. "But you have had some bad experience, Darya Lang. Did the man seek to hurt you?"

"No. Not a physical hurt." *But he hurt me anyway.* "He made me angry and upset. I'm sorry, J'merlia. He wanted to talk, and so we went outside. I thought you were asleep. I didn't realize that you would be threatened by that horrible animal of his."

J'merlia was staring at her and shaking his thin mantis-head in a gesture he had picked up from the humans. "Threatened? By that?" He pointed to the door. "By the Hymenopt?"

"Yes."

"I was not threatened. Kallik and I were beginning a protoconverse—a first learning of each other's language."

"Language?" Darya thought of the whipping cane and the halter. "Are you telling me that it can *talk*? It's not just a simple animal?"

"Honored Professor Lang, Kallik can certainly talk. She never had the chance to learn more than Hymenopt speech, because she met few others and her master did not care for her to know. But she is learning. We began with less than fifty words in common; now we have more than one hundred." J'merlia moved to the door, his wounded leg still trailing. "Excuse me, honored Professor. I must leave now and find Atvar H'sial. It is a pity that Kallik is leaving this place. But maybe we will have an opportunity to talk and learn again when they arrive."

"Arrive? Where are they going?"

"Where everyone is going, it seems." J'merlia paused on the threshold. "To Quake. Where else?"

CHAPTER 11

Summertide
minus thirteen.

VIOLENT RESISTANCE IS a problem, but nonresistance can be harder to handle.

Hans Rebka felt like a boxer, braced for a blow that never came. At some level he was still waiting.

"Didn't they fight it?" he asked.

Max Perry nodded. "Sure. At least, Louis Nenda did. But then he said he'd had it with the Dobelle system, and we could take his access request and stuff it, he was getting the hell out of here as soon as he could. And he already left."

"What about Darya Lang and Atvar H'sial?"

"Lang didn't say a word. There's no way of knowing what Atvar H'sial *thinks*, but what came out of J'merlia didn't have much steam in it. They went off to sulk on another Sling. I haven't seen them for two days—haven't had time to bother with them, to be honest. Think we ought to be worried?"

The two men were in the final moments of waiting as the capsule taking them to Quake was coupled to the Umbilical. They were carrying their luggage, one small bag for each man. Julius Graves was over by the aircar that had brought them from Starside, fussing with his two heavy cases.

Rebka considered Perry's question carefully. His own assignment to Dobelle involved only the rehabilitation of Max

Perry. In principle it had nothing to do with members of other clades, or how they were treated. But as far as everyone on Opal was concerned, he was a senior official, and he had the duties that went with the position. He had received a new coded message from Circle headquarters just before they left Starside, but he had no great hopes that it would help him much, whatever it said. Advice and direction from far away were more likely to add to problems than to solve them.

"People ought to be protesting a lot more," he said at last. "Especially Louis Nenda. What's the chances that he might leave Opal and try for a direct landing on Quake from space? He came in his own ship."

"There's no way we could stop him *trying*. But unless his ship is designed for takeoff without spaceport facilities, he'll be in trouble. He might get down on Quake, but maybe he'd never get off it."

"How about Darya Lang and Atvar H'sial?"

"Impossible. They don't have a ship available, and they won't be able to rent one that will fly interplanetary. We can forget about them."

And then Perry hesitated. He was not sure of his own statement. There was that feeling in the air, a sense of final calm before a great storm. And it was not just the cloudbursts that threatened Opal within twenty-four hours.

It was Summertide, hanging over everything. With thirteen Dobelle days to go, Mandel and Amaranth loomed larger and brighter. Average temperatures were already up five degrees, under angry clouds like molten copper. Opal's air had changed in the last twelve hours. It was charged with a metallic taste that matched the lowering sky. Airborne dust left lips dry, eyes sore and weeping, noses itching and ready to sneeze. As the massive tides brought the seabed close to the surface, undersea earthquakes and eruptions were blowing their irritant fumes and dust high into the atmosphere.

Julius Graves had finally stowed the cases to his satisfaction in the bottom level of the Umbilical's car. He walked over to the other two men and stared up at the lambent sky.

"Another storm coming. A good time to be leaving Opal."

"But a worse time to be going to Quake," Perry said.

They climbed into the car. Perry provided his personal ID and keyed in a complex command sequence.

The three men maintained an uneasy formality as the ascent began. When Perry had quietly informed Graves that access to Quake was denied until after Summertide, Graves had just as coolly asserted the authority of the Council. He would be going to Quake anyway.

Perry pointed out that Graves could not prevent planetary officials from accompanying him. They had a responsibility to stop him from killing himself.

Graves nodded. Everyone was polite; no one was happy.

The tension eased when the capsule emerged from Opal's clouds. The three men had something else to occupy their minds. The car had been provided with sliding viewing ports in its upper level, as well as a large window directly overhead. The passengers had an excellent view of everything above and about them. As Quake appeared through the thinning clouds, any attempt at small talk faded.

Julius Graves stared around, gasped, and gaped, while Max Perry took one look up and retreated into himself. Hans Rebka tried to ignore their surroundings and focus his mind on the task ahead. Perry might know all about Quake, and Graves might be a fount of information about every subject under a thousand suns; yet Rebka had the feeling that he would have to carry both of them.

But carry them through what? He looked around, to find a panorama that swept away all rational thoughts. He had traveled the road to Quake just a few days before, but nothing was the same. Mandel, grossly swollen, loomed on the left. The Builder-designed shell of the car detected and filtered out dangerous hard radiation, turning the star's glowing face into a dark image seamed and pocked with faculae, sunspots, and lurid flares. The disk was so large that Rebka felt he could reach out and touch its raddled surface.

Amaranth—a dwarf no longer—stood beyond Quake. The companion was transformed. Even the color was changed. Rebka recognized that as an artificial effect. When the car windows altered their transmission properties to screen radiation from Mandel, they also modified the transmitted spectrum of Amaranth. Orange-red was transformed to glowering purple.

Even Gargantua was well on the way to its final rendezvous. Reflecting the light of both Mandel and Amaranth, the gas-giant had swelled from a distant spark to a thumbnail-sized glow of bright orange.

The partners were there; gravity was calling the changes, and the cosmic dance was ready to begin. In the final hours of Summertide, Mandel and Amaranth would pass within five million kilometers of each other—the thickness of a fingernail, in stellar terms. Gargantua would hurtle close by Mandel on the side opposite to Amaranth, propelled in its orbit by the combined field of both stellar companions. And little Dobelle, caught in that syzygy of giants, would gyrate helplessly through the warp and woof of a dynamic gravitational tapestry.

The Dobelle orbit was stable; there was no danger that Opal and Quake would separate, or that the doublet might be flung off to infinity. But that was the only assurance the astronomers would provide. Summertide surface conditions on Opal and Quake could not be calculated.

Rebka stared up at Quake. That ball of dusky blue-gray had become the most familiar feature in the sky. It had not changed perceptibly since the last ride up the Umbilical.

Or had it? He stared harder. Was the planet's limb a little fuzzier, where dust in the peel-thin layer of air surrounding Quake had become thicker?

There were few distractions to draw a traveler's mind away from the outside view. Their ascent was at a constant rate, with no sense of motion inside the car. Only a very careful observer would notice the golden knot of Midway Station slowly increasing in size, while the apparent gravity within the capsule was just as gradually diminishing. The journey did not take place in free-fall. The body forces were decreasing steadily, but the only weightless part of the journey would be two thousand kilometers beyond Midway Station, where all centrifugal and gravitational forces were in balance. After that came the real descent to Quake, when the capsule would truly be falling toward that planet.

Rebka sighed and stood up. It would be easy to allow the skyscape to hypnotize him, as Quake hypnotized Max Perry. And not just Perry. He glanced across at Graves. The councilor was totally absorbed in a reverie of his own.

Rebka walked over to the ramp and went down its turning path to the lower level of the capsule. The galley was a primitive one, but there had been no chance of a meal since they left Starside. He was hungry and not choosy, and he dialed without looking. The flavor and contents of the container of soup that he ordered did not matter.

With its opaque walls, the lower level of the capsule was depressingly bland. Rebka went to the table and selected a private music segment. Pre-Expansion music, complex and polyphonic, sounded within his head. The intertwining fugal voices suggested the coming interplay of Mandel and its retinue. For ten minutes Rebka ate and listened, enjoying two of the most basic and oldest pleasures of humanity. He wondered. Did the Cecropians, lacking music, have some compensating art form of their own?

When the piece ended he was surprised to find Julius Graves standing there watching him.

"May I?" The councilor sat down at the table and gestured at the empty bowl. "Can you recommend it?"

Rebka shrugged. Whatever Julius Graves wanted from him, opinions on soup were low on the list.

"Has it ever occurred to you," Graves said, "how improbable it is that we are able, with very little assistance, to eat and digest the foods of a thousand different worlds?

The ingredients of that soup were produced on Opal, but your stomach will have no trouble handling it. We and the Hymenopts and the beings of the Cecropian clade are totally different biologically. Not one of them is DNA-based. And yet, with the help of a few strains of single-celled bacteria in our gut, we can eat the same food as each other. Surprising, is it not?"

"I guess so."

Rebka hated one-on-one conversations with Graves. Those mad blue eyes scared him. Even when the conversation seemed general he suspected an undercurrent, and to add to the confusion he was never sure how much input was coming from the mnemonic twin. Steven had a fondness for endless facts and stupid jokes, Julius for subtlety and indirection. The present conversation could be simple speculation from the one, or a devious probing from the other.

Graves was grinning to himself. "I know, you don't think it's significant that we can eat Opal's food, or Quake's. But it is. For one thing, it disposes of a popular theory as to why Cecropians and humans did not fight when first they met. People say they avoided combat because they were not competing for the same resources. But that is nonsense. They not only compete for the same *inorganic* resources of metals and raw materials; they are also—with a little assistance at the bacterial level—able to eat the same food. A human could eat a Cecropian, if the need arose. Or vice versa. And that introduces a new mystery."

Rebka nodded to show that he was listening. It was better to play the straight man than say too much.

"We look at a Cecropian," Graves continued, "or a Lo'tfian, or a Hymenopt, and we say, how *alien* they are! How different from us! But the mystery is surely the other way round. We should say, why are we all so *similar*? How is it possible that beings derived from different clades, seeded on different worlds, warmed by suns of other stellar types, of totally disjoint biology, without one item of common history—how can it be that they are so alike that they *can* eat the same foods? That they are so close in body shape that we can use Earth-analogs—Cecropians, Hymenopts, Chrysemides—in beings from the most distant stars. That we can all *talk* to each other, one way or another, and understand each other amazingly well. That we share the same standards of behavior. So much so, that a single ethical council can agree on rules to apply through the whole of the spiral arm. How can these things be?

"But then, the spiral arm is filled with mysteries."

Graves was heading somewhere, Rebka was sure. But the other had a long way to go before he made any kind of sense. For the moment, all he seemed to offer was a philosophical lecture.

"Many mysteries," Graves went on. "The Builders, of course. What happened to them? What was their physiology, their history, their science? What is the function of the Lens, or of Paradox, or of Flambeau, or of the Phages? Of all the constructs of the Builders, surely the Phages are the most useless. Steven, if permitted, will discourse for many hours on this subject."

Rebka nodded again. But, pray God, he won't.

"And there are other, more recent mysteries, ones that puzzle me extremely. Think of the Zardalu. A few millennia ago they ruled more than a thousand worlds. We hear from their subject species that they were tyrannical, ruthless, merciless. But as their empire crumbled, those same vassal species rebelled and exterminated every Zardalu. Genocide. Was that not an action more barbaric than any practiced by the Zardalu themselves? And *why* did they choose to rule as they did? Did they have a different idea of ethical behavior, one unrecognizable to us? If so, they were truly alien, but we will never know in what way. What would an ethical council have made of the Zardalu?"

. . . a single ethical council can agree on rules . . . Rebka saw the sudden agony on Graves's lined face, and his mind flicked back to that earlier comment. By talking alternative moralities for the Zardalu, was Graves questioning the rules

set up by his own council? Was he preparing to disobey his own instructions?

Graves would not meet Rebka's eye. "I sometimes wonder if the ethics we favor are just as local and as limited as our common set of body shapes and thought patterns. The Builders had science truly alien to us. It does not match our worldview. We do not know how they built, or why they built. And yet our scientists tell us that there is only one set of physical laws that govern the whole universe—just as our philosophers tell us that we have one system of universal ethics! I wonder if Builder ethics would prove as alien as their science. Or if they, able to see how we treat our many different species, would not be appalled at our bias and misjudgment.

"I propose that we all have a lesson to learn, Captain, and it is as simple as this: the rules set up by any council must be *dynamic*. Regardless of the way they are viewed by the average person, they cannot be forever the same, set in stone and steel. We must study them constantly. And we must always ask if they can be improved."

Graves glared suddenly at Rebka, turned, and ascended the ramp to the upper level of the capsule.

Rebka remained seated and stared after him. There had been a counterpoint in those final sentences, almost of two voices. Was it possible that Julius and Steven Graves were holding some kind of interior dialog, with Rebka as no more than bystander? Maybe Julius wanted to do one thing, and Steven another.

It was preposterous; but no more unlikely than the development of individual consciousness in the mnemonic twin. And if working with Julius Graves on the surface of Quake would be bad, working with an unstable mixture of Julius and Steven would be impossible.

Twins, squabbling for dominance within one braincase? Rebka stood up, noticing as he did so that the deck offered much less pressure on the soles of his feet. His weight was down to a few pounds. They must be closing on Midway

Station. He headed for the ramp, wondering if Max Perry was still sitting in frozen contemplation of Quake. More and more, he felt like the keeper of a bunch of talented lunatics.

On his first trip to Quake, Rebka had been quite keen to enter and examine Midway Station. Humans had modified and cannibalized it, but it was still Builder technology, and that made it fascinating. Yet when Max Perry had chosen to bypass it—had been *driven* to bypass it—Rebka, in his own curiosity about Quake, had not argued with that decision.

Now the urgency to reach Quake was far greater—thirteen Dobelle days to Summertide, according to Rebka's internal clock; only one hundred and ten hours! Keep moving!—but now Perry insisted on stopping at Midway.

"Take a look for yourself." Perry pointed at the status board on their capsule. "See the power consumption? It's too high."

Rebka looked and could deduce nothing. Nor could Graves. If Perry said things did not seem right, the others had to believe him. There was no substitute for experience, and when they were on the Umbilical, Perry's knowledge reigned supreme.

"Are we in danger?" Graves asked.

"Not immediate danger." Perry was rubbing his nose thoughtfully. "But we can't risk heading down to Quake until we know why the power use is up. We daren't risk power loss for our own approach. And the central controls are all on Midway Station. We have to stop there and find out what's happening."

Under his direction, the capsule had already left its invisible guides and turned toward the misshapen bulk that filled half the sky on their left.

When humans had first discovered it, Midway Station had been an airless, arching vault, three kilometers across and almost empty. The walls were transparent. A man in a space suit could fly to the side facing Opal and detect that he was falling gently in that direction; one strong kick off the glassy outer wall would carry him through the open interior. He would then drift on and on, gradually slowing, until the opposite outer wall finally arrested his motion. The station marked the exact center of mass of the Quake/Opal coupled system.

The Builders' uses for Midway Station were not understood. That did not matter to most humans. They had filled the open sphere with a set of interlocking pressurized chambers, making it a temporary habitat and a storage facility for everything from thermal boots to freeze-dried food. Responding to some old cave instinct that favored enclosed spaces, they had also covered the external walls with a shiny, opaque monolayer. After four thousand years of Expansion, humans were apparently still uncomfortable with the open endlessness of space.

The capsule moved through a first airlock, then nosed molelike along a dark corridor just wide enough to permit its passage. Two minutes later it came to a cylindrical chamber filled with racks of display equipment and control boards.

Perry waited for a couple of minutes while the interior and exterior pressures were almost matched, then forced open the capsule's hatch and floated out. By the time the others had followed him he was already at work on one of the displays.

"Here." He pointed. "Straightforward enough. That's the problem. Another car was traveling the Umbilical at the same time as us."

"Where?" Rebka stared at the displays. They showed cameras and monitors all along the length of the Umbilical. He saw nothing.

"No, you won't see it." Perry had noticed where Rebka was looking. "The power drain is over now. That means the other capsule isn't on the Umbilical anymore."

"So where is it?" Graves asked.

Perry shrugged. "We'll find out. I hope there's someone

on duty down there. I'm sending an emergency signal." He was already moving across to a communications unit and tapping in entry codes.

Within twenty seconds Birdie Kelly's face came onto the screen. He was panting, and his hair was tousled. "Max? Commander Perry? What's wrong?"

"You can tell us, Birdie. Look at your power draw for the past few hours. We've had two capsules in use."

"That's right. No problem; we checked and there's plenty in reserve."

"Maybe. But there is a problem. That other car didn't have authorization."

Birdie's face was puzzled. "It certainly did. The woman had authorization from *you*. Personally. Hold one second."

He disappeared for a few moments from the screen and returned holding a marked sheet. "That's your sigil—see it?—right there."

"You let her have a car?"

"Of course I did." Birdie's tone switched from defensive to annoyed. "She had authorization, and she must have known the exact Umbilical command codes. If she hadn't, they'd never have risen one meter above sea level."

"They?"

"Sure. We assumed you knew all about this. The woman." Birdie Kelly peered at the sheet. "Darya Lang. With the two aliens. A Cecropian, and another form I didn't recognize. What's going on up there?"

"That authorization was bogus, Birdie. My sigil was faked." Perry glanced at another control board. "We show they're not on the Umbilical anymore."

"Right. They'll be on Quake. I hope they're having a better time up there than we are here." The wall behind Kelly shivered and tilted, and a scream of wind sounded through the link. He turned to glance away from the screen for a split second. "Commander, unless there's something else I can tell you, I have to get off right now."

"Another storm?"

"Worst ever. We just had a call through the Sling Network, five minutes ago. Spidermonkey is starting to break up. We have an airlift going in, but they're having trouble landing on the Sling to get people off."

"Go help there. We're on our way. Good luck, Birdie."

"Thanks. We're going to need it. Same to you."

Birdie Kelly was gone.

And so was Perry. By the time Rebka and Graves caught up with him he was starting to seal the capsule.

"Nine hours ahead of us," he said. "This near Summertide, that's more than enough to kill them all."

He touched a final command sequence, and the capsule started them back out along the narrow corridor.

Hans Rebka lay back in his seat and stared ahead, waiting for the first sight of Quake as they emerged from Midway Station.

He felt tense, yet oddly satisfied. His instincts had not let him down. The blow that he had been waiting for since Max Perry told the others that Quake was off-limits had been delivered.

Or at least, *one* blow had been struck.

His feeling of impending revelations had not gone away completely. The old inner voice assured him that there was more to come.

ARTIFACT: PHAGE.
UAC#: 1067
Galactic Coordinates: Not applicable
Name: Phage
Star/planet association: Not applicable
Bose Access Node: All
Estimated age: Various. 3.6 to 8.2 Megayears

Exploration History: The first Phages were reported by humans during the exploration of Flambeau, in E. 1233. Subsequently, it was learned that Phages had been observed and avoided by Cecropian explorers for at least five thousand years. The first human entry of a Phage maw was made in E. 1234 during the Maelstrom conflict (no survivors).

Phage avoidance systems came into widespread use in E. 2103, and are now standard equipment in Builder exploration.

Physical Description: The Phages are all externally identical, and probably internally similar though functionally variable. No sensor (or explorer) has ever returned from a Phage interior.

Each Phage has the form of a gray, regular dodecahedron, of side forty-eight meters. The surface is roughly textured, with mass sensors at the edge of each face. Maws can be opened at the center of any face, and can ingest objects of up to thirty meters' radius and of apparently indefinite length. (In E. 2238, Sawyer and S'kropa fed a solid silicaceous fragment of cylindrical cross-section and twenty-five meters' radius to a Phage of the Dendrite Artifact. With an ingestion rate of one kilometer per day, four hundred and twenty-five kilometers of material, corresponding to the full length of the fragment, were absorbed. No mass change was detected in the Phage, nor any change in any other of its physical parameters.)

Phages are capable of slow independent locomotion, with a mean rate of one or two meters per standard day.

No Phage has ever been seen to move at a velocity in excess of one meter per hour with respect to the local frame.

Intended Purpose: Unknown. Were it not for the fact that Phages have been found in association with over three hundred of the twelve hundred known artifacts, and only in such association, any relationship to the Builders would be questioned. They differ greatly in scale and number from all other Builder constructs.

It has been speculated that the Phages served as general scavengers for the Builders, since they are apparently able to ingest and break down any materials made by the clades, and anything made by the Builders with the single exception of the structural hulls and the paraforms (e.g., the external shell of Paradox, the surface of Sentinel, and the concentric hollow tubes of Maelstrom).

—From the *Lang Universal Artifact Catalog,*
Fourth Edition.

CHAPTER 12

Summertide
minus eleven.

DARYA LANG HAD the terrible suspicion that she had wasted half her life. Back on Sentinel Gate she had believed it when her family told her that she lived in the best place in the universe: "Sentinel Gate, half a step from Paradise," the saying went. And with her research facilities and her communications network, she had seen no need to travel.

But first Opal, and now Quake, taught her otherwise. She *loved* the newness of the experience, the contact with a world where everything was strange and exciting. From the moment she stepped out of the capsule onto the dry, dusty surface of Quake, she felt all her senses intensify by a factor of a hundred.

Her nose said it first. The air of Quake held a powerful mixture of odors. That was the scent of flowers, surely, but not the lush, lavish extravagances that garlanded Sentinel Gate. She had to seek them out—and there they were, not five paces in front of her, tiny bell-shaped blooms of lilac and lavender that peeped out from a gray-green cover of wiry gorse. The plants hugged the sides of a long, narrow crevice too small to be called a valley. From their miniature blossoms came an urgent midday perfume, out of all proportion to their size. It was as though flowering, fertilization, and seeding could not wait another hour.

And maybe it can't, Darya thought. For overlaid on that heady scent was a sinister, sulfurous tinge of distant vulcanism: the breath of Quake, approaching Summertide. She paused, breathed deep, and knew she would remember the mixture of smells forever.

Then she sneezed, and sneezed again. There was fine dust in the air, irritant powdery particles that tickled the nose.

She raised her eyes, looking beyond the miniature valley with its carpet of urgent flowers, out beyond the plain to a smoky horizon fifteen kilometers away. The effects of dust were easy to see there. Where the nearby surface stood out in harsh umbers and ochres, in the distance a gray pall had darkened and softened the artist's palette, painting everything in muted tones. The horizon itself was not visible, except that to the east her eye traced—or imagined—a faint line of volcanic peaks, cinnamon-hued and jagged.

Mandel stood high in the sky. As she watched, it began to creep behind the shielding bulk of Opal. The brilliant crescent shrank, moment by moment. At the present time of year there would be no more than partial eclipse, but it was enough to change the character of the light. The redder tones of Amaranth bled into the landscape. Quake's surface became a firelit landscape of subterranean gloom.

At that moment Darya heard the first voice of Summertide. A low rumble filled the air, like the complaining snore of a sleepy giant. The ground trembled. She felt a quiver and a pleasant tingle in the soles of her feet.

"Professor Lang," J'merlia said from behind her. "Atvar H'sial reminds you that we have far to go, and little time. If we might proceed . . ."

Darya realized that she had not yet completed her first step onto Quake's surface, and Atvar H'sial and J'merlia were still standing on the ladder from the capsule. As Darya moved out of the way the Cecropian crept past her and stood motionless, broad head sweeping from side to side. J'merlia came to crouch beneath the front of the carapace.

Darya watched the trumpet-horn ears as they swept across the scene. What did Atvar H'sial "see" when she listened to Quake? What did those exquisite organs of smell "hear," when every airborne molecule could tell a story?

They had talked about the world as it was perceived by echolocation, but the explanation was unsatisfying. The best analogy that Darya could create was of a human standing on the seabed, in a place where the water was turbid and the light level low. Everything was monochrome vision, with a range of only a few tens of meters.

But the analogy was inadequate. Atvar H'sial was sensitive to a huge range of sound frequencies, and she could certainly "see" the distant mutter of the volcanoes. Those signals lacked the fine spatial resolution offered by her own sonar, but they were definite sensory inputs.

And there were other factors, perhaps even other *senses,* that Darya was only vaguely aware of; for instance, at the moment the Cecropian was lifting one forelimb and pointing off to the middle distance. Was she sensing the waft of distant odors, with olfactory lobes so acute that every trace of smell told a story?

"There is animal life here," J'merlia translated. "And winged forms. This suggests another possible method of surviving Summertide, unmentioned by Commander Perry. By remaining in Quake's Mandel-shadow, and always aloft, these would be safe."

Darya could see the flying creatures—just. They were half a meter long, with dark bodies and gauzy, diaphanous wings; too delicate, surely, to survive the turbulence of Summertide. Far more likely, they had already laid their eggs and would die in the next few days. But Atvar H'sial was right about one thing: there were many facts about Quake that humans did not know, or Max Perry was not telling.

The thought came to her again: this was a whole planet, a world with its own intricate life-balance; hundreds of millions of square kilometers of land and small lakes, empty of humans or other intelligence, spread out for their inspection. Infinite diversity was possible there, but it would take a lifetime to explore and know it.

Right, her more practical side said. But we don't have a whole lifetime. In eighty hours we'd better be finished with our exploration and on our way.

Leaving Atvar H'sial to her sightless sweep of the landscape, Darya moved around the foot of the Umbilical to the line of aircars. There were eight of them, sitting under the lee of their protective sheet of Builder material. The apron they stood on was connected by silicon fiber cables to the Umbilical itself and would lift with it at Summertide.

Darya climbed into one of the cars and inspected its controls. As Atvar H'sial had foretold, the vehicle was human-made and identical with the one that they had used for travel on Opal. It was fully charged, and Darya could fly it with no problem, provided—and at the thought, her collarbone gave a twinge of reminder—that they did not hit a storm like the one that had wiped them out last time.

She held up an open hand to test the wind. At the moment it was no more than a stiff breeze, nothing to worry about. Even allowing for the twisting pockets of dust, visibility was at least three or four kilometers. That was ample for a landing, and they could fly far above any sandstorm.

At her urging, Atvar H'sial and J'merlia climbed into the car and settled in for the flight. Darya took them up at once, heading for an altitude that would clear any turbulence. J'merlia squatted by her side in the front of the car. Darya had explained the aircar controls to him when they were flying on Opal, and if necessary he could probably pilot the craft. But apparently he would never dream of trying to do so without direction from Atvar H'sial.

Darya tried to talk with him and failed. She had imagined that he might behave differently toward her after their conversations while they were recuperating from the crash. She was wrong. When Atvar H'sial was present he refused to make an independent move, and for the first three hours of the trip he spoke only at Atvar H'sial's direction.

But in the fourth hour J'merlia made a move of his own, unprompted by his mistress. He suddenly sat upright and pointed. "There. Above."

They were cruising on autopilot at twenty thousand meters, far above most of Quake's atmosphere and out of reach of surface storms. Darya had not been looking up. She had been surveying the ground ahead of them, using the car's imaging sensors. At top resolution she could see plenty of evidence of life on Quake. The lake-dotted hill ranges bore great herds of white-backed animals, moving away from the high ground and heading for water as steadily and inexorably as a retreating wave. She watched their compact mass divide and break around bare ridges and massive boulders. A few kilometers farther on, the hill country ended, and she saw wriggling lines of dark green, following and defining the moist gravel of streambeds. The dry streams ended in dense pockets of vegetation, impenetrable from above, lining the bottom of hollows of uncertain depth.

As Darya looked up at J'merlia's words, he leaned over her shoulder and pointed with a thin, multijointed arm into the blue-black and starlit sky.

Atvar H'sial hissed. "Another car," J'merlia translated. "We have been pursued up the Umbilical, and much more quickly than we expected."

The moving light was right above them, following their own ground track but at much greater altitude. It was also rapidly outdistancing them. Darya allowed the autopilot to continue the flight while she rotated the high-mag sensor to take a closer look at the newcomer.

"No," she said after a few moments. "It's not an aircar." She set the car's little on-board computer to work, computing a trajectory. "It's too high, and it's moving much too fast. And look—it's growing brighter. We're not looking at an aircar's lights."

"Then what is it?"

"It's a spaceship. And that bright glow means it's entering Quake's atmosphere." Darya glanced at the computer output, providing a first estimate of the other ship's final trajectory. "We'd better put down for a while and consider what we do next."

"No." Atvar H'sial's thoughts came as a mutter of protest from J'merlia.

"I know; I don't want to, either," Darya said. "But we have to, unless you know something I don't. The computer needs a few more points of tracking data to be sure, but it's already giving us a preliminary result. That ship is landing. I don't know who is in it, but it will touch down just where we don't want it—a few kilometers from our own destination."

Twilight on Quake—if so sudden and ominous a nightfall, red as dragon's blood, could justify that description.

Mandel would rise in three hours. Amaranth lay low on the horizon, its ruddy face obscured by clouds of dust. Gargantua alone shone in full splendor, a banded marble of orange and salmon-pink.

The aircar stood on a level patch of gravel, readied for rapid takeoff. Darya Lang had set them down between two small water bodies, in an area shown on the map to be liberally scattered with miniature freshwater lakes.

The map had lied in at least one respect. Atvar H'sial, crouched down by one of the ponds, had sucked water noisily through her proboscis. J'merlia pronounced it potable. But Darya, tasting the same pool, spat in disgust and wondered about Cecropian metabolism. The lake water was harsh and bitter to the tongue, filled with strong alkalines. She could not drink it, and would have to rely on the car's supplies.

Darya walked back past the car and prepared for sleep. Even with the help of the autopilot, the journey around Quake had been a strain. Harmless as the planet below her seemed, she had not dared to lower her concentration for more than a moment; and now finally free to relax, she could not do so.

There was too much to see, too much to speculate on.

According to Perry, Quake so close to Summertide should have been an inferno. The crust ought to have been heaving and shattered, surface ablaze with brush fires, plants shriveled and dying in air burning hot and close to unbreathable. The animals should have been long gone, already dead or estivating far below the surface.

Instead she could breathe and walk and sit in moderate comfort, and there were ample signs all about her of energetic life. Darya had set her camp bed outside, close to one of the pools and in the shade of a thicket of horsetails. She could hear animals scuttling through them, ignoring her presence, and the ground by the water was riddled with holes of all different sizes, as a variety of small creatures tunneled underground. When the distant growl of thunder or vulcanism died away, she could hear those workers, scrabbling steadily deeper into the drying earth.

But it was *warm,* she would admit that. The disappearance of Mandel from the sky had brought little relief. Sweat stained her suit and ran down the hollow of her neck.

She lay down on her camp bed. Although Quake seemed safe enough, she was worried about what they should do next. That spaceship must be from Opal, and it had probably been sent to drag them back there. If they went on, they might be captured and forced to leave Quake. But if they did not keep going, they would not reach their destination.

While she was pondering that, Atvar H'sial surprised her by coming across and offering a meal of Opal fruit and bottled water. Darya took it and nodded her thanks. That was a shared gesture. The Cecropian nodded back and retreated to the interior of the aircar.

As Darya ate she wondered about her two companions. She had never seen either of them eat. Perhaps, like the people on some Alliance worlds, they regarded the taking of food as a private function. Or maybe they were like the tortoises on Opal, who according to the crewmen at Starside Port could survive quite happily for a full year on just water. But then why would Atvar H'sial think to feed the human of the group?

She lay back on the camp bed, pulled the waterproof sheet up to her neck, and watched the heavens reeling above her. The stars moved so fast . . . on Sentinel Gate, with its thirty-eight-hour day, the swing of the starry vault was almost imperceptible. Which direction in space did her homeworld lie? She puzzled over the unfamiliar constellations. That way . . . or that. . . . Her mind drifted off toward the stars. She wrenched her thoughts back with an effort to the present. She still had a decision to make.

Should they proceed to the place that her calculations pointed to as the focus of activity at Summertide? They could go, knowing that others would be there also. Or should she hang back and wait? Or should they go just partway, pause for a while . . .

Go partway, pause . . .

Darya Lang passed easily into a deep sleep, a dreamless slumber so profound that nearby noise and vibration did not wake her. Brief dawn came; day passed, and again it was night and flaming day. The sounds of tunneling animals ended. Opal and Quake had made two complete turns about each other before Darya drifted back to consciousness.

She woke slowly to the half day of Amaranth's light. It was a full minute before she knew where she was, another before she felt ready to sit up and look around her.

Atvar H'sial and J'merlia were nowhere to be seen. The aircar was gone. A small heap of supplies and equipment had been placed under a thin rainproof sheet next to the camp bed. Nothing else, from horizon to horizon, suggested that humans or aliens had ever been there.

She dropped to her knees and scrabbled through the pile, searching for a message. There was no note, no recording, no sign. Nothing that might help her except a few containers of food and drink, a miniature signal generator, a gun, and a flashlight.

Darya looked at her watch. Nine more Dobelle days. Seventy-two hours to go before the worst Summertide ever. And she was stranded on Quake, alone, six thousand kilometers from the safety of the Umbilical . . .

The panic that she had felt on first leaving Sentinel Gate crept back into her heart.

CHAPTER 13

    . . . *the orange glow on the horizon was continuous, the burning ground reflecting from high dust clouds. As they watched, a new burst of crimson arose, no more than a kilometer from where they stood. It developed smoky tendrils and grew taller. Soon it stretched from earth to sky. As the lava bubbled to the summit of the crater he turned to Amy.*

In spite of his warning she still stood outside the car. When the flash of the explosion was replaced by a glow of red-hot lava she clapped her hands, entranced by the colors and the shapes. Shock waves of sound rolled and echoed from the hills behind. The stream of fire crested the cone and began to roll toward them, as easy-flowing and fast as running water. Where it touched the cooler earth, white flux sputtered and sparked.

Max stared at her face. He saw no fear, only the rapt entrancement of a child at a birthday party.

That was what it was. She saw it all as a fireworks display. Caution had to come from him. He leaned forward from the car seat to pluck at her sleeve.

"Get in." He was forced to shout to be heard. "We have to start back for the Stalk. You know it's a five-hour journey."

She glared at him and pulled away. He knew the pout very

well. "Not now, Max." He read the words from her lips, but he could not hear her. "I want to wait until the lava reaches the water."

"No!" He was yelling. "Absolutely not. I'll take no more risks! It's boiling hot out there, and it's getting nearly as bad in the car."

She was walking away, not listening to him. He felt tight-chested and overheated despite the air curtain that held a sheath of cooler air at the open hatch. It was mostly in his mind, he knew that—the fiery furnace of his own worries that consumed him. And yet the outside heat was real enough. He stumbled out of the car and followed her across the steaming surface.

"Stop pestering me. I'll come in a minute." Amy had turned around to look at the whole infernal scene. There was—thank God!—no sign yet of another eruption, but one could happen at any second.

"Max, you have to relax." She came close, shouting right into his ear. "Learn to have fun. All the time we've been here, you've sat like a lump of Sling underside. Let yourself go— get into the swing of things."

He took her hand and began to pull her toward the car. After a moment of resistance she allowed herself to be steered along. With her eyes still on the volcano's bright fury, she did not look where they were going.

And then, when they were no more than a few meters from the car, she broke loose and ran laughing across the flat, steaming surface of heat-baked rock. She was ten paces ahead of him before he could start after her. By then it was too late.

Summertide
minus ten.

GRAVES AND PERRY made it sound simple. Rebka argued that it was impossible.

"Look at the arithmetic," he said as the Umbilical's capsule lowered them gently to the surface of Quake. "We have a planetary radius of fifty-one hundred kilometers, and a surface that's less than three percent covered by water. That gives over three hundred million square kilometers of land. Three hundred million! Think how long it can take to search *one* square kilometer. We could look for years and never find them."

"We don't have years," Perry said. "And I know it's a big area. But you seem to assume we'll do a random search, and of course we won't. I can rule out most areas before we start."

"And I know that the Carmel twins will avoid all open spaces," Graves added.

"How can you possibly know that?" Rebka was being the pessimist.

"Because Quake is usually cloud-free." Graves was unmoved by the other's skepticism. "Their homeworld of Shasta has a high-resolution spaceborne system that gives continuous surveillance of the surface."

"But Quake doesn't."

"Ah, but the twins don't know that. They'll assume that if they're out on the open surface, they'll be spotted and picked up. They'll have run for deep cover and stayed there."

"And I can tell you now," Perry said, "that cuts the problem way down. There are only three places that a sane human would take refuge on Quake. We'll start with these three areas—and we'll have to finish with them, too."

"But if we don't find them there," Graves began, "we can broaden—"

"No, we can't," Perry said, cutting him off. "Summertide, Councilor. It will hit maximum strength in less than eighty hours. We'd better not be here then—not you, not me, and not the twins."

Max Perry listed the three most likely areas: in the high forests of the Morgenstern Uplands; upon—or probably *within*—one of the Thousand Lakes; or in the deep vegetation pockets of the Pentacline Depression.

"Which reduces the area to be searched by a factor of thousands," he said.

"And still leaves tens of thousands of square kilometers to be examined," Rebka replied. "In detail. And don't forget, this isn't your standard search-and-rescue problem. Usually, the missing persons *want* to be found. They cooperate, as best they can. But the twins won't send distress signals until conditions are intolerable. If they signal then, it will probably be too late."

If his arguments impressed Julius Graves, no one would have known it from the other's grinning face. While Max Perry was busy checking the aircars, Graves dragged Rebka away in the direction of the smoke-edged line of volcanic hills.

"I need a quiet word with you, Captain," he said confidentially. "Just for a moment or two."

Warm ash drifted down like pale-gray snow, settling onto their heads and shoulders. The ground was already covered a centimeter deep. Of the low-growing plants and the peaceful herbivores of Rebka's first visit to Quake there was no sign. Even the lake itself had vanished, hidden beneath a scummy layer of volcanic ash. Instead of the predicted rumble and roar of seismic violence, the planet held a hot, brooding silence.

"You realize," Graves continued, "that we don't need to stay together? There are aircars here to spare."

"I know we could cover three times as much ground if we split up," Rebka replied. "But I'm not sure I want to do it. Perry has unique knowledge of Quake, while you have never been here before."

"Aha! Your thoughts parallel my own." Graves brushed a flake of ash from the end of his nose. "The logical course of action is quite clear: Perry has identified three areas of Quake where fugitives will naturally seek to hide. Those regions are widely separated; but there are enough aircars for each of us to tackle one of them. Therefore, we can all go separately, and examine one area each. That's what logic says. But I say, phooey, who wants *logic*? Not you, and not me. We want *results.*"

He leaned closer to Rebka. "And frankly, I worry about the stability of Commander Perry. Say 'Quake' and 'Summertide' to him, and his eyes almost roll out of his head. We can't let him go off on his own. What do you think?"

I think that you and Perry both need keepers, is what I think, but I don't want to come right out and say it. Rebka knew what was on the way. He was going to be saddled with Perry—the same stupid assignment that had brought him to Dobelle—while Graves charged off uncontrolled into the Quake wilderness and probably killed himself.

"I agree, Councilor, Perry should not go alone. But I don't want to waste—"

"Then we agree that I must go with Perry," Graves went on, ignoring Rebka. "You see, if he gets into trouble, I can help him. No one else is able to do that. So he and I will tackle the Morgenstern Uplands, while you do the Thousand Lakes—Perry says that's the quickest and easiest. And if neither of us finds the twins, then whoever gets through first takes on the Pentacline Depression."

What does one do when a madman suggests an appealing course of action? One worries—but probably goes along with it. In any case, Graves was in no mood to listen to an argument. When Rebka pointed out again how low the chances were that they would find the twins at all, the councilor snapped his fingers.

"Piffle. I *know* we'll find them. Think positive, Captain Rebka. Be an optimist! It's the only way to live."

And a likely way to die, Rebka thought. But he gave up. Graves would not be dissuaded, and maybe he and Perry deserved each other.

It was also one of the first rules of life, something Rebka had learned as a six-year-old in the hot saline caverns of Teufel. When someone gives you what you want, *leave*—before he has time to think again and take it back.

"Very well, Councilor. As soon as a car is ready I'll be on my way."

Rebka had half an hour's start on the other two. The cargo space of the fastest aircars was not designed to carry large and heavy cases, and Julius Graves dithered over his luggage for a long time before he finally left behind everything except a little bag. The rest he put back in an Umbilical capsule. At last he pronounced himself ready to leave.

After takeoff Max Perry set the craft to cruise on autopilot and headed for the Morgenstern Uplands. When they were within scanning range, both men crouched over the displays.

"Primitive equipment," Graves said. He was grimacing and twitching with concentration as he pored over images. Checking the displays was a long and tedious process. "If this were an Alliance car, we wouldn't have to watch—we'd sit back and wait for the system to *tell* us when it found the twins. As it is it's the other way round. I have to sit and peer at this thing and tell it what it's seeing. Primitive!"

"It's the best we have on Opal or Quake."

"I believe you. But do you ever ask yourself why all the worlds of the spiral arm are not as wealthy as Earth and the other old regions of Crawlspace? Why isn't *every* planet using the latest technology? Why don't all worlds have more service robots than people, like Earth? Why aren't they all *rich,* everyone on every colony? We know how to *make* advanced equipment. Why doesn't every planet have it, instead of just a few?"

Perry had no answers, but he grunted to show that he was listening.

He was not. With Julius Graves busy looking at images, that had to be Steven chattering on. And Perry was busy himself, with the radio receiving equipment. Graves did not believe that the Carmel twins would send a distress call. Perry disagreed. As Summertide came closer the twins ought to be more than ready to be arrested and rescued.

"It's a simple reason," Graves continued, "the cause of Dobelle's poverty. It is built into the basic nature of humanity. A rational species would make sure that one world was fully developed and perfect for humans before going on to another. But we don't know how to do that! We have the outward urge. Before a planet is half settled, off go the new ships, ready to explore the next one. And very few people say, wait a moment, let's get this one right before we go on."

He took a closer look at a couple of false alarms on the image, then shook his head in dismissal.

"We're just too nosy, Commander," he went on. "Most humans have their patience level set a little too low, and their curiosity a bit too high. The Cecropians are as bad as we are. So almost all the wealth of the spiral arm—and *all* the luxury—finds its way into the hands of the stay-at-homes. It's the old paradox, one that predates the Expansion: the groups that do nothing to *create* wealth manage to gain possession of most of it. Whereas the ones that do all the work finish up with very few possessions. Perhaps one day that will change. Maybe in another ten thousand years—"

"Radio beacon," Perry interrupted. "A weak one, but it's there."

Graves froze in position and did not look up. "Impossible." His voice was sharp. Julius Graves was back in charge.

"They would not advertise their presence on Quake. Not after running so far and for so long."

"Take a look for yourself."

Graves slid across the seat. "How far away is it?"

"Long way." Perry studied the range and vector settings. "In fact, too far. That signal isn't coming from anywhere within the Morgenstern Uplands. The source is at least four thousand kilometers beyond the edge. We're getting ionospheric bounce, or we wouldn't hear them at all."

"How about the Thousand Lakes?"

"Could be. The vector isn't quite right, but there's a lot of noise in the signal. And the range is spot on."

"Then it's Rebka." Graves slapped his hand flat on the table. "It must be. He goes off to look, and no sooner do we get down to work than he's in trouble. Before we even—"

"Not Rebka."

"How do you know?"

"It's not his aircar." Perry was running comparisons with the signal templates. "Not any of ours. Wrong frequency, wrong signal format. Looks like a portable send unit, low power."

"Then it's the Carmel twins! And they must be in terrible trouble, if they're willing to ask for help. Can you take us there?"

"Easy. We just home on the beacon."

"How long from here?"

"Six or seven hours, top speed."

As he spoke Perry was looking at the car's chronometer.

"How long?" Graves had followed his look.

"A bit more than eight Quake days to Summertide; say, sixty-seven hours from now."

"Seven hours to Thousand Lakes, eight more back to the Umbilical. Then up and away. Plenty of time. We'll escape from Quake long before the worst."

Perry shook his head. "You don't understand. Quake is inhomogeneous, with variable internal structure. The earthquakes can pop up anywhere, long before Summertide. We're not seeing much activity here in the Uplands, but the Thousand Lakes area could be a nightmare."

"Come on, man, you're as bad as Rebka. It can't be all that unpleasant, if the Carmel twins are still alive there."

"You said it right. *If* they're still alive there." Perry was at the controls, and already the car was turning. "There's one thing you're forgetting, Councilor. Radio beacons are made tough—a whole lot tougher than human beings."

CHAPTER 14

Summertide minus nine.

THE WEAPONS SENSORS had been tracking the car for a long time. When it came within line-of-sight range, Louis Nenda placed the starship's concealed arsenal on Full Alert.

The approaching aircar slowed, as though aware of the destructive power poised a few kilometers in front of it. It moved sideways, then sank to a vertical landing on a seamed shelf of rock, well away from the ship.

Nenda kept the weapons primed for action, watching as the car's hatch eased open.

"Who's it gonna be, then?" he said softly in Communion patois, more to himself than to Kallik. "Place your bets, ladies and gentlemen. Name them visitors."

A familiar pair of figures climbed out onto the steaming, rubble-strewn shelf. Both wore breathing masks, but they were easily recognizable. Louis Nenda grunted in satisfaction and flipped every weapon to standby mode.

"They'll do fine. Open the hatch, Kallik. Show the guests some hospitality."

Atvar H'sial and J'merlia were steadily approaching, picking their way carefully past rounded blue-gray boulders and across a scree of loose gravel. Louis Nenda had chosen his landing site carefully, on the most solid-seeming and permanent surface that he could find; still there were drifts of blown dust and signs of recent earth movement. A deep, jagged crack ran from the shelf where the aircar had just landed, halfway to the much bigger ship. Atvar H'sial was following the line of the fissure, occasionally peering over the edge to sniff the air and estimate the bottom depth. That trench was her only possible refuge. Nothing lived in this region of Quake, and there was no shred of cover within ten kilometers. The ship's weapons, thirty meters high in the dome of the vessel, enjoyed a three-hundred-and-sixty-degree prospect.

Atvar H'sial entered the lower hatch, bowing low—not from any idea of respect for Louis Nenda, but because she was squeezing in through an entrance designed for something half her height. Inside, she pulled off her breathing mask. J'merlia followed, with an odd little whistle of greeting to Kallik, then scurried forward to crouch in front of his owner.

The Cecropian straightened and moved closer to Nenda. "You chose not to use your weapons on us," J'merlia translated. "A wise decision."

"From your point of view? I'm sure it was. But what's this talk of weapons?" Nenda's voice was mocking. "You'll find no weapons here."

"You may be right," Atvar H'sial said through J'merlia. "If the inspection facility on Opal could not find them, it may be that we could not." Atvar H'sial's broad white head turned up to look at the ceiling. "However, if you will permit me half an hour for inspection of your starship's upper deck . . ."

"Oh, I don't think so." Louis Nenda grinned. "It might be fun, but we really don't have half an hour to play around. Not with Summertide breathing down our necks. Suppose we stop fencing for a while? I'll not ask what tools and weapons you're carrying on you, if you'll stop worrying about what's on this ship. We've got more important things to talk about."

"Ah. A truce, you suggest." The words came from J'merlia, but it was Atvar H'sial who held out a long foreleg. "Agreed. But where do we begin? How do we discuss cooperation, without revealing too much of what we each know?"

"For a start, we send them"—Nenda pointed at J'merlia and Kallik—"outside."

Atvar H'sial's yellow trumpet-horns turned to scan the Hymenopt, then moved down to the Lo'tfian crouched beneath her carapace.

"Is it safe there?" J'merlia translated.

"Not specially." Nenda raised bushy eyebrows. "Hey, what do you want, carnival time on Primavera? It's not safe anywhere on Quake right now, and you know it. Is your bug extrasensitive to heat and light? I don't want to fry him."

"Not particularly sensitive," J'merlia translated, with no sign of emotion. "Given water, J'merlia can survive heat and bad air for a long period, even without a respirator. But the communication between you and me . . ."

"Trust me." Nenda pointed to J'merlia and Kallik and jerked a thumb toward the hatch. "Out. Both of you." He switched to Communion talk. "Kallik, take plenty of water with you for J'merlia. We'll tell you when to come back in."

He waited until the two aliens were outside and the hatch was closed, then moved forward to sit in the shadow of Atvar H'sial's carapace. He took a deep breath and opened his shirt, revealing a chest completely covered with an array of gray molelike nodules and deep pockmarks. He closed his eyes and waited.

"Be patient." The coded pheromones diffused slowly into the air. "It is not easy . . . and I lack . . . recent practice."

"Ah." Atvar H'sial was nodding her blind head and pointing her receptors to the chest array. "A Zardalu augmentation, I assume? Heard of but never encountered by me. May I ask, at what physical price?"

"The usual." Louis Nenda's face showed a harsh ecstasy.

"Pain—the going rate for every Zardalu augment. That's all right, I'm getting there. I'm going to talk in human style as we go, if you don't mind. It helps me frame my thoughts."

"But there is no need for this!" In addition to the literal meaning, Louis Nenda's pheromone receptors picked up Atvar H'sial's disdain and contemptuous amusement. "J'merlia is totally loyal to me, as I assume Kallik is to you. They would die before they would reveal any conversation of ours."

"They certainly would." Louis Nenda managed to chuckle. "I'd make sure of that. But I don't know how smart J'merlia is. Things can always come out by accident, specially if someone tricky asks the questions. Only way to be really safe is if they're not here to listen." The laugh changed to a grunt of discomfort. "All right, let's get down to business and finish this as quick as we can. It's hard on me."

"We need a protocol for the exchange of information."

"I know. Here's my suggestion. I'll make a statement. You can agree, disagree, or make a statement of your own, but no one is obliged to answer any question. Like this. Fact: You have no interest at all in environmentally stressed lifeforms on Quake. That's all bull. You came here because you are a specialist on the Builders."

"To you, I will not deny it." Atvar H'sial reared up to full height. The red-and-white ruffles below the head expanded. "I am more than a specialist. I am *the* specialist on the Builders in the Cecropia Federation." The pheromones carried a message of pride more powerful than words ever could. "I was the first to fathom the mystery of Tantalus; the first—and only—Cecropian to survive a transit of Flambeau. I realized the significance of Summertide before Darya Lang was foolish enough to publish her findings. I—"

"All right. You're smart, I hear you." Nenda's breathing was becoming easier. "Tell me something I need to know, or we'll be here till Summertide and we'll all fry."

"Very well. You are here because you want to know what will happen at Summertide. But I say that you did not initiate that idea. You know too little science or history. Someone else applied Darya Lang's idea and told you the significance of this time and place. It would be of interest to know who that someone is."

"That sure sounds like a question to me, even if it's not phrased like one. But I'll tell you." Nenda jerked his thumb to the ship's hatch. "Kallik."

"Your Hymenopt? A slave!" Atvar H'sial was more than surprised. She was outraged. "It is not fitting for a slave species to perform such high-level work."

"Ah, nuts." Nenda was grinning. "She has a brain—might as well let her use it for my benefit. Anyway, it keeps her happy when she can read and calculate in her spare time. She saw Lang's work, then did the computing herself. She decided this was the special time and place. Then she got all excited, wanted to tell somebody. I said no way. We'll tell no one—and we'll go to Quake ourselves. And here we are. But I want to compare notes with you on something more specific. Let's talk about what will happen here at Summertide."

"That sounds like a question to me. I do not choose to answer."

"So I'll make a statement instead. Let me tell you what Kallik says, based on her analysis, and you can comment if you want to. She says the Builders are going to return—here, and at Summertide. The secret of their technology and the reason for their disappearance will be revealed to those present. How's that grab you?"

"That is also a question, not a statement, but I will answer it. Kallik's suggestion is plausible. However, it is not certain. There is no actual evidence for an appearance of the Builders."

"So it's a bet you have to make. And what Kallik didn't say—but what I think, and it won't surprise me if you're way ahead of me—is that anyone who gets the keys to

Builder technology will be plenty powerful in this spiral arm."

"I agree. The technology will be the prize."

"For some people. But it's still not the only reason you're here." Nenda moved closer and went so far as to tap Atvar H'sial's shiny abdomen with his index finger. "Fact: You're another Builder fanatic, as much as Lang and Kallik. You all think you're going to *meet* the Builders, seventy hours from now. Know what Kallik calls this Summertide? The *Epiphany*—when the gods will appear."

"My own term is the Awakening. Do you accept that there will be some momentous event?"

"Hell, I don't know. What do you mean by momentous? I'm damn sure the gods won't appear. The whole thing's a long shot, but it's for super-big stakes. That's my game. I'm a gambler, and I play long shots."

"You are wrong. It is not a long shot. *It will happen.*"

Atvar H'sial's conviction was unmistakable in the pheromonal message. Nenda knew that subtlety of communication technique was beyond him. He wondered if the Cecropians had mastered the means of *lying* with their chemical messengers.

"Already there is evidence of it," Atvar H'sial went on. "All through the spiral arm, the artifacts are restless. And they point here."

"Hey, you don't have to persuade me. I flew eight hundred light-years to land on this crapheap—and I don't give a damn about the artifacts. You can have them all—you're as bad as Kallik. Me, I'll settle for a few new bits of Builder technology. But I've another question for you. Why did you come here to see me, knowing I might blow you away? Not just to compare notes with me and Kallik, that's for sure."

"Ah. That is true. I came because you need me. And because I need you." Atvar H'sial gestured to the port, and to the bare expanse of Quake beyond it. "If you and I were the only people on this world, we would enjoy sole knowledge of any new Builder techniques. We might battle later over who should enjoy the powers of the Builders, but I would accept such a contest."

"That would be your mistake. But I still don't know why you came to me."

"Because today we are *not* the only ones on Quake. Others are here, who would make new knowledge generally available for the sake of science. Now, you are not a scientist, you are an adventurer. You are here for personal gain."

"Damn right. And so are you."

"Perhaps." There was amusement in Atvar H'sial's message, now that Louis Nenda knew how to read it. "And we do not want the Builders' powers shared still further. Rebka, Graves, and Perry are on Quake. They traveled the Umbilical just after us. They will not keep new knowledge to themselves. We might do something about that, but we have no way of knowing where they are."

"I assumed they would follow. What about Darya Lang? She came with you."

"No problem. She has . . . already been taken care of."

Chill certainty in the pheromones. There was a long pause.

"Well, all right," Louis Nenda said at last. His voice was soft. "You are a cold-blooded son of a bitch, aren't you?"

The Cecropian's proboscis trembled. "We attempt to give satisfaction."

"And you're taking a risk, telling me this."

"I think not." Atvar H'sial was silent for a moment. "There is no risk. Not to someone who has read and remembered the Lascia Four files. May I refresh your memory? A medical-supply capsule was plundered en route to Lascia Four. It never reached the planet, and without the viral inhibitors it carried, three hundred thousand people died. An augmented human, accompanied by a Hymenopt slave, was guilty of that atrocity. The Hymenopt died, but the human escaped and was never captured."

Louis Nenda said nothing.

"But about the other humans," Atvar H'sial continued.

"We cannot locate them. I am especially worried about Graves."

"He's a madman."

"True. And he reads me and you—even without augmentation, he understands what I am thinking. He is too dangerous. I want him out of the way. I want *all three* out of the way."

"Understood. But I can't find them on Quake, any more than you can. So what are you proposing?"

"Before Summertide they will leave Quake. Their escape route is the Umbilical. That would have been my own line of retreat, until I saw your ship arriving and realized that it is equipped for space travel."

"To the edge of the galaxy, if I want to go. I can see how that might be useful to you, getting off Quake with no risk of running into Graves. But what do you have to offer *me*? I don't want to be crude about this, but I'm not your fairy godmother. Why should I provide you with free transportation off Quake? I told Kallik, we can have a good look around her site on the surface, but come Summertide, we'll be watching from orbit. But that's for *us*. I'm not running a bus service. Why should I help you?"

"Because I know the codes for control of the Umbilical. The *complete* codes."

"But why should I care . . ." Louis Nenda slowly looked up at the Cecropian, at the same time as the sightless head swung down close to him.

"You see?" The pheromones added a message more strong and yet more subtle than any words: pleasure, triumph, the touch of death.

"I do. It's pretty damned clear. But what about *them*?" Nenda gestured at the window. J'merlia and Kallik were huddled together on the hot ground, trying to find shelter behind the starship from Mandel's searing summer rays. They were both shaking, and J'merlia seemed to be trying to comfort the Hymenopt. "I'll go along with what you propose, but there's no way I'm going to drag them along to watch."

"Agreed. And we do not *need* them. Anything that requires J'merlia's sensitivity to half-micrometer radiation, you can perform in his place."

"I can *see*, if that's what you mean." Nenda was already at the hatch, calling to Kallik. "Look, I'm not willing to leave them with my ship, either. In fact, I'm not willing to leave the ship here at all. We'll fly it around to the Umbilical. And we'll leave J'merlia and Kallik to wait for us here."

"Not quite that, I suggest." Atvar H'sial was moving her legs to full extension, towering over Louis Nenda. "We do not want them to have access to the aircar, either."

"Kallik won't touch it if I tell her not to." Nenda waited while the Cecropian stared at him. Even the pheromonal overtones were silent. "Oh, all right. I agree with you. We won't leave them here. No risk is better than a small one—and I'm not too sure of your Lo'tfian. How do you want to handle it?"

"Very simple. We will give them a beacon and some supplies, and drop them off at a convenient point between here and the foot of the Umbilical. When we have done our work there we will home on them, pick them up, look at the site for the Awakening—and head for orbit before it gets too wild on the surface."

"Suppose surface conditions get bad, right where we leave them? Perry swore they will, and I don't think he was lying."

"If things become bad too soon, that would be a pity." Atvar H'sial stood with her head turned, as J'merlia and Kallik waited at the open hatch. Both the slaves were quivering with fear and tension. "But you can always find another Hymenopt. And although J'merlia has been an adequate servant—more than adequate; I would be sorry to lose his services—that may be the price . . . of a larger success."

CHAPTER 15

Summertide
minus eight.

DARYA LANG DID the natural thing: she sat down and cried. But as House-uncle Matra had told her, long before, weeping solved no problems. After a few minutes she stopped.

At first she had been merely bewildered. Why would Atvar H'sial choose to drug her and maroon her in the middle of nowhere, in a region of Quake that they had chosen only because it seemed like a good place for a landing? She could think of no explanation for the Cecropian's disappearance while she slept.

Darya was thousands of kilometers away from the Umbilical. She had only a vague idea of its direction. She had no way to travel except walking. The conclusion was simple: Atvar H'sial intended that she should be stranded on Quake, and die when Summertide hit.

But in that case, why leave a supply of provisions? Why provide a mask and air filter, and a primitive water purifier? Most baffling of all, why leave behind a signal generator that could be used to broadcast a distress call?

Her confusion had been succeeded by misery; then by anger. It was a sequence of emotions that she would never have anticipated, back in the quiet days before she left Sentinel Gate. She had always thought of herself as a reasonable person, a scientist, a citizen of an orderly and logical universe. Rage was not a reasonable reaction; it clouded the thought processes. But her world had changed, and she had been forced to change with it. The intensity of her own emerging feelings amazed her. If she had to die, she would not do it without a struggle.

She squatted on the soft soil by the nearest lake and systematically inspected every item in the heap of materials. The purifier was a little flash-evaporation unit, one that would produce clean, drinkable water from the most bitter alkalines of any lake. At maximum production the unit would give two pints of water a day. The food in the heap was simple and bland, but it was self-heating, nutritious, and enough to last for weeks. The signal generator, so far as she could tell, was in perfect working order. And the waterproof quilted sheet that covered everything would provide insulation against heat, cold, or rain.

Conclusion: If she died, it would not be from hunger, thirst, or exposure.

That was small comfort. Death would be more immediate and much more violent. The air was hot and steadily becoming hotter. Every few minutes she could feel the earth stirring beneath her, like a sleeper unable to find a comfortable position. Worst of all, a stiffening breeze was carrying in a fine white powder that stung her eyes and gave everything an unpleasant metallic taste. The mask and air filter provided only partial protection.

She walked back to the edge of the lake and saw the ghostly reflection of Gargantua in the dark water. The planet grew more bright and bloated with every hour. It was still far from closest approach to Mandel, but looking up she could already see its three largest moons, moving around Gargantua in strangely perturbed orbits. She could almost feel the forces that Gargantua, Mandel, and Amaranth exerted on those satellites, pulling them in different directions. And the same gravitational forces were at work on Quake. The planet she stood on was enduring terrific stress. Its surface must be ready to disintegrate.

So why had Atvar H'sial left her, then fed her and given her protection, when Summertide would get her anyway?

There had to be an explanation of what had happened. She had to *think*.

She crouched down by the water, seeking a spot partly shielded from the blowing dust. If Atvar H'sial had wanted to kill her, the Cecropian could have done it very easily while she still slept. Instead she had been left alive. Why?

Because Atvar H'sial *needed* her alive. The Cecropian did not want her at the moment for whatever intrigue was being arranged, but Atvar H'sial needed her later. Maybe for something she knew about Quake, or about the Builders. But what? Nothing Darya could imagine.

Change the question. What did Atvar H'sial *think* Darya knew?

Darya could make no rational suggestion, but at the moment she did not need the answer. The new Darya insisted that reasons for actions were less important than actions themselves. The thing that mattered was that she had been left here in cold storage—or hot storage—for an indefinite period; someone, sometime, might be coming back for her. And if she did nothing, she would quickly die.

But it would not happen that way. She would not *let* it happen.

Darya stood up and surveyed her surroundings. She had been Atvar H'sial's dupe once, arranging for the trip up the Umbilical. That was the last time.

The lake she was standing by was the highest of half a dozen connected bodies of water. Their sizes ranged from less than a hundred meters across to maybe four hundred. The outflow of the nearest pool, forty paces away from her, splashed down a little cataract of one or two meters' height into the next lake in the sequence.

She searched the shoreline for some type of shelter. Judging from the weather, it would have to be something pretty substantial. The wind was strengthening, and fine sand was seeping into every open space—including her *own* open spaces; the sensation was not pleasant.

Where? Where to hide, where to find sanctuary? The determination to survive—she was going to live!—had been growing.

She brushed fine talc from her arms and body. Earthquakes might be a long-term danger, but at the moment the biggest threat was this intrusive, hard-blown powder. She must get away from it. And it was not clear that anywhere was safe.

What do the native animals do?

The question popped into her head as she was staring down at the lake shore, riddled with what seemed to be animal bore holes. Quake life-forms didn't stay on the surface at this time of year. They went underground, or better yet underwater. She recalled the great herds of white-backed animals, heading single-mindedly for the lakes.

Could she do the same thing? The bottom of an alkaline pond was not an enthralling prospect, but at least it would get her away from the dust.

Except that she could not survive on a lake bed. She needed to breathe. There was no way to carry an air supply down with her.

She waded into the water until she was up to her knees. The water was pleasantly warm, and increased a little in temperature as she went deeper. Judging from the bottom slope, the middle of the pool would take her over her head. If she went in until the water came to her neck, the seals of her mask and air filter would be below the waterline and only her head would be above it. That would keep out the dust.

But how many hours could she stand like that? Not enough.

It was a solution that solved nothing.

She began to follow the flow-line of the chain of lakes, descending from one step-like level of rock to the next. The first cataract dropped two meters through a series of half a dozen small rapids, running over smooth lips of stone until they finally discharged into the largest of the lakes. If anything, the blowing dust was worse here at the lower level.

She walked on. This lake was roughly elliptical, at least three hundred meters across and maybe five hundred long. Its outfall was correspondingly larger, a substantial cataract that she could hear when she was still forty paces away from it.

When she came to the noisy waterfall she found a wall of water, three meters high, dropping almost vertically into the next lake of the chain. Spray from the foot of it blew up and fogged her mask, but at least it washed some of the dust from the air. If she could find nothing better, this might be a place to return to.

She was ready to head for the next pool when she saw that the waterfall actually flowed over an overhang in the ledge of rock. There was a space behind. If she could step through the fall without being carried away by the water torrent she would be in a shielded enclosure, protected from blowing dust by a rock wall on one side and running water on the other.

Darya moved to the side of the waterfall, pressed herself as close as she could to the rock face, and edged sideways into the rush of water. As soon as she was partway into the foaming white spray she knew she could get through it. The main force of the fall was missing her, arching out over her head in a torrent that sent only noise and blown droplets back to the hidden rock wall. And as she had thought, there was a space behind.

The trouble was, that ledge and shielded space were too small. She could not stand up without poking her head into the torrent. She could not lie down flat. The ledge was lumpy and uneven. And there was not one square inch of wall or floor undrenched by the continuous spray.

She began to feel dismay, then caught herself. What had

she been expecting, an Alliance luxury apartment? This wasn't a matter of *comfort;* it was one of survival.

With the quilt to protect her, she could curl up with her back to the rock. She could stack most of her food and drink outside, and whenever necessary she could leave her cave long enough to bring in more to eat, or to stretch her legs. She could wash out the mask and air filter when she was inside, to keep it free of dust. And she would be warm enough, even if she was never totally dry or rested. If she had to, she could survive here for many days.

She went back and made three trips to her cache of supplies. In the first two she carried everything except the beacon over to the waterfall, and spent a long time deciding which items should be inside with her, and which would be left just outside.

The third trip involved the most difficult decision.

She could carry the beacon signal generator over to a point of high ground near the lake. She could put it on a heap of stones, to maximize its range. She could make sure that it had adequate power. But would she do something else?

She thought about it, and knew she had no choice. If and when Atvar H'sial came back, Darya would still be at her mercy, to be used, rescued, or discarded, as the Cecropian chose. Two months ago Darya might have bowed to that as inevitable; now it was not acceptable.

She wrapped the generator in the quilt and carried it through into the waterfall cave. There she rearranged the waterproof sheet so that she and the beacon were shielded from blown water droplets. It was close to Mandel-noon, and enough light diffused in through the rush of water.

Slowly and carefully, she switched off the generator and partly disassembled it. It would be a mistake to rush, and time seemed to be the one thing she had in abundance. She knew the basic circuits she needed, but she had to improvise to achieve the impedance that would do the trick. She took the high-voltage alternating leads, and ran their output in parallel to the r/f stage, through the transformer, and on to the message box. Then it was a test of memory, and of long-ago courses in neural electronics. The convolver that she needed was little more than a nonlinear oscillator, and there were resistors and capacitors in the signal generator that could perform dual functions. She could not test the result, but the changes she had made were simple enough. It ought to work. The main danger was that it might be too powerful.

Mandel was setting before she was finished. The modified beacon went back outside, into the ruddy light of Amaranth and the driving dust storm, and onto its little cairn of stones. Darya activated it, and nodded in satisfaction as the function light blinked to indicate that the beacon was working again.

She inched her way back into the waterfall cave, swathed herself completely in the quilt, and curled up on the ledge of rock. Stony lumps stuck into her side. The splashing fall provided a continuous spray of droplets and the noise of rushing water. Underneath that was the uneasy movement of Quake itself, groaning as the planet was stretched harder on the rack of tidal forces.

No one could expect to be able to sleep in such conditions. Darya nibbled on dry biscuits, closed her eyes, and fixed her mind on one thought: *she was fighting back.* What she had done was little enough, but it was all that she *could* do.

And tomorrow, she would find some new idea to save herself.

With that thought in her head and uneaten biscuits still in her hands, she drifted off into the most restful sleep since she had left Sentinel Gate.

Hans Rebka had another reason for wishing to be alone. Just before they had left Opal, another encrypted message had arrived from Phemus Circle headquarters. There had been no time to examine it in the haste of their departure, but while the capsule was descending the Umbilical toward

Quake he had taken a first look. He had been able to decipher just enough to make him uncomfortable by the time they landed. As the aircar took him north away from Opalside and toward the starside of Quake, the message was burning a hole in his jacket pocket. He put the plane on autopilot, ignored the brooding scene below him, and set out in earnest to work on the message.

Headquarters had switched from prime numbers and cyclic ideals as the basis for their codes, to an invariant-embedding method. The messages were supposedly almost uncrackable—and vastly more difficult to read, even when you knew the key. Rebka appropriated most of the car's on-board computer power and began to grind out the message, symbol by symbol. It did not help at all that there were occasional data losses in transmission at the Bose Transitions, adding their own random garbling to the cipher.

The received signal contained three independent messages. The first, deciphered after three quarters of an hour of patient work, made him want to throw the whole facsimile record out of the car's window.

. . . THE ALLIANCE COUNCIL MEMBER WHO IS HEADING FOR DOBELLE USES THE NAME *JULIUS GRAVES*, OR APPARENTLY SOMETIMES *STEVEN GRAVES*. HE IS AUGMENTED WITH AN INTERIOR MNEMONIC TWIN, DESIGNED AS AN EXTENDED SUPPLEMENTARY MEMORY, BUT THAT UNION IS NOT FOLLOWING NORMAL PATTERNS. OUR ANALYSTS SUGGEST A POSSIBILITY OF INCOMPLETE INTEGRATION. THIS MAY LEAD TO VOLATILE OR INCONSISTENT BEHAVIOR. SHOULD GRAVES ARRIVE ON DOBELLE, AND SHOULD HE EXHIBIT BEHAVIORAL IRREGULARITIES, YOU WILL COMPENSATE FOR THESE TENDENCIES AND NEUTRALIZE ANY ILLOGICAL DECISIONS THAT HE MAY SEEK TO MAKE. PLEASE NOTE THAT A MEMBER OF THE COUNCIL HAS PERSONAL DECISION POWERS THAT EXCEED THOSE OF ANY PLANETARY GOVERNMENT CONTROLS. YOU MUST WORK WITHIN THIS CONSTRAINT . . .

"Thanks, guys." Rebka crumpled the message into a ball and threw it over his shoulder. "He's crazy and he can do anything he likes—but it's my job to control him and stop him. And if I don't, my head rolls! Just perfect."

It was another fine example of action at a distance, of government trying to control events a hundred light-years away. Rebka set to work on the next message.

That took another hour. It did not seem much use when he had it, but at least it provided information and did not ask for outright impossibilities.

. . . PERHAPS OF NO DIRECT RELEVANCE TO YOUR SITUATION, BUT THERE ARE WIDESPREAD AND INDEPENDENT REPORTS OF CHANGES IN BUILDER ARTIFACTS THROUGH THE WHOLE OF THE SPIRAL ARM. STRUCTURES THAT HAVE BEEN STABLE AND INVARIANT THROUGHOUT HUMAN AND CECROPIAN MEMORY AND IN ALL REMAINING ZARDALU RECORDS ARE EXHIBITING FUNCTIONAL ODDITIES AND MODIFIED PHYSICAL PROPERTIES. THIS IS ENCOURAGING MANY EXPLORATION TEAMS TO REEXAMINE THE POSSIBILITY OF PROBING THE UNKNOWN INTERIORS OF A NUMBER OF ARTIFACTS . . .

"Tell me about it!" Rebka glared at the computer that was displaying the offending transcript. "And don't you remember that I was all set to explore Paradox, before this idiot assignment? Before you dummies pulled me away!"

. . . WHILE PERFORMING YOUR OTHER DUTIES YOU SHOULD OBSERVE CLOSELY THE ARTIFACT OF THE DOBELLE SYSTEM KNOWN AS THE UMBILICAL, AND DETERMINE IF THERE HAVE BEEN SIGNIFICANT CHANGES IN ITS FUNCTION OR APPEARANCE. NONE HAVE SO FAR BEEN REPORTED . . .

Rebka turned to stare back the way he had come. The Umbilical was long since invisible. All he could see was a broken line on the planet's terminator, like a glowing string of orange beads on the curving horizon. A major eruption had begun there. He looked down to the surface over which he was flying—all quiet below—and skipped to the third message.

Which made up for the other two. It was the answer to Rebka's own query.

... A CECROPIAN ANSWERING YOUR DESCRIPTION. SHE IS INTERESTED IN LIFE-FORM EVOLUTION UNDER ENVIRONMENTAL PRESSURE, AS YOU SUGGEST, BUT SHE IS ALSO KNOWN AS A SPECIALIST IN BUILDER TECHNOLOGY ...

... SHE GOES UNDER A VARIETY OF NAMES (AGTIN H'RIF, ARIOJ H'MINEA, ATVAT H'SIAR, AGHAR H'SIMI) AND CHANGES OF EXTERNAL APPEARANCE. SHE MAY BE RECOGNIZABLE BY AN ACCOMPANYING SLAVE INTERPRETER OF THE LO'TFIAN FAMILY. SHE IS DANGEROUS TO BOTH HUMANS AND CECROPIANS, RESPONSIBLE FOR AT LEAST TWELVE DEATHS OF KNOWN INTELLIGENCES AND TWENTY-SEVEN DEATHS OF PROBATED INTELLIGENCE.

ADDED NOTE: LOUIS NENDA (HUMAN, REPUTED AUGMENTATION), FROM KARELIA IN THE ZARDALU COMMUNION, IS ALSO HEADED FOR DOBELLE. HE IS ACCOMPANIED BY A HYMENOPT SLAVE. NO DETAILS ARE AVAILABLE, BUT THE KARELIA NET SUGGESTS THAT NENDA MAY ALSO BE DANGEROUS.

NEITHER THE CECROPIAN NOR THE KARELIAN SHOULD BE ADMITTED TO THE DOBELLE SYSTEM ...

Rebka did not throw the printout from the car—it was moving too high and too fast for that. But he did crumple the message and toss it over his shoulder to join the other two. He had spent more than three hours deciphering those missives from Circle headquarters, and all they offered was bad news.

He lifted his head and stared out of the window ahead. Amaranth was behind him, and the car's roof shielded its light. He looked west, ready to catch the last gleam of Mandel-set before the primary was lost behind the dark crescent of Quake. The sun's rim dipped below the horizon.

His eyes adjusted. And as they did so they picked up a faint, blinking light flashing from a tiny red bead next to the control console. At the same moment an insistent beep started within the cabin.

Distress circuit.

The skin on the back of his neck prickled with anticipation. Sixty hours to Summertide. And someone or something, down on the looming dark surface of Quake ahead of him, was in big trouble.

The line of the beacon would bring him down on the fringes of the Thousand Lakes area, not far from the region Max Perry favored for the location of the Carmel twins. Rebka checked the car's power supply. It was ample—each aircar could make a trip right around Quake and still have something in reserve. No reason for worry there. He sent a brief message to Perry and Graves, then increased the car's speed and set his new course without waiting for either acknowledgment or approval.

Mandel was still hidden, but Gargantua was high in the sky and providing enough light to land by. Rebka stared ahead. He was skimming low over a chain of circular lakes, waters steaming and churning. Their turbulent surfaces matched his own mood. Nowhere, from horizon to bleak horizon, was there a sign of life. For that, he would have to look into the waters of the Thousand Lakes themselves, or in the deepest hollows of the Pentacline Depression. Or deeper yet—the most tenacious life-forms would burrow far under Quake's shifting surface. Would the Carmel twins have had the sense to do the same?

But maybe he was already too late. The twins were no specialists in harsh-environment survival, and every second the tidal forces at work on the planet below him grew bigger.

Rebka increased speed again, pushing the car to its limits.

There was nothing else he could do. His mind wandered away into troubled speculation.

Gravity is the weakest force in nature. The strong interaction, the electromagnetic interaction, even the "weak" interaction that governs beta decay, are many orders of magnitudes more powerful. Two electrons, one hundred light-years apart, repel each other with an electric force as great as the attractive gravitational force of two electrons half a millimeter apart.

But consider the gravitational *tidal* force. That is weaker yet. It is caused only by a *difference* of gravitational forces, the difference in the pull on one side of a body from the pull on the other. While gravity is governed by an inverse square law—twice the distance, a quarter the force—gravity tides are governed by an inverse *cube* law. Twice the distance, one *eighth* the force; thrice the distance, one twenty-seventh the force.

Gravity tides should be negligible.

But they are not. They grip a billion moons around the galaxy, forcing them to present the same face always to their master planets; tides worry endlessly at a world's interior, squeezing and pulling, releasing geological stresses and changing the figure of the planet with every tidal cycle; and they rip and rend any object that falls into a black hole, so that, no matter how strong the intruder may be, the tides will tear it down to its finest subatomic components.

For that inverse-cube distance relationship can easily be *inverted:* one half the distance, eight times the tidal force; one-third the distance, twenty-seven times the tidal force; one-tenth the distance . . .

At closest approach to Mandel, the Dobelle system was one eleventh of its mean distance from the primary. One thousand three hundred and thirty-one times the mean tidal force was exerted upon its components.

That was *Summertide.*

Hans Rebka had been told those basic facts by Max Perry, and he thought of them as he overflew the surface of Quake. Every four hours, the vast invisible hand of Mandel and Amaranth's gravity squeezed and pulled at Opal and Quake, trying to turn their near-spherical shapes into longer ellipsoids. And close to Summertide, tidal energy equivalent to a dozen full-scale nuclear wars was pumped into the system—not just *once,* but twice every Dobelle day.

Rebka had visited worlds where global nuclear war had recently taken place. Based on that experience he expected to see a planet whose whole surface was in turmoil, a seething chaos where the existence of life was impossible.

It was not happening. And he was baffled.

There were local eruptions—that was undeniable. But when he looked at the ground speeding beneath him, he could see nothing to match the scale of his imaginings.

What was wrong?

Rebka and Perry had overlooked a fact known since the time of Newton: gravity is a *body force.* No known material can shield against it; every particle, no matter where it may be in the universe, feels the gravitational force of every other particle.

And so, whereas nuclear war confines its fury to the atmosphere, oceans, and top few tens of meters of a planet's land surface, the tidal forces squeeze, pull, and twist every cubic centimeter of the world. They are *distributed* forces, felt from the top of the atmosphere to the innermost atom of the superheated, superpressured core.

Rebka examined the surface but saw little to suggest a coming Armageddon. His mistake was natural, and elementary. He should have been looking much deeper; and then he might have had his first inkling of the true nature of Summertide.

A wind of choking dust was screaming across the surface as the aircar came in to land. Rebka brought the car directly into that gale, relying on microwave sensors to warn of rocks big enough to cause trouble. The final landing was smooth enough, but there was an immediate problem. The search-and-rescue system told him that the distress beacon was right in front of him, less than thirty meters away. But the mass detector insisted that nothing the size of an aircar or a ship was closer than three hundred. Peering into the dust storm did not help. The world in front of the car ended with a veil of driving dust and sand, no more than a dozen paces beyond the car's nose.

Rebka checked the SAR system again. No doubt about the location of the beacon. He gauged its line and distance from the door of the car. He forced himself to sit down and wait for five minutes, listening to the sandstorm as it screamed and buffeted at the car and hoping that the wind would drop. It blew on, as strongly as ever. Visibility was certainly not improving. Finally he pulled on goggles, respirator, and heat-resistant clothing, and eased open the door. At least the combination was a familiar one. Howling wind, superheated atmosphere, foul-tasting and near-poisonous air—just like home. He had grappled with all that in his childhood on Teufel.

He stepped outside.

The wind-driven sand was unbelievable, so fine-grained that it could find a way through the most minute of gaps in the suit. It blasted and caught at his body. He could taste powdery talc on his lips in the first few seconds, somehow creeping in through the respirator. Millions of tiny, scrabbling fingers touched him and tugged at his suit, each one eager to pull him away. His spirits dropped. This was *worse* than Teufel. Without the shelter of a car, how could anyone survive such conditions for even an hour? It was a side of Quake that Perry, in his preoccupation with volcanoes and earthquakes, had not warned about. But given enough atmospheric disturbance, interior activity of a planet was not necessary to make it inhospitable to life. Blown sand that would allow a person to neither breathe nor escape would do the trick nicely.

Rebka made sure that he had a return line attached firmly to the body of the aircar, then leaned into the wind and crept forward. The beacon finally appeared when it was less than four meters in front of him. No wonder the mass sensors had not registered it! It was tiny—a stand-alone unit and the smallest one he had ever seen. It measured no more than thirty centimeters square and a few centimeters thick, with a stubby antenna sticking up from its center. The solid cairn of stones on which it nestled stood at the top of a small rise in the ground. Someone had taken the trouble to make sure that, weak as it was, the beacon would be heard over the maximum possible range.

Someone. But who, and where? If they had left the beacon and headed for refuge on foot, their chances were grim. An unprotected human would not make a hundred meters. They would suffocate, unable to avoid that choking, driving dust.

But maybe they had recorded what they were doing. Every distress beacon carried a message cache in its base. If they had been gone just a few minutes . . .

Wishful thinking, Rebka told himself as he removed his glove and reached for the sliding plate at the bottom of the beacon. He had been receiving the distress signal for an hour. And who knew how long it had been sending out its cry for help before he heard it?

He put his hand in the narrow opening. As his fingertips touched the base, a gigantic bolt of pain shot up his hand, along his arm, and on through his whole body. His muscles convulsed and knotted, too quickly and tightly to permit a scream. He could not pull his hand free. He doubled up, helpless, over the distress beacon.

Neural convolver, his mind said in the moment before the next shock hit him, harder than the first. He could no longer draw breath. In the seconds before he became unconscious, Rebka's mind filled with anger. Anger at the whole stupid assignment, anger at Quake—but most of all, anger at *himself.*

He had done something supremely dumb, and it was going to kill him. Atvar H'sial was dangerous, and at large on the surface of Quake. He had known that before he landed. And still he had blundered along like a child at a picnic, never bothering with the most elementary precautions . . .

But I was trying to help.

So what? His brain rejected that excuse as the jolting current twisted his body and scrambled his brains for a third and final time. You've said it often enough: people who are stupid enough to get themselves killed never help anybody . . .

And now, damn it, he would never know what Quake looked like at Summertide. The planet had won; he had lost . . .

The dust-filled wind screamed in triumph about his unconscious body.

ARTIFACT: ELEPHANT.
UAC#: 859
Galactic Coordinates: 27,548.762/16,297.442/−201.33
Name: Elephant
Star/planet association: Cam H'ptiar/Emserin
Bose Access Node: 1121
Estimated age: 9.223 $\pm$ 0.31 Megayears

Exploration History: Discovered by remote observation in E. −4553, reached and surveyed by a Cecropian exploration fleet in E. −3227. Members of the same fleet performed the first entry to Elephant and measured its physical parameters (see below). Subsequent survey teams performed the first complete traverse of Elephant (E. −2068), attempted communication with Elephant (E. −1997, E. −1920, E. −1883, all unsuccessful), and removed and tested large samples from the body (E. −1882, E. −1551). Slow changes in physical parameters and appearance were reported on each successive visit, and a permanent Cecropian observation station (Elephant Station) was established on Emserin, four light-minutes distant, in E. −1220. Human observers were added to Elephant Station for the first time 2,900 years later, in E. 1668. This artifact has been continuously monitored for more than five thousand standard years.

Physical Description: Elephant is an elongated and amorphous gaseous mass, approximately four thousand kilometers in maximum dimension and nowhere wider than nine hundred kilometers. It is in fact not a true gas, but a wholly interconnected mass of stable polymer fibers and transfer ducts. The interior is highly conducting (mainly superconducting) of both heat and electricity.

Applied stimuli suggest that the whole body reacts to any external influence but begins the return to its original condition with a first response time of about twenty years. Physical repair is by subsection replication, and any incident materials (e.g., cometary fragments) are employed catabol-

185

ically and anabolically to synthesize needed components. Local temperature changes are corrected to the mean body temperature of 1.63 Kelvins, consistent with the use of liquid helium II as a heat-transfer agent. The necessary cooling mechanism to maintain subunits of Elephant below 2 Kelvins is unclear.

Holes in Elephant (including excised fragments up to twenty kilometers long and complete longitudinal transects) are replaced from within, with a small matching reduction of overall dimensions. The external shape is held constant, and the impression of an amorphous body is obviously misleading. Unless material is added or removed from the body, both the size and shape of Elephant are invariant to within fractions of a millimeter in any direction.

Intended Purposes: Is Elephant alive? Is Elephant conscious? That debate continues. Today's consensus is that Elephant is a single active artifact with a limited self-renewal capability. Any removed section slowly becomes inert, its conductivity diminishes, and the system loses its homeostatic character. If Elephant is alive, the full response time to external stimuli is very long (hundreds of years) and the implied metabolic rate correspondingly slow.

Regardless of this artifact's overall self-awareness, it is certainly true that Elephant can function, as a whole or in part, as a general-purpose computing device. Following the pioneering work of Demerle and T'russig, Elephant has been used extensively in applications requiring enormous storage and moderate computing speed.

If Elephant is an intelligent and self-aware entity, the notion of purposes and uses is inappropriate. More sophisticated tests for self-awareness are clearly needed.

> —From the *Lang Universal Artifact Catalog,*
> Fourth Edition.

CHAPTER 16

Summertide minus seven.

"IT'S LIKE A treasure hunt," Graves said. He was walking on ahead, slow and steady. With his hands clasped behind him and his relaxed manner, he was like a thoughtful skeleton out for a midday stroll. "The old party game. You remember?"

Max Perry stared after him. He had grown up on a world too harsh and marginal to permit the luxury of children's games and children's parties. Food had been his best treasure. And the best game that he could think of at the moment was survival.

"You get clues," Graves went on. "First the beacon. Then the pointer, then the mystery caves. And then—if you're lucky—the treasure!"

The aircar had landed on a crumbling and eroded plateau in the wilderness area between the Thousand Lakes and the outer boundary of the Pentacline Depression. In that no-man's-land the soft rock had been eaten away into deep tunnels and smooth-sided sinkholes, like soft putty that an aged giant had kneaded and poked with bent, arthritic fingers. The meters-wide holes ran haphazardly at all angles from the surface. Some dived almost vertically; others sloped so shallowly that they could be walked down with ease.

"Be careful!" Perry hated Graves's casual attitude. "You

don't know how shaky the edges might be—and you don't know what could be at the bottom! This whole area is an estivation zone for Quake wildlife."

"Relax. It's perfectly safe." Graves took a step closer to the edge of one of the holes, then had to jump smartly backward as the rock crumbled and slid away beneath his feet. "Perfectly safe," he repeated. "This isn't the hole that we want anyway. Just follow me."

He led the way forward again, skirting the dangerous area. Perry followed at what he hoped was a safe distance. Expecting another car, perhaps a crashed one, at the site of the distress call, both men had been surprised to find nothing there but an isolated radio beacon. Next to it, marked as a black line in the chalky white rock, was an arrow. It pointed straight toward the dark, steep tunnel on whose brink Graves was currently poised and leaning precariously forward. Alongside the arrow, in an ill-formed scrawl, were the words "In Here."

"Fascinating." Graves leaned farther. "It seems to me—"

"Don't go so *near*!" Perry exclaimed when Graves moved forward again. "That edge there, if it's like the other one . . ."

"Oh, phooey." Graves jumped up and down. "See, solid as the Alliance. And I read the report before I came to Do-belle—there are no dangerous animals on Quake."

"Sure, you read the report, but I *wrote* the damned thing. There's a lot we don't know about Quake." Perry advanced cautiously to the brink of the tunnel and peered down. The rock seemed firm enough, and quite old. On Quake that was a good sign. The surface here at least had a certain permanence, as though it had avoided the turmoil that hit the planet at Summertide. "Anyway, it's not just animals. Mud pools can be just as bad. You don't even know how deep this hole is. Before you start charging down there, at least take a sounding."

He picked up a fist-sized chunk of chalky stone and lobbed it down the line of the tunnel. Both men leaned forward, listening for an echo where it struck the bottom. There was a two-second silence, then a thud, a whoof of protest, and a surprised whistle.

"Ah-ha! That's not a rock or a mud pool." Graves snapped his fingers and started to scramble on his bottom down the steep-sided hole. He had a flashlight, and he was shining it along in front of him. "That's the Carmel twins down there. I told you what to expect, Commander—the beacon, the arrow, the cave, and then the—" He halted. "And then . . . well, well, well. We were wrong."

Perry, a few steps behind, craned to see past Graves. The narrow beam of the flashlight reflected from a line of bright black eyes. As Graves held the light steady a small body, its black fur dusted to gray by a coating of fine powder, moved slowly up the incline. The Hymenopt was rubbing her tubby midsection with a foreleg, and while they watched she shook herself like a drenched dog and threw off a cloud of white dust.

There was another whistle, and a click-click-click of jointed hind limbs.

"Kallik offers respect and obedience," a familiar, sibilant voice said. J'merlia was emerging from around the curve of the tunnel. He, too, was completely coated with fine talc. "She is a loyal slave and servant. She asks, why do you throw stones at her? Did her master command it?"

The Lo'tfian's narrow face was not equipped to register human emotions, but there was a puzzled and worried tone in his voice. Instead of answering, Graves slithered farther along the tunnel to where it leveled off as a small cave whose floor was covered with powdered gypsum. He stared at the cleared area, and then at the little pile of objects standing in the middle of it.

"You were here in the dark?"

"No." J'merlia's compound eyes glittered in the flashlight beam. "It is not dark. We can both see here fairly well. Do you need our assistance?"

Perry, who had followed Graves down the tunnel at his

own pace, pushed past the other man and reached up high to touch the tunnel's roof. "See those? Cracks. Recent ones. I'm sure we shouldn't stay any longer. What are you doing down here, J'merlia?"

"Why, we are waiting. As we were instructed to do." The Lo'tfian offered a rapid set of whistles to Kallik, then continued. "Our masters brought us here and told us to await their return. Which we are doing."

"Atvar H'sial and Louis Nenda?"

"Of course. Owners never change."

"So Nenda didn't fly home in a huff. When did your masters leave?"

"Two days ago. We stayed at first on the surface, but we did not like conditions there—too hot, too open, too hard to breathe. But here, snug underground—"

"Snug, while the roof is ready to fall in. When did they say they would be back?"

"They did not say. Why should they? We have food; we have water; we are safe here."

"Don't bother to ask any more, Commander." Graves, done with his inventory of the little cavern, sank to his knees and began rubbing at eyes irritated by the fine dust that flew up at every movement. "Atvar H'sial and Louis Nenda would not have provided their itinerary, or anything else, to J'merlia. Why should they, as J'merlia says? To make it easy for you or me to follow them? No." His voice dropped to a stage whisper. "If they ever intended to come back for them at all! Maybe they have abandoned them. But even that is not the right question. The real question, one that I ask myself and do not like the answer to, is this: Where did H'sial and Nenda *go*? Where did they go, on Quake near Summertide, where they could not or would not take J'merlia and Kallik with them?"

As though answering his question, there was a tremor through the floor of the cave. The minor quake left the roof intact, but a cloud of fine white powder flew up to cover all of them.

"I don't care—*ough!*—where they went." Perry had trouble holding back his coughs. "I care about us, and where we go next."

"We go to find the Carmel twins." Graves rubbed the white powder away from his eyes again and looked like a circus clown.

"Sure. Where? And when?" Perry was aware of the running clock, even if Graves was not. "It's only fifty-five hours to Summertide."

"Ample time."

"No. You think, fifty-five hours, and you imagine that you'll be all right until then. That's totally wrong. Anybody who is still on the surface of Quake five hours or even fifteen hours from Summertide is probably dead. If we don't find the twins soon—in the next ten to twelve hours—they're dead, too. Because we'll have to give up the search and head back to the Umbilical."

Perry was finally getting through to the councilor. Graves stood, bald head bowed, and sighed in agreement. "All right. We don't have time to argue. Let's look for the twins."

"What about these two?" Perry gestured at Kallik and J'merlia.

"They come with us. Naturally. Atvar H'sial and Louis Nenda may never come back, or they may be too late, or they may not be able to track that beacon—you said it was running low on power."

"It is. I agree, we can't just leave the aliens. There's enough room in the car for all of us." Perry turned to J'merlia and Kallik. "Come on. Let's get out of here."

When the others did not move, he reached out for one of J'merlia's slender black forelimbs and started toward the tunnel entrance. Surprisingly, the Lo'tfian resisted.

"With respect, Commander Perry." J'merlia dug in six of his feet and cowered down until his slender abdomen was touching the rocky floor. "Humans are much greater beings than me or Kallik, we know that, and we will seek to do whatever you tell us. But Atvar H'sial and Louis Nenda gave us orders to stay in this area. We must wait until they return."

Perry turned in frustration to Graves. "Well? They won't do what I tell them. Do you think they'll obey a direct order from you?"

"Probably not." The councilor looked calmly at J'merlia. "Would you?"

The Lo'tfian shivered and groveled lower on the powdery floor.

Graves nodded. "That's answer enough. You see, Commander, we are placing them in an impossible position. Although they are trained to obey us, they cannot disobey the orders of their owners. They also have strong instincts to save their own lives, but they do not see the danger here. However, I have an alternative proposal—one that may be acceptable to them. We can leave them here—"

"We can't leave them. They'll die."

"We don't leave them *indefinitely.* But we are close to the Pentacline Depression. We can explore that for the twins. And if we provide a new power source for this beacon we can come back here afterward, whether we succeed or fail. By that time, perhaps Nenda and Atvar H'sial will also have returned. If not, the surface of Quake will surely be more obviously dangerous, and we can try again to persuade the aliens to leave."

Perry was still hesitating. At last he shook his head. "I think we can do better." He turned to J'merlia. "Were you told not to leave the place where Atvar H'sial and Louis Nenda dropped you off?"

"That is correct."

"But you *already* left that place—to come down into this tunnel. So you must have some freedom of movement. How far are you and Kallik willing to roam?"

"One moment, please." J'merlia turned away from Perry and held a whistling dialog with the Hymenopt, who had been squatting on the floor completely immobile. Finally he nodded.

"It is not so much a question of distance, as of time. A few kilometers would be all right; Kallik and I are agreed that we could go so far on foot. But if you are sure we can return here in three or four hours, we would be willing to travel a longer distance by aircar."

Graves was shaking his head. "Four hours is not long enough. How big is the Pentacline Depression, Commander?"

"Roughly a hundred and fifty kilometers across."

"And the twins may be in there, but they could be way over on the other side. I'm sure we can find them, given enough time, but we can't make an adequate scan for a starship in a few hours. We'll have to do it my way; leave these two here, and then come back."

Kallik interjected a whistle and a series of agitated clicks.

"But coming back will cut further into the search time." Perry ignored the Hymenopt. "If the two aliens would—"

"With great respect, Captain," J'merlia cut in—the first time he had ever interrupted a human. "But in all the time since Kallik and I met on Opal, I have been teaching her human talk. Already she understands some, though she cannot yet speak. Now she asks me, did she hear what she thought she heard? Are you searching for other human presence, here on the surface of Quake?"

"We sure are—if we can ever get out of here! So no more talk, we have to—"

This time it was Kallik herself who interrupted. The Hymenopt ran up close to Perry, raised herself onto the points of her toes, and produced a rapid series of whistling screams.

"With great respect," J'merlia gabbled before Perry could speak again, "she wants you to know that there is a starship on the surface of Quake."

"We know. The one that Kallik and Louis Nenda used to come over from Opal."

"Not that one. Before they landed, Master Nenda did a precautionary scan, because he was worried that there might be a trap. He picked up the trace of a ship's Bose Drive. Kallik says it was an Alliance design, able to do Bose Network transfers. She thinks, maybe it brought the humans you seek."

Kallik grunted and whistled again. J'merlia nodded.

"She says it is only a hundred kilometers from here—a few minutes' flight time. Kallik asks, Would you have any interest in knowing where it is?"

CHAPTER 17

"WHAT SINS MUST a man commit, in how many past lives, to be born on Teufel?"

The water-duty for seven-year-olds was precise and unforgiving.

Suit on, check air tank, seal respirator, walk to the lock. Warning: Opening takes place as the surface wind drops, five and a half minutes before first light, after the night predators retreat to their caves. Be there in time, or forfeit one day's food.

Outside. Empty yesterday's wastes (time allocation, 24 seconds); climb the twenty-four stone steps to the pure-water stream that gushes halfway up the cliffside (33 seconds); wash out plastic containers (44 seconds); rinse filters (90 seconds); fill water cans (75 seconds); descend (32 seconds); reenter lock and perform closing sequence (25 seconds).

Margin for error: seven seconds. If you are caught on the steps or with the lock wide open you are hit by the *Remouleur*—the Grinder, the dreaded dawn wind of Teufel. And you are dead.

Rebka knew that. And suddenly he knew that he was late. He could hardly believe it. Usually when his turn came for water-duty he was the one who hurried down the cliff ahead of schedule, the only one with the time and confidence to stand in the open lock and look out on Teufel's stark scenery and spiky, eccentric vegetation for a few seconds as lock closure began. The strata of the cliff face were still too dark to be seen, but he knew they were a muted purple interleaved with gray and faded reds. The strip of sky above the canyon already showed the signs of coming dawn. He could watch as the stars began to fade and streaks of high cloud turned from black to rosy gray. The sight had an indescribable beauty. It excited him.

But not today. The trickle of spring water was weaker, and the cans refused to fill at their usual speed. Nearly five minutes were already gone. He was still on the top step, and his face mask was fogging over. He had to leave, with half-filled containers. *Right now.*

Descent time allocation is 32 seconds; reenter lock and perform closing sequence, 25 seconds.

He headed down the steps blind and fast, risking a fall. He knew from experience the possible fates. If the *Remouleur* hit when he was on the top few steps, he would be carried out of the canyon like a dry leaf and no one would ever see him again. That had happened to Rosamunde. Halfway down, the dawn wind was less strong, but it blew its victims right down the canyon and dashed them against the rock chimneys. They had retrieved Joshua's body from there, what was left of it after the day predators were finished. If he almost made it, say to the bottom three or four steps, the wind could not carry him away completely. But it still would rip away his respirator, break his grip no matter how he clung to the rocks or the support rail, and roll him into the poisonous, boiling-water cauldron that seethed and churned below the spring. Lee had floated there for nine hours before she could be retrieved. Some of her had been lost forever. The cooked flesh had flaked from her bones and escaped the nets.

Twelve steps to go. And the Remouleur *is coming, no more than twenty seconds away, and the dust devils are stirring along the canyon, and now there is the preliminary scream of far-off wind and the chatter of torrential rain. The steps feel greasy under your feet.*

If someone was actually in the lock when the wind hit, he might have a chance. Teufel lore said that if one dropped the water containers and flattened oneself to the floor, one might—just might—keep the respirator on and survive until the lock closed all the way. But Rebka had never met anyone who had actually done it. And the penalty for returning without water—or, worse, without containers—was severe.

But not as severe as death.

Six steps to go.

Time had run out. He dropped the water containers.

There was a strange, moaning cry in his ears, and his body was lifted and pulled across a rocky surface. Cold water drenched his exposed arms and legs. His respirator was pulled away from his face. Death would at least be quick.

But he was not ready to die. He writhed against the force that held him, reaching up to grab the respirator straps and hold it in position.

His clawing fingers met human hands. The shock was so great that for a couple of seconds he could do nothing.

"Hans! Hans Rebka!" The cry came again, and this time he could understand it.

He opened his eyes for a last look at Teufel's dark skies. Instead of rosy streaks of wind-torn cloud he found himself staring at a shimmering blur of running water. Framed in front of the torrent, mouth open and panting with effort, was a dusty and droplet-streaked face.

It was Darya Lang.

When she realized what she had done, Darya was ready to sit down and start weeping again.

She had crawled out and hurried over to check the beacon as soon as she woke up. And when she peered through the shrouding dust and saw a figure huddled over the cairn, her first reaction was pure delight. That would teach Atvar

H'sial a lesson! The Cecropian would not do that again, callously leaving someone to live or die without even telling her why.

And then as Darya came closer she realized that it was not a Cecropian. It was a human—it was a man—dear God, it was Hans Rebka!

Darya screamed and ran forward. The dust of Quake was as lethal to him as it would be to her. If he were dead, she would never forgive herself.

"Hans. Oh Hans, I'm sorry . . ."

He was unconscious and not listening. But it *was* unconsciousness, not death. Darya found the strength to hoist him over her shoulder—he weighed less than she did—and carry him back through the waterfall. And as she laid him gently on the rock, his eyes opened. That puzzled look up at her was the most satisfying expression she had ever seen on a human face.

For twenty minutes she had the pleasure of tending him, watching him curse and spit up dust and snort out gray powder through his nose. It was delight, simply to know he was *alive*. And then, before she could believe that he was able to function, he was on his feet and forcing her back out onto the surface.

"You're not safe here, even if you think you are." He was still wringing his hand and arm at the pain that the neural convolver had left in the nerves. "Another few hours, and that waterfall might be steam. Summertide's coming, Darya, and there's only one road to safety. Come on."

He hurried her across the arid surface, and at the aircar he made a quick inspection. Within a couple of minutes he shook his head and sat back on his haunches. "It doesn't matter where Atvar H'sial went, or if she's coming back. We won't go far in this." He leaned in under the car to rub his hand over the intake units. "See for yourself."

The dust storm was easing, but the inside of the vents was still clogged. Worse than that, where Rebka brushed the dust away the liner metal showed bright and eroded.

"That was from flying in and landing here." He placed the grille back in position. "I think we ought to be able to make one more trip without major servicing and overhaul, but I wouldn't want to try beyond that. And we can't risk flying in any more dust storms. If we run into one, we'll have to go up and over and bide our time coming down. Assuming we don't run out of power, too—no extreme head winds, or we're done for."

"But what about the Carmel twins? You were supposed to be looking for them." Darya Lang remained crouched by the aircar's intakes. She had explained to Rebka why she had set her trap, and how Atvar H'sial had deserted her. He seemed to accept what she said, brushing it all off as an unimportant detail. But she had trouble looking him in the eye.

She knew why. That trap had been more than a desire to protect herself when Atvar H'sial came back. She had been looking for *revenge* for what Atvar H'sial had done. And then her unguided missile had gone astray and hit the wrong person.

"We can't do anything to help the twins," Rebka replied. "We'll have to hope that Graves and Perry had better luck than I did. Maybe they'll find them, or maybe the spaceship that you and J'merlia saw will be able to help them. I doubt it, though, if it's who I think it is."

"Louis Nenda?"

He nodded and turned away. He had his own reasons for wanting to appear calm and casual. First, he had fallen into Darya Lang's trap so easily that it dismayed him. He was supposed to be the smart and cautious one, but he had become soft and casual. Five years ago he would have tested *everything* for traps. This one he had fallen into like a baby.

Second, over the years he had found that dreams of his childhood on Teufel were a useful indicator. They were his own unconscious, trying to tell him something important. He had experienced those dreams only when he was in desperate trouble, and always when he did not know what that trouble might be.

Third—and maybe the driving force for the other two worries—Quake had changed since he had landed at the radio beacon. Superficially it was a change for the better. The winds had dropped, the blown sand was reduced to no more than an irritating half-centimeter blanket that lay over everything, and even the distant grumble of volcanic action was quiet.

But that was *impossible*. It was less than forty hours to Summertide. Amaranth was directly overhead, a huge, bloodshot eye glaring across five degrees of sky; Mandel, off to the west, was half as big again, and Gargantua was bright enough to be seen at Mandel-noon. The tidal energies pouring into the interiors of Quake and Opal were prodigious, enough to produce continuous and severe planetary distortions.

So where were they?

Energy had to be conserved, even on Quake, but it might be changed to another form. Was it being accumulated by some unknown physical process in the planet's deep interior?

"I guess we could stay here and tough it out," Darya Lang was saying, staring around them. "This is as quiet as it's been for a long time. If it doesn't get much worse than it was . . ."

"No. It will get a lot worse."

"How bad?"

"I'm not sure."

That was an understatement. He had no idea how bad, and it did not matter. We have to get off Quake, a tiny voice was saying in his ear, or we are dead. He was glad that Darya could not hear that voice, but he had learned never to ignore it.

"We have to leave," he added. "This minute, if you're ready."

"And go where?"

"To the Umbilical, and then to Midway Station. We'll be safe there. But we can't wait too long. The Umbilical is programmed to lift away from the surface before Summertide."

She climbed into the car and consulted the chronometer. "It lifts twelve hours before Summertide Maximum. That's twenty-seven hours from now. And we can be over there in one Dobelle day. We have plenty of time."

Rebka closed the car door. "I *like* to have plenty of time. Let's go."

"All right." She smiled at him. "But you've seen more of Quake than I have. What do you think will happen here at Summertide?"

Rebka took a deep breath. She was trying to be nice to him, but worse than that, she assumed that he was tense and needed to be calmed down. And the trouble was, she was right. He was *too* tense. He could not explain it—except that he had been badly fooled once on Quake, by assuming that something was safe when it was not. He did not want to do it again. And every nerve in his body urged him to get away from Quake *soon*.

"Darya, I'd love to compare notes about Summertide." He was not annoyed that she had trapped him, he told himself; he was impressed. "But I'd rather do it when we're on the Umbilical, and well on our way to Midway Station. You may think I'm a coward, but this place scares me. So if you'll just move over, and let me get at those controls . . ."

CHAPTER 18

Summertide minus five.

THE *SUMMER DREAMBOAT* was well hidden.

The Pentacline Depression formed the most highly visible feature on the surface of Quake. One hundred and fifty kilometers across, packed with a riot of vivid and strongly growing vegetation, it could be seen from half a million kilometers away in space as a starfish splash of lurid green on Quake's dusty gray surface. The Pentacline was also the lowest point on the planet. Its five valleys, radiating up and out like stretching arms from the central low, had to rise over eight hundred meters to reach the level of the surrounding plain.

The little starship had landed close to the middle of the Pentacline's north-pointing arm, at a point where dense vegetation was broken by a small flat island of black basalt. But the ship had flown in to the bare outcrop on an angled descent and skated to its very edge. It was shielded from overhead inspection by vigorous new growth. Scarcely bigger than an aircar, the *Summer Dreamboat* was tucked neatly away under a canopy of five-meter leaf cover. It was empty, with all its life-support systems turned off. Only residual radiation from the Bose Drive betrayed its presence.

Max Perry stood inside the abandoned ship and stared

around him with amazement. His head nearly touched the roof, and the whole living space was no more than three meters across. One step took him from the main hatch to the tiny galley; another, and he was at the control console.

He inspected the panel's simple displays, with their couple of dozen brightly colored switches and indicators, and shook his head. "This is a damned *toy*. I didn't know you could even get into the Bose Network with something this small."

"You are not supposed to." Graves had himself under firm control. He did not look quite sane, but the twitching of his fingers was less, and his bony face no longer boiled in a turmoil of emotion. "This was built as a small tourist vessel, for in-system hops. The designers didn't expect a Bose Drive to be added, and certainly no one ever thought it might be used for so many Bose Transitions. But that's Shasta for you—the children rule the planet. The Carmel twins talked their parents into it." He turned to J'merlia. "Would you kindly tell Kallik to stop that, before she does something dangerous?"

The little Hymenopt was over by the ship's drive. She had removed the cover and was peering inside. She turned at Graves's words.

"It is not dangerous," J'merlia interpreted, listening to the series of clicks and whistles. "With great respect, Kallik says that it is the opposite of dangerous. She is aware that someone as ignorant as she can know little about anything so difficult as the Bose Drive, but she is quite sure that this one's power unit is exhausted. It cannot be used again. It is debatable that this ship could even make it from here to low orbit. She already suspected this, from the weak signal that her master's ship received in its survey of the surface."

"Which explains why the twins never left Quake." Perry had turned on the display and was examining the computer log. "It makes sense of their peculiar itinerary, too. This shows a continued Bose Network sequence that brings them to Dobelle and then takes them right into Zardalu territory in two more transitions; but they couldn't do that without a new Bose power source. They could have picked one up at Midway Station, but naturally they didn't know it. So the only other place they could have gone in this system would have been Opal, and we'd have tracked their arrival there at once."

"Which is unfortunately not the case *here*. So how will we find them?" Graves walked across to the door and peered out, snapping his finger joints. "I deserve censure, you know. I assumed that once we found the ship they came in, the hard task was over. It never occurred to me that they might be foolhardy enough to *leave* the ship and roam the planet's surface."

"I can help with that. But even if you find them, how will you handle the twins themselves?"

"Leave that to me. It is the area of my experience. We are creatures of conditioning, Commander. We assume that what we know is easy, and we find mysterious whatever we do not." Graves waved a skinny, black-clad arm out toward the Pentacline. "All that to me is mysterious. They are hidden somewhere out there. But why would they leave this ship, and relative safety, to go to *that*?"

What could be seen from the ship was a green mass of vines, lush and intertwined. They trembled continuously to ground tremors, giving an illusion of self-awareness and nervous movement.

"They went there because they thought it was safe, and so they wouldn't be found. But I can find them." Perry glanced at his watch. "We have to be quick. It's already hours since we left the beacon. J'merlia." He turned to the apprehensive Lo'tfian. "We promised we'd have you back where we came from in four hours. And we will. Come on, Councilor. I know where they'll be—alive or dead."

Outside the ship the atmosphere of the depression felt thicker and more oppressive, ten degrees hotter than the plain. Black basalt quivered underfoot, hot and pulsing like the scaly hide of a vast beast. Perry walked along the edge of the rock, carefully examining it.

Graves followed, mopping at his perspiring brow. "If you are hoping to see footprints I hate to be discouraging, but—"

"No. *Water* prints." Perry knelt down. "Runoff patterns. Quake has a lot of small lakes and ponds. The native animals manage fine, but they make do with water that you or I couldn't drink. And once the Carmel twins left their ship, they'd need a supply of fresh water."

"They might have had a purifier."

"They would have, and they'd need it—fresh water on Quake is a relative term. You and I couldn't drink it, nor could Geni and Elena Carmel." Perry ran his hand over a smooth indented wedge in the rock. "If they're alive, they'll be within reach of water. And it doesn't matter where they headed first, if they started out from this rock—and they must have, because the *Summer Dreamboat* is here—they'll finish up along one of the runoff lines. Here's one of them, a good strong one. There's another over there, just about as well defined. But this rock slab is tilted and we're on the lower side. We'll try this one first."

He lowered himself carefully over the edge. Graves followed, wincing as his hand met the basalt. The bare rock was beyond blood heat, almost hot enough to blister. Perry was moving away fast, scrambling along on his backside down a thirty-degree slope that plunged through a trailing curtain of purple-veined creepers.

"Wait for me!" Graves raised one arm to protect his eyes. Saw-edged leaves cut into the back of his hand and left their scratch marks along the top of his unprotected skull. Then he was through, under the tree-floor of vegetation that marked the first level of the Pentacline.

The light of Mandel and Amaranth was muted here to a blue-green shadow. Small creatures flew at them. Julius Graves thought at first that they were insects or birds, but a query to Steven brought the information that they were pseudocoelenterates, more like flying jellyfish than any other Earth or Miranda form. The creatures chittered in panic and flew away from Graves into the gloom. He hurried on after Max Perry. Within a few meters the air temperature beneath the canopy had jumped another few degrees.

Perry was following the rocky watercourse, squeezing his way past sticky yellow trunks and upthrusting mushroom structures two meters high. Clouds of minute winged creatures burst from the overhead leaves and flew for his unprotected face and hands.

"They don't bite," Perry said over his shoulder. "Just keep going."

Graves swatted at them anyway, trying to keep them out of his eyes. He wondered why Perry had not brought masks and respirators with them. In his concentration he was not looking where he was going, and he walked into the other man's back.

"Found something?"

Perry shook his head and pointed down. Two steps ahead the streambed dropped into a vertical hole. Graves leaned recklessly forward and could see no sign of the bottom.

"Let's hope they're not down there." Perry was already turning back. "Come on."

"What if the other one dead-ends, too?" Graves was snapping his finger joints again.

"Bad news. We'll need a new idea, but we won't have time for one even if we think of it. We'll have to worry about ourselves."

Rather than climbing back up the rock face, he led the way to one side, working his way slowly around the foot of the outcropping to where a second runoff flowed. Away from the watercourse the lower-level vegetation grew more strongly. Tough bamboo spears jutted up to knee level, scoring their boots and cutting through the cloth of their trousers. Irritant sap from broken leaves created lines of stinging cuts along their calves. Perry swore, but did not lessen his pace.

In another twenty meters he stopped and pointed. "There's the other runoff. And something has been this way quite a few times." The gray-green sedges at the side of the streambed had been flattened and broken. Their crushed stems were coated with a brown layer of dried sap.

"Animals?" Graves leaned down to rub at his scraped shins and calves, which had begun to itch maddeningly.

"Maybe." Perry lifted his foot and pressed down on an unbroken stem, gauging its strength. "But I doubt it. Whatever flattened these wasn't far from human body weight. I've never heard of anything in the Pentacline that massed more than a quarter as much. At least this makes it easy to track."

He began to walk down the stream side, following the line of broken vegetation. The verdurous gloom had deepened, but the path was easy to follow. It ran parallel to the dry watercourse and then inched over into it. Thirty meters farther on, the bottom of the path became veiled by a thicket of tough ferns.

Graves put his hand on Perry's shoulder and moved on past him.

"If you're right," he said quietly, "then from this point on it's my show. Let me go in front, and alone. I'll call you when I want you."

Perry stared for a moment, then allowed Graves to step ahead of him. In the past five minutes the other had changed. Every sign of instability had vanished from his face, leaving in its place strength, warmth, and compassion. It was the countenance of a different man—of a councilor.

Graves stepped cautiously along the streambed until he was no more than a couple of paces from the veil of ferns. He paused, listening, then after a few seconds nodded and turned to Perry. He winked grotesquely, parted the ferns, and stepped through into the dark interior of the thicket.

It was the Carmel twins, it had to be; they had been located, although Perry would have given high odds against it when he, Graves, and Rebka had left Opal. But what was Graves saying to them, hidden away in the darkness?

A few minutes in the Pentacline so close to Summertide felt like hours. The heat and humidity were horrible. Perry looked again and again at his watch, hardly able to believe that time was passing so slowly. Though it was full day, and Mandel must still be rising, his surroundings grew less and less visible. Was there a dust storm brewing far overhead in the atmosphere? Perry stared straight up, but he could see nothing through the thick multiple layers of vegetation. Underfoot, however, there was plenty of evidence of Quake's activity. The root-tangled forest floor was in continuous, steady vibration.

Thirty-five hours to Summertide Maximum.

The clock kept running in Perry's head, along with a question. They had promised to return J'merlia and Kallik to where they had found them. That promise had been made in good faith and without reservations. But could they allow such a thing to be done, knowing that Quake would soon be a death trap to everything except its own uniquely selected organisms?

Perry was startled by a sudden bright light in front of him. The curtain of ferns had been pulled aside, and Graves stood behind it gesturing him forward.

"Come on in. I want you to hear this and serve as an additional witness."

Max Perry eased his way in through the bristly fronds of the ferns. Lit from the interior, the dark thicket was revealed to be less than it seemed. The ferns formed only an outer framing web, a convenient natural fence within which stood a flexible tent supported by pneumatic ribbing. Graves was holding a door panel open, and when Perry stepped through he was astonished by the size of the interior. The floor area was at least ten meters square. Even with the inward-sloping walls the living area was substantial. And the furnishings were amazingly complete, everything that was needed for normal pleasant living. Some form of cooling and humidity-control unit was operating, to hold the internal conditions at a comfortable level. And it was well hidden from any normal searcher. No wonder the twins preferred to stay here, rather than in the cramped quarters of the *Summer Dreamboat.*

The tent must also have been totally lightproof, or else the lights had only just been turned on. But Perry had time for only one look at the line of glowing cylinders around the walls, before his attention was drawn to the tent's occupants.

Elena and Geni Carmel were sitting over by the far wall, side by side, their hands on their knees. They were dressed in russet jumpsuits and wore their auburn hair hanging low over their foreheads. Perry's first impression—an overwhelming one—was of two identical people, with the same resemblance to Amy that had left him unable to breathe when he had first seen their pictures back on Opal.

But in the flesh, under the bright lights of the tent, reason quickly asserted itself. If the twins looked like Amy, it was through their dress and hairstyle. Elena and Geni Carmel seemed weary and crushed, as far as one could be from Amy's perky and invincible self-confidence. The tan that he had seen in the image cubes was long gone, replaced by a tired pallor.

And the twins were *different,* one from the other. Although their features might be structurally identical, their expressions were not. One was clearly the dominant twin—born a few minutes earlier, maybe, or a fraction bigger and heavier?

She was the one meeting Max Perry's eyes. The other kept her gaze downcast, shooting only one shy and lightning glance at the new arrival from large, heavy-lidded eyes. Yet she seemed at ease with Graves, turning her face to him as he closed the tent's panel and moved to sit opposite them.

He waved Perry to a seat by his side. "Elena"—he indicated the more self-confident twin—"and Geni have been through a very difficult time." His voice was gentle, almost subdued. "My dears, I know it is a painful memory, but I want you to repeat to the commander what you just told me . . . and this time we will make a recording of it."

Geni Carmel gave Perry another hooded glance and looked to her sister for direction.

Elena gripped her knees more tightly with her hands. "From the beginning?" Her voice was deep for her slender frame.

"Not the very beginning. You don't need to tell how you won the trip on Shasta—we have all that on record. I'd like you to begin with your arrival on Pavonis Four." Graves held forward a small recording unit. "Whenever you are ready, we can begin."

Elena Carmel nodded uncertainly and cleared her throat several times. "It was going to be the last planet," she began at last. "The last one that we visited before we went back to Shasta. Before we went home." Her voice cracked on the final word. "So we decided we would like to stay out on the surface, away from people. We bought special equipment"—she gestured around her—"this equipment, so we could live comfortably away from everything. And we took the *Summer Dreamboat* out to one of the dryland turf hummocks in the middle of the marshes—Pavonis Four is mostly marshes. We wanted to get right away from civilization, and we wanted to camp away from the ship."

She paused.

"That was my fault," Geni Carmel said, in a beaten voice a tone higher than her sister's. "We'd seen so many people, on so many worlds, and the ship was smaller than we realized before we started. I was tired of living cramped up in it."

"We were both tired." Elena was defending her little sister. "We camped maybe thirty meters from the ship, close to the edge of the hummock. When twilight came we thought it would be a great idea to go really primitive, just as if we were back on Earth ten thousand years ago, and light a fire. We did that, and it was nice and warm, with no threat of rain. So we decided that we would even sleep outside. When it was completely dark, we put out sleeping bags next to each other, and lay looking up at the stars." She frowned. "I don't know what we talked about."

"I do," Geni said. "We talked about that being our last stop, and how dull it would be to go back to school on Shasta. We tried to see our own sun, but the constellations looked too different, and we weren't sure where home was . . ." Her voice trailed off, and she glanced again at her sister.

"So we fell asleep." Elena was speaking less easily. "And while we were asleep, they came. They—the—"

"The Bercia?" Julius Graves prompted. Both twins nodded.

"Wait a moment, Elena," he went on. "I want to note for the record here a number of facts about the Bercia. These facts are well established and easily verified. The Bercia were large, slow vertebrates. As nocturnal amphibians, native to and unique to Pavonis Four, they were highly photophobic. In life-style they resembled Earth's extinct beavers. Like beavers, they were communal and largely aquatic, and they built lodges. The main reason they were credited with possible intelligence is because of the complex structure of those lodges. And to make them, they employed mud and the trunks of the only treelike structures on Pavonis Four. Those grow only close to the dryland turf hummocks. It was therefore almost inevitable that the Bercia would appear at night by the hummock where the Carmel camp stood."

He turned to Elena. "Did anyone ever tell you about the Bercia before you set out to camp? Who they were, what they looked like?"

"No."

"Or you?" he asked, switching his attention to Geni Carmel.

She shook her head, then added, "No," in an almost inaudible voice.

"So I would like to add the physical description of the

Bercia to this record. All human experience with these beings suggests that they were gentle and totally herbivorous.
However, to chew through the xylem of the tree trunks, the
Bercia were equipped with heavy jaws and big, strong
teeth." He nodded to Elena Carmel. "Please continue. De-
scribe the rest of your night on Pavonis Four."

"I'm not sure when we went to sleep, or how long we
slept." Elena Carmel glanced at her sister. "I only woke up
when I heard Geni cry out. She told me—"

"I want to hear it directly from Geni." Graves pointed
his finger at the other sister. "I know this is painful, but tell
us what you saw."

Geni Carmel looked terrified. Graves leaned forward and
took her hands in his. He waited.

"Pavonis Four has one big moon," Geni said at last. "I
don't sleep as soundly as Elena, and the full moonlight woke
me up. At first I didn't look around me—I just lay in my
sleeping bag and stared up at the moon. I remember that
it had a dark pattern on it, like a curved cross on top of a
pyramid. Then something big moved in front of the moon.
I thought it must be a cloud or something, and I didn't realize how close it was until I heard it breathing. It was leaning
over me. I saw a flat, dark head, and a mouth full of pointed
teeth. And I screamed for Elena."

"Before we continue," Graves said, "I would like to make
another easily verified addition to this record. The planet
Shasta, homeworld of Elena and Geni Carmel, has no dangerous carnivores. But at one time it did. The largest and
most dangerous of those animals was a four-legged inverte-
brate known as a Skrayal. Although anatomically it in no
way resembles a Bercia, it possessed the same superficial appearance and was roughly the same size and weight. Elena
Carmel, what did you think when you realized that a Bercia
was leaning over your sister, with a ring of them surrounding both your beds?"

"I thought—I thought that they were Skrayal. Just at
first." She hesitated, then words came in a rush. "Of course,

when I got a good look at them and thought about it, I knew they couldn't be, and anyway we had never seen Skrayal—they were gone before we were born. But all our stories and pictures were filled with them, and when I first woke up I didn't even know where I was—all I saw were big animals, and the teeth of the one next to Geni."

"What did you do?"

"I screamed, and picked up the light, and turned it on all the way."

"Did you know that the Bercia were strongly photophobic and would go into terminal shock at high illumination levels?"

"I had no idea."

"Did you know that the Bercia were possibly intelligent?"

"I told you, we'd never even heard of the Bercia. We found all that out later, after we checked the planetary data base on the *Summer Dreamboat.*"

"And so you also had no way of knowing that those Bercia were the *only* surviving mature members of the species? And that the infant forms could not survive without adult care?"

"We didn't know any of that. We learned it after we returned to Capra City and heard that we were being looked for so we could be arrested."

"Councilor," Perry interrupted. He was looking again at his watch. "We've been gone three hours. We have to get back."

"Very well. We can pause here." Graves picked up the recording instrument and turned to Elena and Geni Carmel. "There will have to be an inquiry and trial back on Shasta, in controlled conditions, and also a hearing on Miranda. But I can assure you, what you have told me is already enough to establish innocence of intent. You killed by accident, not knowing that you were killing, when you were terrified and half-asleep. There is still one mystery to me—*why* you fled. But that can wait for explanation." He stood up. "Now I must take you both into my custody. From this moment, you are under arrest. And we must leave this place."

The twins flashed split-second glances at each other.

"We won't go," they said in breathless unison.

"You must. You are in danger. We are all in danger."

"We'll stay here and take our chances," Elena said.

Graves frowned at them. "You don't understand. Commander Perry can give you details, but I'll put it simply: you may feel safe enough just now, but there is no way you can survive Summertide if you stay here on Quake."

"Leave us, then." Elena Carmel was close to tears. "We'll stay. If we die, that ought to be enough punishment to satisfy everybody."

Graves sighed and sat down again. "Commander Perry, you must go. Get back to the others and take off. I cannot leave."

Perry remained standing, but he took a sidearm from his belt and pointed it at the twins. "This can kill, but it can also be used at stunner setting. If the councilor chooses, we can take you to the aircar unconscious."

The young women stared apprehensively at the weapon, but Graves was shaking his head. "No, Commander," he said wearily. "That is no solution. We'd never drag the pair of them up that slope, and you know it. I will stay. You must leave, and tell J'merlia and Kallik what has happened." He leaned back and closed his eyes. "And go quickly, before it's too late."

A rumble of thunder, far overhead, added weight to his words. Perry looked up, but did not leave.

"Tell me *why*," Graves went on. He opened his eyes, stood up slowly, and began to pace the length of the tent. "Tell me why you won't come back with me. Do you think that I'm your enemy—or that the governors of the Alliance are all cruel monsters? Do you believe that the whole system of justice is set up to torment and torture young women? That the Council would condone any mistreatment of you? If it would help, I can give you my personal promise that you will not be harmed if you go with me. But please, tell me what you are so afraid of."

Elena Carmel looked questioningly at her sister. "Can we?" And then, at Geni's nod, she spoke. "There would be treatment for us. *Rehabilitation.* Wouldn't there?"

"Well, yes." Graves paused in his pacing. "But only to help you. It would take away the pain of memory—you don't want to go through the rest of your life reliving that night on Pavonis Four. Rehab isn't punishment. It's *therapy.* It wouldn't hurt you."

"You can't guarantee that," Elena said. "Isn't rehab supposed to help with mental problems—any mental problems?"

"Well, it's always focused on some particular incident or difficulty. But it helps in all areas."

"Even with a problem that we might not *think* is a problem." Geni Carmel took the lead for the first time. "Rehab would make us 'saner.' But we're *not* sane, not by the definition you and the Council will use."

"Geni Carmel, I have no idea what you are talking about, but no one is totally sane." Graves sighed and rubbed the top of his bald head. "Least of all me. But I would undergo rehab willingly, if it were judged necessary."

"But suppose you had a problem you didn't *want* cured?" Elena asked. "Something that was more important to you than anything in the world."

"I'm not sure I can imagine such a thing."

"You see. And you represent Council thinking," Geni said. "*Human species* thinking."

"You are human, too."

"But we're *different,*" Elena said. "Did you ever hear of Mina and Daphne Dergori, from our world of Shasta?"

There was a puzzled pause. "I did not," Graves replied. "Should I have?"

"They are sisters," Elena said. "Twin sisters. We knew them since we were little children. They are our age, and we have lots in common. But they and their whole family were involved in a spaceship accident. Almost everyone was killed. Mina and Daphne and three other children were thrown into the pinnace at the last moment by a crew member, and they survived. When they got back home they were given rehab. To help them forget."

"I'm sure they were." Graves glanced at Perry, who was gesturing again at his watch. "And I'm sure it worked. Didn't it?"

"It helped them forget the accident." Geni was pale, and her hands were shaking. "But don't you see? *They lost each other.*"

"We knew them well," Elena said. "We understood them. They were just like us; they had the same *closeness* to each other. But after rehab, when we saw them again . . . it was gone. Gone completely. They were no more to each other than other people."

"And you would do it to us," Geni added. "Can't you understand that's *worse* than killing us?"

Graves stood motionless for a few moments, then flopped loose-limbed into a chair. "And *that's* why you ran away from Pavonis Four? Because you thought we would take you away from each other?"

"Wouldn't you?" Elena said. "Wouldn't you have wanted to give us 'normal' and 'independent' lives, so we could live apart? Isn't that included in rehab?"

"Lord of Lords." Graves's face was back to its spastic twitching. He covered it with his hands. "*Would* we have done that? Would we? We would, we would."

"Because closeness and dependence on each other is 'unnatural,'" Elena said bitterly. "You would have tried to *cure* us. We can't stand that idea. That's why you'll have to kill us before we will go with you. So go now, and leave us with each other. We don't want your cure. If we die, at least we die together."

Graves did not seem to be listening. "Blind," he muttered. "Blind for years, filled with my own hubris. Convinced that I had a gift, so sure that I could understand any human. But can an individual relate fully to a compound being? Is there that much empathy? I doubt it."

He straightened up, walked across to the two women, and put his open hands together in a gesture of prayer. "Elena and Geni Carmel, listen to me. If you will come with me now and agree to rehabilitation for what happened on Pavonis Four, you will not be separated. Never. There will never be an attempt to 'treat' your need to be together, or to break your closeness. You will continue to share your lives. I swear this to you, with every atom of my body, with my full authority as a member of the Alliance Council."

He dropped his hands to his sides and turned away. "I know I am asking you to trust me more than is reasonable. But please do it. Discuss this with each other. Commander Perry and I will wait outside. Please talk . . . and tell me that you will come."

The Carmel twins smiled for the first time since Perry had entered the tent.

"Councilor," Elena said quietly, "you are right when you say that you do not understand twins. Don't you understand that you do not need to leave, and we do not need to talk to each other? We both *know* what the other feels and thinks."

The two women stood up in unison and spoke together. "We will come with you. When must we leave?"

"Now." Perry had been a silent bystander, glancing from the three people before him to his watch and back. For the first time, he accepted the idea that Julius Graves had a gift for dealing with people that Perry himself would never have. "We all have to leave this minute. Grab what you absolutely need, but nothing else. We've been down here longer than we expected. Summertide is less than thirty-three hours away."

The aircar rose from the black basalt surface.

Too slow, Max Perry said to himself. Too slow and sluggish. What's this car's load limit? I bet we're close to it.

He said nothing to the others, but his internal tension willed them upward, until they were cruising at a safe height back the way they had come.

Apparently the others did not share his worries. Elena and Geni Carmel appeared exhausted, lying back in their seats at the rear of the car and staring wearily out at the glowing sky. Graves was back to his old manic cheerfulness, querying J'merlia, and through him Kallik, about the Zardalu clade and Kallik's own homeworld. Perry decided that it was probably Steven again, busy in simple information gathering.

Perry had little time himself for watching the others, or for conversation. He was tired, too—it was more than twenty-four hours since he had slept—but nervous energy kept him wide awake. In the past few hours Quake's atmosphere had passed through a transition. Instead of flying under a dusty but sunlit sky, the aircar sped beneath continuous layers of roiling cloud, black and rusty-red. They needed to be safely above those clouds, but Perry dared not risk the force of unknown wind shears. Even at the car's present height, well below the clouds, violent patches of turbulence came and went unpredictably. It was not safe to fly the car at more than half its full speed. Jagged bolts of lightning, showing as dusky red through windblown dust, ran between sky and surface. Every minute the lower edge of the cloud layer crept closer toward the ground.

Perry looked down. He could see a dozen scattered lakes and ponds, steaming and shrinking, giving up their stored moisture to the atmosphere. Quake needed the protection of that layer of water vapor to shield it from the direct rays of Mandel and Amaranth.

What could not be shielded were the growing tidal forces. The ground around the shrinking lakes was beginning to fracture and heave. Conditions were steadily worsening as the car flew closer to the place where J'merlia and Kallik had been found.

Perry wrestled the car's controls and wondered. A landing in these conditions would be difficult. How long would it take to drop J'merlia and Kallik at their car and move back to the relative safety of the air? And if there was no sign of Atvar H'sial and Louis Nenda, could they leave the two slaves alone on the surface?

They had not much farther to go. In ten more minutes he would have to make the decision.

And in thirty hours, Summertide would be here. He risked a slight increase in airspeed.

A glow of ruddy light began to appear in the sky ahead. Perry peered at it with tired eyes.

Was it Amaranth, seen through a break in the clouds? Except that no cloud break was visible. And the bright area was too low in the sky.

He stared again, reducing speed to a crawl until he was sure. When he was finally certain, he turned in his seat.

"Councilor Graves, and J'merlia. Would you come forward, please, and give me your opinion on this?"

It was a formality. Perry did not need another opinion. In the past few hours there had been intense vulcanism in the area ahead. Right where J'merlia and Kallik had been picked up, the surface glowed orange-red from horizon to horizon. Smoking rivers of lava were creeping through a blackened and lifeless terrain, and nowhere, from horizon to horizon, was there a place for an aircar to land.

Perry felt a shiver of primitive awe at the sight—and a great sense of relief.

He did not have to make a decision after all. Quake had made it for him. They could head at once for the safety of the Umbilical.

The arithmetic was already running in his head. Seven hours' flight time from their current location. Add in a margin for error, in case they had to fly around bad storms or reduce airspeed, and say it might take as much as ten. And it would be eighteen hours before the Umbilical withdrew from the surface of Quake.

That was an eight-hour cushion. They would make it with time to spare.

CHAPTER 19

Summertide
minus two.

NOISE MEANT INEFFICIENCY. So did mechanical vibration. The motors of an aircar in good shape were almost silent, and its ride was silky smooth.

Darya Lang listened to the wheezing death rattle behind her and felt the floor tremble beneath her feet. There was no doubt about it, the shaking was getting worse. Getting worse *fast*, noticed easily above the buffeting of the wind.

"How much farther?" She had to shout the question.

Hans Rebka did not look up from the controls, but he shook his head. "Fourteen kilometers. May be too far. Touch and go."

They were churning along no more than a thousand meters above the surface, just high enough to escape added dust in the intake vents. The ground below was barely visible, ghostly and indistinct beneath a fine haze of swirling powder.

Lang looked higher. There was a thin vertical strand far off in front of them. She cried out, "I can see it, Hans! There's the foot of the Stalk!" at the same moment Rebka was shouting, "No good. We're losing lift."

The aircar engine began to sputter and gasp. Spells of smooth flight at close to full power were followed by grinding vibration and seconds of sickening descent. They dropped into the dust layer. The silver thread of the Umbilical vanished from Darya's view.

"Six kilometers. Four hundred meters." Rebka had taken a last sighting before they entered the storm and was flying on instruments. "I can't see to pick the landing site. Check your harness and make sure your mask and respirator are tight. We may be heading for a rough one."

The aircars were sturdy craft. They had been designed to fly in extreme conditions; but one thing they could not guarantee was a soft landing with an engine worn to scrap by corundum dust. The final gasp of power came when the instruments showed an altitude of twenty meters. Rebka changed flap setting to avoid a stall and brought them in at twice the usual landing speed. At the last moment he shouted to Darya to hold tight. They smacked down hard, bounced clear over a rock outcrop big enough to remove the car's belly, and slithered to a stop.

"That's it!" Rebka had hit the release for his own harness and was reaching over to help Darya while they were still moving. He took a last look at the microwave sensor and turned to give her a grin of triumph. "Come on, I've got the bearing. The foot of the Umbilical's less than half a kilometer ahead."

Ground conditions were much better than Darya had expected. Visibility was admittedly down to a few tens of meters, and wind sounds were punctuated by the boom of distant explosions. But the ground was calm, flat, and navigable, except where a row of house-sized boulders jutted up like broken teeth. She followed Rebka between two of them, thinking how lucky they were that the engine had failed when it did, and not a few seconds later. They would have flown on and smashed straight into those rocks.

She was still not convinced that Quake was as dangerous as Perry claimed, and she had a lingering desire to stay and explore. But having flown so far to reach the Umbilical, it made sense to use it. She peered ahead. Surely they had walked at least half a kilometer.

Not looking where she was going, she slipped on a thick layer of powder, slick and treacherous as oil. Rebka in front of her fell down in a cloud of dust, rolled over, and staggered to his feet. Instead of shuffling onward he halted and pointed straight up.

They had emerged into a region shielded from the wind. Visibility had improved by a factor of ten. A circular disk, blurred in outline by high-level windblown dust, hung above them in the sky. As they watched, it lifted higher and shrank a fraction in apparent size.

His cry coincided with her understanding of what she was seeing. "The foot of the Stalk. It's going up."

"But we got here earlier than we expected."

"I know. It shouldn't be doing that. It's rising way ahead of time!"

The Umbilical was fading as they watched, its club-shaped bottom end receding into the clouds and blown dust. Around its rising base stood the apron supporting the air-cars. She knew their size and tried to judge the height. Already the lower end must have risen almost a kilometer above the surface.

She turned to Rebka. "Hans, our car! If we can get back there and take it up—"

"Won't work." He moved to put his head close to hers. "Even if we could get the car into the air, there's nowhere to land on the base of the Umbilical. I'm sorry, Darya. This mess is my fault. I brought us, and now we're stuck here. We've had it."

He was speaking louder than necessary—as if to make nonsense of his words the wind had dropped completely. The dust in the air began to thin, the surface was quiet, and Darya could see right back to their aircar. Above them the foot of the Umbilical was visible, hovering tantalizingly close.

It was the worst possible time for such a thought, but Darya decided that a little anguish in Hans Rebka's voice made him nicer than ever. Self-confidence and competence were virtues—but so was mutual dependence.

She pointed. "It's not going any higher, Hans. Who's controlling it?"

"Maybe nobody." He was no longer shouting. "The control sequences can be preset. But it could be Perry and Graves—they may have taken it up just to get clear of the surface. Maybe they're holding it there, waiting to see if we show up. But we can't reach them!"

"We'll have to try." While he was still staring at the Umbilical, Darya was already slipping and sliding across the layer of talc, heading toward the aircar. "Come on. If we can make our car hover next to the apron on the bottom of the Stalk, maybe we can jump across onto it."

She listened in amazement to her own words. Was it really Darya Lang proposing that? Back on Sentinel Gate she had avoided all heights, telling friends and family with a shiver that she was terrified by them. Apparently everything in the universe was relative. At the moment, the prospect of leaping from a moving and malfunctioning aircar to an Umbilical, a kilometer or more above the ground, did not faze her at all.

Hans Rebka was following, but only to grip her arm and swing her around. "Wait a minute, Darya. Look."

Another aircar was cruising in from the northwest, just below cloud level. It was in a descent pattern, until its pilot apparently saw the Umbilical. Then the car banked and started to ascend in a slow and labored spiral.

But the foot of the Stalk had begun to rise again, and more rapidly. The two on the ground gazed up helplessly as the Umbilical gradually vanished into the clouds, the pursuing aircar laboring upward after it. As they both disappeared it seemed that the car was losing the race.

Darya turned to Hans Rebka. "But if Graves and Perry are up there on the Stalk, who's in the aircar?"

"It must be Max Perry. I was wrong about him and Graves being on the Umbilical. The Stalk ascent is performing its automatic Summertide retraction, but it's taking place ahead of time. It has been reprogrammed." He shook his head. "But that doesn't make sense, either. Perry is the only one who knows the Umbilical control codes." He saw her stricken look. "Isn't he?"

"No." She stared away and would not look at him. "Atvar H'sial knew them. All of them. I told you, that's how we got over from Opal. This is all my fault. I should never have agreed to work with her. Now we're stuck here, and she's safe up there on the Umbilical."

Hans Rebka glared up at the overcast. "I'll bet she is. That damned Cecropian. I wondered as we were flying here if she was still on Quake. And J'merlia will be with her. So the aircar up there has to be Perry and Graves."

"Or maybe the Carmel twins."

"No. They didn't have access to an aircar. Anyway, we can stop speculating. Here it comes again."

The car was spiraling down from the clouds, searching for a good place to touch down. Darya ran toward it and waved her arms frantically. The pilot saw her and carefully banked closer. The aircar flopped to a heavy landing no more than fifty meters away, creating a minor dust storm with its jets of downward air.

The car door slid open. Hans Rebka and Darya Lang watched in astonishment as two identical and identically dressed humans climbed out, followed by a Lo'tfian and a dusty-looking Hymenopt. Last of all came Julius Graves and Max Perry.

"We thought you were dead!" "We thought *you* were on the Umbilical!" "Where did you find them?" "How did you get here?"

Perry, Rebka, Lang, and Graves were all speaking at once, standing in a tight inward-facing group by the aircar door. The two aliens and the Carmel twins stood apart, staring around them at their desolate surroundings.

"No active radio beacons—we listened all the way here,"

Graves went on. He stared at Darya Lang. "Do you have any idea what has happened to Atvar H'sial?"

"I'm not sure, but we think she's probably up there on the Umbilical."

"No, she isn't. No one is. We couldn't catch it, but we could tell that no capsules are in use. And it's out of aircar altitude range now. But what about you? I thought Atvar H'sial left you behind on the surface."

"She did. Hans Rebka rescued me. But Atvar H'sial must have intended to come back for me, because she gave me supplies and a signal beacon."

"No, she didn't. That was J'merlia's doing." Graves gestured at the Lo'tfian. "He says that Atvar H'sial did not forbid him to help you, and so he did. He was very worried about your safety when they left you behind. He said that you seemed poorly equipped for survival on Quake. But then he thought you must be dead, anyway, because when we listened there was no sign of your beacon. I feel sure that Atvar H'sial didn't intend to go back for you. You were supposed to die on Quake."

"But where is Atvar H'sial now?" Rebka asked.

"We just asked *you* that question," Perry said. "She must be with Louis Nenda."

"Nenda!"

"He came here on his own ship," Graves said. "And did you know he can talk to a Cecropian directly? Kallik told J'merlia that Nenda had a Zardalu augment that lets him use pheromonal communication. He and Atvar H'sial left J'merlia and Kallik behind, and went off somewhere by themselves."

"We think they came here. Atvar H'sial had help. Somehow she obtained the control sequences, and she must have set the Umbilical for earlier retraction from the surface." Hans Rebka gave Darya Lang a "say-no-more" look and went on. "She wants us all dead, stranded on Quake at Summertide. That's why she left J'merlia and Kallik behind— she didn't want witnesses."

"But we heard their distress signal and picked them up." Perry nodded to the silent aliens. "I think Nenda and H'sial may have intended to come back for them, but they would have been too late. The landing area was molten lava. We had to keep J'merlia and Kallik with us."

"But if Nenda made it back to his own ship," Graves said, "he and Atvar H'sial can still leave the planet."

"Which is more than we can do." After his earlier depression, Rebka had bounced back and was full of energy. "The Umbilical is gone, and it won't be back until after Summertide. We only have one aircar between the lot of us—ours died as we arrived here. And they can't achieve orbit anyway, so they're no answer. Commander Perry, we need a plan for survival here. We're stuck on Quake until the Umbilical returns."

"Can I say it one more time? That's *impossible.*" Perry spoke softly, but his grim tone carried more weight than a bellow. "I've been trying to impress one fact on you since the day you all arrived at Dobelle: *Humans can't survive Summertide on the surface of Quake.* Not even the usual Summertide. Certainly not *this* Summertide. No matter what you think, there's no 'survival plan' that can save us if we stay on Quake. It's still pretty quiet here, and I don't know why. But it can't last much longer. Anyone on the surface of Quake at Summertide will die."

As though the planet had heard him, a distant roar and groan of upthrust earth and grinding rocks followed his words. Moments later a series of rippling shocks blurred the air and shook the ground beneath their feet. Everyone stared around, then instinctively headed for the inside of the aircar and an illusion of safety.

Darya Lang, the last one in, surveyed the seven who had preceded her.

It was not a promising group for last-ditch survival schemes. The two Carmel sisters had the look of people already defeated and broken. They had been through too much on Quake; from this point on they would act only as they were directed. Graves and Perry were filthy and battered, clothes torn and rumpled and covered with grime and dust and sweat. They both had bloody and inflamed scratches on their calves, and Graves had another set of scabby wounds along the top of his bald head. Worse than that, he was acting much too cheerful, grinning around him as though all his own troubles were over. Maybe they were. If anyone could save them, it would be Max Perry and not Julius Graves. But after Perry's gloomy prediction, he had returned to a brooding, introverted silence, seeing something that was invisible to everyone else.

J'merlia and Kallik seemed fairly normal—but only because Darya did not know how to read in their alien bodies the signs of stress and injury. J'merlia was meticulously removing white dust from his legs, using the soft pads of his forelimbs. He seemed little worried by anything except personal hygiene. Kallik, after a quick shiver along her body that threw a generous layer of powder away from her and produced protests from the rest of the aircar's occupants, was stretching up to full height and staring bright-eyed at everything. If anyone was still optimistic, maybe it was the little Hymenopt. Unfortunately, only J'merlia could communicate with her.

Darya looked at Hans Rebka. He was obviously exhausted, but he was still their best hope. He had deep red lines on his face, scored by his mask and respirator, and there were owlish pale circles of dust around his eyes. But when he caught her look he managed a grin and a wink.

Darya squeezed in and had just enough room to slide the door closed. She had never expected to see so many beings, human or alien, in one small aircar. The official capacity was four people. The Carmel twins had managed to fit into one seat, but J'merlia was crouched on the floor where he could see or hear little, and Darya Lang and Max Perry had been left standing.

"What's the time?" Rebka asked unexpectedly. "I mean, how many hours to Summertide?"

"Fifteen." Perry's voice was expressionless.

"So what's next? We can't just sit here and wait to die. Anything's better than that. Let's look at our options. We can't reach the Umbilical, even if it goes no higher. And there's no place on Quake that we can go to be safe. Suppose we fly as high as we can and ride it out in this car?"

Kallik gave a series of whistling snorts that sounded to Darya Lang very like derision, while Perry roused himself from his reverie and shook his head. "I went through all those ideas, long ago," he said gloomily. "We're down to an eight-hour power supply for the aircar, and that's with normal load. If we get off the ground—it's not clear that we can, with so many on board—we'll be down again before Summertide Maximum."

"Suppose we sit here and wait until four or five hours before Summertide," Rebka suggested. "And *then* take off? We'd be clear of the surface during the worst time."

"Sorry. That won't work, either." Perry glared at Kallik, who was bobbing up and down to an accompaniment of clicks and whistles. "We'd never manage to stay in the air. The volcanoes and earthquakes turn the whole atmosphere into one mass of turbulence." He turned to the Lo'tfian. "J'merlia, tell Kallik to keep quiet. It's hard enough to think without that noise."

The Hymenopt bobbed even higher and whistled, "Sh-sh-sheep."

"Kallik asks me to point out," J'merlia said, "with great respect, you are all forgetting the ship."

"Louis Nenda's ship?" Rebka asked. "The one that Kallik came in? We don't know where it is. Anyway, Nenda and Atvar H'sial will have taken it."

Kallik let loose a louder series of whistles and wriggled her body in anguish.

"No, no. Kallik says humbly, she is talking about the *Summer Dreamboat,* the ship that the Carmel twins came in to Quake. We know exactly where that is."

"But its drive is exhausted," Perry said. "Remember, Kallik looked at it when we first found it."

"One moment, please." J'merlia wriggled his way past Julius Graves and the Carmel twins, until he was crouched close to the Hymenopt. The two of them grunted and whistled at each other for half a minute. Finally J'merlia bobbed his head and straightened up.

"Kallik apologizes to everyone for her extreme stupidity, but she did not make herself sufficiently clear when she examined the ship. The power for the Bose Drive is certainly exhausted, and the ship cannot be used for star travel. But there could be just enough power for one local journey—maybe for one jump to orbit."

Rebka was maneuvering past Julius Graves to the pilot's seat before J'merlia had finished speaking. "How far to that starship, and where is it?" He was examining the car's status board.

"Seven thousand kilometers, on a great circle path to the Pentacline Depression." Perry had emerged from his gloom and was pushing past the Carmel twins to join Rebka. "But this close to Summertide we can expect a sidewind all the way, strong and getting worse. That will knock at least a thousand off our range."

"So there's no margin." Rebka was doing a quick calculation. "We have enough power for about eight thousand, but not if we try for full speed. And if we slow down, we'll be flying closer to Summertide, and conditions will be worse."

"It is our best chance." Graves spoke for the first time since entering the aircar. "But can we get off the ground with this much load? We had a hard time getting here, and that was with two people less."

"And can we stay in the air, so close to Summertide?" Perry added. "The winds will be incredible."

"And even if Kallik is right," Graves said, "and there is a little power still in the starship, can the *Summer Dreamboat* make it to orbit?"

But Rebka was already starting the engine. "It's not our

best chance, Councilor," he said, as the downjets blew a cloud of white dust up to cover the windows. "It's our *only* chance. What do you want, a written guarantee? Get set and hold your breath. Unless someone has a better idea in the next five seconds, I'm going to push this car to the limit. Hold tight, and let's hope the engine wants to cooperate."

CHAPTER 20

Summertide minus one.

AS THE AIRCAR lurched from the ground and struggled upward, Darya Lang felt useless. She was supercargo, added load, a dumb weight unable to help the pilot or navigator in front of her. Helpless to contribute and unable to relax, she took a new look at her fellow passengers.

This was the group who would live or die together—and soon, before the rotating dumbbell of Quake and Opal had completed one more turn.

She studied them as the car droned onward. They were a depressed and depressing sight. The situation had turned back the clock, revealing them to Lang as they must have been long years earlier, before Quake entered their lives.

Elena and Geni Carmel, sitting cheek to cheek, were little girls lost. Unable to find their way out of the wood, they waited to be saved; or, far more likely, for the monster to arrive. In front of them Hans Rebka was crouched over the controls, a small, worried boy trying to play a game that was too grown-up for him. Next to him sat Max Perry, lost in some old, unhappy dream that he would share with no one.

Only Julius Graves, to Perry's right, failed to fit the pattern of backward-turning time. The councilor's face when he turned to the rear of the car had never been young. Thousands of years of misery were carved in its lines and roughened surface; human history, written dark and angry and desperate.

She stared at him in bewilderment. That was not the Council member of Alliance legend. Where was the kindness, the optimism, the crackling manic energy?

She knew the answer: snuffed out, by simple exhaustion.

For the first time, Darya realized the importance of fatigue in deciding human affairs. She had noticed her own gradual loss of interest in deciphering the riddle of Quake and the Builders, and she had attributed it to her concentration on simple survival. But now she blamed the enervating poisons of weariness and tension.

The same slow drain of energy was affecting all of them. At a time when thought and prompt action could make the difference between life and death, they were mentally and physically flat. Every one—she was surely no exception—looked like a zombie. They might rise for a few seconds to full attention and alertness, as she had at the moment of takeoff, but as soon as the panic was over they would slump back to lethargy. The faces that turned to her, even with all the white dust wiped off them, were pale and drawn.

She knew how they were feeling. Her own emotions were on ice. She could not feel terror, or love, or anger. That was the most frightening development, the new indifference to living or dying. She hardly cared what happened next. Over the past few days Quake had not struck her down with its violence, but it had drained her, bled her of all human passions.

Even the two aliens had lost their usual bounce. Kallik had produced a small computer and was busy with obscure calculations of her own. J'merlia seemed lost and bewildered without Atvar H'sial. He swiveled his head around constantly, as though seeking his lost master, and kept rubbing his hand-pads obsessively over his hard-shelled body.

Perry, Graves, and Rebka were wedged into the front

row, in a seat meant for two. The twins and J'merlia sat behind them, probably more comfortable than anyone else, while Darya Lang and Kallik had squeezed into an area at the rear designed only for baggage. It was tall enough for the Hymenopt, but Kallik had the reflex habit of shaking like a wet dog to remove residual powder from her short black fur. She had Darya sneezing and bending her head forward all the time to avoid contact with the car's curved roof.

Worst of all, those in the back could see only a sliver of sky out of the forward window. Information on progress or problems had to come from the warnings and comments of those in front.

And sometimes they arrived too late.

"Sorry," Perry called, two seconds after the car had been slewed, tilted, and dropped fifty meters by a terrific gust of wind. "That was a bad one."

Darya Lang rubbed the back of her head and agreed. She had banged it on the hard plastic ceiling of the cargo compartment. There would be a nasty bruise—if she lived so long.

She leaned forward and cradled her head on her arms. In spite of noise and danger and sickening instability of motion, her thoughts began drifting off. Her previous life as an archeo-scientist on Sentinel Gate now seemed wholly artificial. How many times, in assembling the Lang catalog of artifacts, had she placidly written of whole expeditions, "No survivors"? It was a neat and tidy phrase, one that required no explanation and called for no thought. The element that was missing was the *tragedy* of the event, and the infinite subjective time that it might have taken to happen. Those "No survivors" entries suggested a clean extinction, a group of people snuffed out as quickly and impartially as a candle flame. Far more likely were situations like the present one: slow extinction of hope as the group clutched at every chance and saw each one fade.

Darya's spirits spiraled down further. Death was rarely

quick and clean and painless, unless it also came as a surprise. More often it was slow, agonizing, and degrading.

A calm voice pulled her up from tired despair.

"Get ready in the back there." Hans Rebka sounded far from doomed and defeated. "We're too low, and we're too slow. At this rate we'll run out of power and we'll run out of time. So we have to get above the clouds. Hold on tight again. We're in for a rough few minutes."

Hold on to what? But Rebka's words and his cheerful tone told her that not everyone had given up fighting.

Ashamed of herself, Darya tried to wedge more tightly into the luggage compartment as the car buffeted its way up through the uneven lower edge of the clouds. The textured glow outside was replaced by a bland, muddy light. More violent turbulence began at once, hitting from every direction and throwing the overloaded vehicle easily and randomly about the sky like a paper toy. No matter what Rebka and Perry did at the controls, the car had too much weight to maneuver well.

Darya tried to predict the motion and failed. She could not tell if they were rising, falling, or heading for a fatal downspin. Bits of the car's ceiling fixtures seemed to come at her head from every side. Just as she felt certain that the next blow would knock her unconscious, four jointed arms took her firmly around the waist. She reached out to grasp a soft, pudgy body, clinging to it desperately as the car veered and dipped and jerked through the sky.

Kallik was pushing her, forcing her toward the wall. She buried her face in velvety fur, bent her legs up to her right, and pushed back. Braced against each other and the car's walls, she and Kallik found a new stability of position. She shoved harder, wondering if the rocky ride would ever end.

"We're almost there. Shield your eyes." Rebka's voice sounded through the cabin intercom a moment before the swoops and sickening uplifts eased. As the flight became smoother, blinding light flooded into the car, replacing the diffuse red-brown glow.

Darya heard a loud, clucking set of snorts from her right. J'merlia wriggled around in his seat to face the back of the car.

"Kallik wishes to offer her humble apologies," he said, "for what she did. She assures you that she would never in normal circumstances dare to touch the person of a superior being. And she wonders now if you might kindly release her."

Darya realized that she was clinging to soft black fur and crushing the Hymenopt in a bear hug, while still pushing her toward the far wall of the car. She let go at once, feeling embarrassed. The Hymenopt was far too polite to say anything, but she must recognize blind panic when she saw it.

"Tell Kallik that it was good that she took hold of me. What she did helped a lot, and no apology is needed." And if I'm a *superior* being, Darya added silently, I'd hate to know what an inferior one feels like.

Embarrassed or not, Darya was beginning to feel a bit better. The flight was smoother, while the whistle of air past the car suggested that they were moving much faster. Even her own aches and fatigue had somehow eased.

"We've just about doubled our airspeed, and it should be smooth sailing up here." Rebka's voice over the intercom seemed to justify her changing mood.

"But we had a hard time coming through those clouds," he went on. "And Commander Perry has recalculated our rate of power use. Given the distance we have to go, we're right on the edge. We have to conserve. I'll slow down a little, and I'm going to turn off the air-conditioning system. That will make it pretty bad here up front. Be ready to rotate seats, and make sure you drink lots of liquid."

It had not occurred to Darya Lang that her limited view of the sky might be an advantage. But as the internal temperature of the car began to rise, she was glad to be sitting in the shielded rear. The people in front had the same stifling air as she did, plus direct and intolerable sunlight.

The full effects of that did not hit her until it was time

to play musical chairs and move around the car's cramped interior. The change of position was a job for contortionists. When it was completed, Darya found herself in the front seat, next to the window. For the first time since takeoff, she could see more than a tiny bit of the car's surroundings.

They were skimming along just above cloud level, riding over individual crests that caught and scattered the light like sea breakers of dazzling gold and crimson. Mandel and Amaranth were almost straight ahead, striking down at the car with a fury never felt on the cloud-protected surfaces of Opal and Quake. The two stars had grown to giant, blinding orbs in a near-black sky. Even with the car's photo-shielding at maximum, the red and yellow spears of light thrown by the stellar partners were too bright to look at.

The perspiration ran in rivulets down Darya's face and soaked her clothing. As she watched, the positions of Mandel and Amaranth changed in the sky. Everything was happening faster and faster. She sensed the rushing tempo of events as the twin suns and Dobelle hurried to their point of closest approach.

And they were not the only players.

Darya squinted off to the side. Gargantua was there, a pale shadow of Mandel and its dwarf companion. But that, too, would change. Soon Gargantua would be the largest object in Quake's sky, sweeping closer than any body in the stellar system, rivaling Mandel and Amaranth with its ripping tidal forces.

She looked out and down, wondering what was going on below those boiling cloud layers. Soon they would have to descend through them, but perhaps the hidden surface beneath was already too broken to permit a landing. Or maybe the ship they sought had already vanished, swallowed up in some massive new earth fissure.

Darya turned away from the window and closed her aching eyes. The outside brightness was just too overwhelming. She could not stand the heat and the searing radiation for one moment longer.

Except that she had no choice.

She looked to her left. Kallik was next to her, crouched down low to the floor. Beyond her, in the pilot's seat, Max Perry was holding a square of opaque plastic in front of his face to give him partial shielding from the sluice of light.

"How much longer?" The question came as a feeble croak.

Darya hardly recognized her own voice. She was not sure what question she was asking. Did she mean how long until they could all change seats again? Or until they arrived at their destination? Or only until they were all dead?

It made no difference. Perry did not answer. He merely handed her a bottle of lukewarm water. She took a mouthful and made Kallik do the same. Then there was nothing to do but sit and sweat and *endure,* until the welcome distraction of changing seats.

Darya lost track of time. She knew that she was in and out of the torture seat at the front at least three times. It felt like weeks, until at last Julius Graves was shaking her and warning, "Get ready for turbulence. We're going down through the clouds."

"We're there?" she whispered. "Let's go down."

She could hardly wait. No matter what happened next, she would escape the roasting torture of the two suns. She would dream of them for the rest of her life.

"No. Not there." Graves sounded the way she felt. He was mopping perspiration from his bald head. "We're running out of power."

That grabbed her attention. "Where are we?"

But he had turned the other way. It was Elena Carmel, in the rear seat, who leaned forward and replied. "If the instruments are right, we're very close. Almost to our ship."

"*How* close?"

"Ten kilometers. Maybe even less. They say it all depends how much power is left to use in hovercraft mode."

Darya said nothing more. Ten kilometers, five kilometers,

what difference did it make? She couldn't walk *one* kilometer, not to save her life.

But a surprise voice inside her awoke and said, Maybe *only* to save your life. If young, bewildered Elena Carmel can find a reserve of strength, why can't you?

Before she could argue the point with herself, they were plunging into the clouds. And within a second there was no time for the luxury of internal debate.

Hans Rebka thought he might need the dregs of aircar power later, and he was not willing to give up any merely to cushion the ride. In its rapid descent, the car was thrown around the sky like a bobbing cork in a sea storm. But it did not last long. In less than a minute they plunged through the bottom of the cloud layers.

Everyone craned forward. Whatever they found below them, they could not go back up.

Was the starship still there? Was there a solid surface around it that they could descend to? Or had they escaped Mandel and Amaranth's searing beams only to die in Quake's pools of molten lava?

Darya stared, unable to answer those questions. Thick smoke blanketed the ground below. They were supposed to be above the slopes of the Pentacline Depression, but they might have been anywhere on the whole planet.

"Well," Hans Rebka said quietly, as though talking to himself, "the good news is that we don't have to make a decision. Look at the power meter, Max. It's redlined. We're going down, whether we want to or not." He raised his voice. "Respirators on."

Then they were floating into blue-gray smoke that swirled and eddied about the car, driven by winds so powerful that Rebka's voice quickly came again. "We're making a negative ground speed. I'm going to take us down as quick as I can, before we blow back all the way to the Umbilical."

"Where's the ship?" That was Julius Graves, sitting behind Darya in the cramped luggage compartment.

"Two kilometers ahead. We can't see it, but I think it's

still there. I'm picking up an anomalous radar reflection. We can't reach the outcrop where the ship was sitting, so we have to land on the valley slope. Get ready. Twenty meters altitude . . . fifteen . . . ten. Prepare for landing."

The gusting wind suddenly died. The smoke around them thinned. Darya could see the ground off to one side of the car. It lay barren and quiet, but steam was emerging like dragon's breath from dozens of small surface vents scattered across the downward slope of the Pentacline's valley. The dense vegetation that Darya expected to see in the depression had gone. It was nothing but gray ash and occasional withered stems.

"One and a half kilometers." Rebka's voice sounded calm and far away. "Five meters on the altimeter. Power going. Looks like we'll have to take a little walk. Three meters . . . two . . . one. Come on, you beauty. Do us proud."

Summertide was just three hours away. The aircar touched down on the steaming slope of the Pentacline Depression, as gently and quietly as an alighting moth.

CHAPTER 21

Three hours to Summertide.

HANS REBKA WAS not happy, but it would be fair to say that for the past few hours he had been content.

Since his assignment to Dobelle he had been unsure of himself and his job. He had been sent to find out what was wrong with Commander Maxwell Perry and rehabilitate the man.

On paper it sounded easy. But just what was he supposed to *do*? He was an action man, not a psychoanalyst. Nothing in his previous career had equipped him for such a vague task.

Now things were different. At the Umbilical he had been thrown in with a helpless group—all aliens, misfits, or innocents, in his mind—and given the job of taking an overloaded, underpowered aircar halfway around Quake and a toy starship up into space, before the planet killed the lot of them.

It might be an impossible task, but at least it was a well-defined one. The rules for performance were no problem. He had learned them long ago on Teufel: you succeed, or you die trying. Until you succeed, you never relax. Until you die, you never give up.

He was tired—they were all tired—but what Darya Lang

had seen as new energy was the satisfying release of a whole bundle of pent-up frustrations. It had carried him so far, and it would carry him through Summertide.

As soon as the aircar touched down, Rebka urged everyone onto the surface. It made no difference how dangerous it might be outside, the car was useless to take them any farther.

He pointed along the blistered downslope of the valley. "That's where we have to go. The direction of the starship." Then he shouted above rumbling thunder to Max Perry, who was staring vacantly about him. "Commander, your group was here a few days ago. Does it look familiar?"

Perry was shaking his head. "When we were here this area was vegetated. But there's the basalt outcrop." He pointed to a dark jutting mass of rock, forty meters high, its upper part obscured by gray smoke. "We have to get over there and climb on top of it. That's where the ship should be."

Rebka nodded. "Any nasty surprises in store for us?" Perry, whatever his faults, was still the expert on conditions on Quake.

"Can't say yet. Quake is full of them." Perry stooped to set the palm of his hand on the rocky floor. "Pretty hot, but we can walk on it. If we're lucky, the brush fires will have burned off the plants around the bottom of the outcrop and we'll have easier going than last time. Things look all different with the vegetation gone. And it's hotter—a lot hotter."

"So let's go." Rebka gestured them forward. The thunder was growing, and their surroundings were too loud for long conversations. "You and Graves lead. Then you two." He pointed to the twins. "I'll tag along last, after the others."

He urged them on without inviting discussion. The aircar trip had been an exhausting trial by fire for everyone, but Rebka knew better than to ask if they could scramble their way over a kilometer or two of difficult terrain. He would learn what they could not do when they collapsed.

The surface had been at rest when they landed, but as

Perry and Graves started forward a new spasm of seismic energy passed through the area. The ground ahead broke into longitudinal folds, rippling down the side of the valley.

"Keep going," Rebka shouted above the grind and boom of breaking rock. "We can't afford to stand and wait."

Perry had halted and put his hand on Graves's arm to stop him. He turned to shake his head at Rebka. "Can't go yet. Earthquake confluence. Watch."

Ground waves of different wavelength and amplitude were converging fifty paces ahead of the party. Where they met, spumes of rock and earth jetted into the dusty air. A gaping trench of unknown depth appeared, then contracted and filled a few seconds later to vanish completely. Perry watched until he was sure that the main earth movements were over, then started forward.

Rebka felt relief. Whatever Perry's problems, the man had not lost his survival instinct. If he could hold on to that for another kilometer, his main job would be done.

They scrambled on. The ground shivered beneath their feet. Hot breaths rose from a hundred fissures in the fractured rock, and the sky above became one rolling tableau of fine ash and bright lightning. Thunder from sky and earth movement snarled and roared around them. A warm, sulfur-charged rain started to fall, steaming where it touched the tide-torn hot ground.

Rebka eyed the rest of the group speculatively from his vantage point at the rear. The Carmel twins were walking side by side, just behind Graves and Perry. After them came Darya Lang, between the two aliens and with one hand on J'merlia's sloping thorax. Everyone was doing well. Graves, Geni Carmel, and Darya Lang were limping, and everyone was weaving with fatigue—but that was a detail.

So they needed rest. He smiled grimly to himself. Well, one way or another they would find it, in the next few hours.

The big problem was the increasing temperature. Another ten degrees, and he knew they would have to slow down or keel over with simple heat prostration. The rain showers, which should have helped, were becoming hot enough to scald exposed skin. And as the party moved lower into the Pentacline Depression, further heat increase seemed inevitable.

But they had to keep descending. If they slowed or went back up, for rest or for shelter, the forces of Summertide would destroy them.

He urged them on, peering ahead as he did so to study the approach to the basalt outcrop. With no more than a few hundred meters to go, the path looked pretty easy. In another hundred paces the jumble of rocks and broken surface that were making walking so difficult would smooth out, providing a brown plain more level than anything that Rebka had seen in the Pentacline. It looked like a dried-out lake bed, the relic of a long, thin water body that had boiled dry in the past few days. They could move across it easily and fast. Beyond the narrow plain, the ground rose with an easy slope to the base of the rocky uplift on whose top they should find the ship.

The two leaders had advanced to within twenty paces of the plain. The hulking, flat-topped rock seemed close enough to touch when Max Perry paused uncertainly. While Rebka looked on and cursed, Perry leaned on a large, jagged boulder and stared thoughtfully at the way ahead.

"Get a move on, man."

Perry shook his head, lifted his arm to halt the others, and crouched low to examine the ground. At the same moment, Elena Carmel cried out and pointed to the top of the rock outcrop.

The sky had turned black, but near-continuous lightning gave more than enough light to see by. Rebka could detect nothing where Perry had been staring, except a slight shimmer of heat haze and a loss of focus in the lake bed ahead. But beyond that blurred area, following Elena Carmel's pointing finger to the top of the rock where the dust clouds rolled, Rebka saw something quite unmistakable: the outline of a small starship. It sat safely back from the rock edge, and it seemed undamaged. The line of ascent was an easy one. In five minutes or less they should be up there.

Elena Carmel had turned and was shouting to her sister, inaudible above the thunder. Rebka could read her lips. "The *Summer Dreamboat*," she was shouting. Her face was triumphant as she went running forward, past Graves and Perry.

She was already onto the dried-mud plain and heading toward the bottom of the outcrop when Perry looked up and saw her.

He froze for a second, then uttered a high-pitched howl of warning that carried even above the thunder.

Elena turned at the sound. As she did so the crust of baked clay, less than a centimeter thick, fractured beneath her weight. Spurts of steam blew pitch-black, steaming slime into the air around her body. She cried out and raised her arms, trying to hold her balance. Under the brittle surface, the bubbling ooze offered no more resistance than hot syrup. Before anyone could move, Elena was waist-deep. She screamed in agony as boiling mud closed around her legs and hips.

"Lean forward!" Perry threw himself flat to spread his weight and started to wriggle forward onto the fragile surface.

But Elena Carmel was in too much pain to take any notice of his cry. He was too slow, and she was sinking too fast. He was still three paces away when the bubbling mud reached her neck. She gave a final and terrible scream.

Perry threw himself across the breaking crust to grab at her hair and one outstretched arm. He could reach her, but he could not support her.

She sank deeper. Far gone in burn-shock, she made no sound as the searing mud bubbled into her mouth, nose, and eyes. A moment later she was gone. The liquid surface swirled into a small whirlpool, then in less than a second became smooth again.

Perry wriggled forward again and plunged his arms to

the elbows in boiling blackness. He roared in agony, groped, and found nothing.

The others in the party had stood rigid. Suddenly Geni Carmel gave a dreadful scream and began to run forward. Julius Graves dived after her, tackling and holding her at the very edge of the boiling quicksand.

"No, Geni. No! You can't help, she's gone." He had her around the waist, trying to pull her toward safety. She resisted with desperate strength. It was all he could do to hold her until Rebka and Darya Lang ran forward to grab her arms.

Geni was still trying to drag herself toward the place where Elena had vanished. She pulled them to the edge of the safe area of rock. As she turned she swiveled Darya with her, forcing the other woman out onto the cracked crust. Darya's left foot broke through and plunged in above the ankle. She screamed and sagged toward Rebka in a near-faint. He had to leave Geni to Graves while he pulled Darya clear.

Geni tried one more time to move to the open area of mud. The surface where Elena had been sucked under spouted and bubbled like escaping breath. But Perry, his face distorted with pain, had come sliding backward across the treacherous mud to the safe region of broken rocks. His hands were useless, but he stood up and used his body weight to push Geni back.

They stumbled together to safety. Geni was quieting. As the first frenzy ended she put her hands to her face and began to sob.

Rebka kept one arm around Darya Lang and surveyed the group. They were all stunned by Elena's death, but still he had to worry about other matters. In thirty seconds, their position had gone from difficult to desperate. The air was almost unbreathable, the heat was increasing, and the surface of Quake was more and more active. The one thing they could not afford to do was slow down.

What now?

He made an unhappy assessment of their new situation. The thunder from ground and sky was a little less, but instead of eight humans and aliens, all fully mobile, they had been reduced to four able-bodied beings: himself, Graves, J'merlia, and Kallik. It was anyone's guess how useful the two aliens would be in a crisis, but so far they had performed as well as any human.

What about the others?

Perry was in deep shock—more than just physical, if Rebka was any judge—and he was standing there like a robot. But he was tough. He could walk, and he would walk. On the other hand, he could no longer help anyone else, and without the use of his hands he would have trouble scrambling up the rock face. His arms hung loose at his sides, burned to the elbows and as useless as rolls of black dough. The pain from them would be awful as soon as the first shock faded. With any luck that would be after they were all in the *Summer Dreamboat*.

Darya Lang would certainly need assistance. Her foot was scalded no worse than Perry's forearms, but she was far less used to physical suffering. Already she was weeping with pain and shock. Tears were running down her grimy, dust-coated cheeks.

Finally there was Geni Carmel. She did not need physical help, but emotionally she had been destroyed. She hardly seemed to realize that the others were there, and she would find it hard to cooperate in anything at all.

Rebka made the assignments automatically. "Councilor Graves, you help Geni Carmel. I'll assist Commander Perry if he needs it. J'merlia and Kallik, Professor Lang needs your aid. Help her, especially when we begin to climb."

And now we'll see just how tough Perry is, he thought. "Commander, we can't go any farther this way. Can you suggest another route to the ship?"

Perry came to life. He shivered, stared down at his burned forearms, and lifted his right hand tentatively away from his body. He pointed to the left side of the outcrop, moving his arm as though the limb had become some alien attachment.

"Last time we were here, we came down a watercourse. It was all rocks, no muddy surface. If we can find that maybe we can follow it back up."

"Good. You lead the way."

As they skirted the deadly patch of boiling mud, Rebka looked up to the top of the rock. It was no more than forty meters above them, but it seemed an impossible distance. The watercourse was not steep. A fit man or woman could scramble up it in half a minute, but Perry would take that long to ascend the first few feet. And that was too slow.

Rebka moved forward from the back of the group and put his hands on Perry's hips.

"Just keep walking. Don't worry about falling, I'll be here. If you need a push or a lift, tell me."

He took one backward glance before Perry began to move. Julius Graves was coaxing Geni Carmel along, and they were doing well enough. J'merlia and Kallik had given up the idea of helping Darya Lang to walk. Instead they had seated her on Kallik's furry back, and the Hymenopt was struggling up the incline with J'merlia pushing them from behind and encouraging Kallik with a selection of hoots and whistles.

The surface beyond the outcrop was shaking with new violence. Rebka saw the aircar that they had arrived in tilt and collapse. A pall of black smoke swallowed it up, then came creeping steadily toward them.

One thing at a time, he told himself. Don't look back, and don't look up.

Rebka focused all his attention on helping Max Perry. If the other man fell, they would all go with him.

They struggled on, stumbling and scrabbling over loose pebbles. There was one critical moment when Perry's feet slipped completely from under him and he fell facedown toward the rock. He groaned as his crippled hands hit the rough surface and their burned palms split open. Rebka held him before he could slide backward. Within a few seconds they were again scrambling up the uneven path of the watercourse.

As soon as Perry came to the easy final steps, Rebka turned to see what was happening behind. Graves was wobble-legged, close to collapse, and Geni Carmel was supporting him. The other three were still halfway down and making slow progress. Rebka could hear Kallik clicking and whistling with the effort.

They would have to manage on their own. Rebka's top priority had to be the starship. Was it in working order, and did it have power for one final flight to orbit? Perry had moved over to the *Summer Dreamboat,* but he was simply standing by the closed door. He raised his hands in frustration as Rebka came up to him. Without working fingers he had no way to get inside.

"Go tell the others to hurry—particularly Kallik." Rebka jerked open the port, suddenly aware of how *small* the ship was. Perry had told him it was more like a toy than a starship, but the size was still a nasty shock. The interior space was not much more than that of the aircar.

He went across to study the controls. At least he would have no trouble with those, even without help from Kallik or Geni Carmel. The board was the simplest he had ever seen.

He turned on the displays. The power level was depressingly low. Suppose it took them only halfway to orbit?

He looked at the chronometer. Less than an hour to Summertide. That answered his question. It was damned if you do, damned if you don't. As the others came squeezing into the ship, he prepared for liftoff.

Darya Lang and Geni Carmel were the last ones in.

"Close the port," Rebka said, and turned back to the controls. He did not watch them do as he said, nor was there time for the long list of checks that should have preceded an ascent to space. Through the forward window he could see a sheet of flame running steadily across the surface toward them. In a few more seconds it would engulf the ship.

"Hold tight. I'm taking us up at three gee."

If we're lucky, he thought. And if we're not . . . Hans Rebka applied full ascent power. The starship trembled and strained on the ground.

Nothing happened for what felt like minutes. Then, as the firestorm ran toward them, the *Summer Dreamboat* groaned at the seams, shivered, and lifted toward Quake's jet-black and turbulent sky.

CHAPTER 22

Summertide.

TEN SECONDS AFTER her foot plunged into that boiling black mud, Darya Lang's nervous system went into suspended animation. She did not feel pain, she did not feel worry, she did not feel sorrow.

She knew, abstractly, that Max Perry was burned worse than she and was somehow leading the way up the rocky slope, but that much effort and involvement was beyond her. If she remained conscious, it was only because she knew no way to slip into unconsciousness. And if she traveled up to the ship with the rest of them, it was only because Kallik and J'merlia gave her no choice. They lifted and carried her, careful to keep her foot and ankle clear of the ground.

Her isolation ended—agonizingly—as they approached the ship's entry port. Darts of pain began to lance through her foot and ankle as Kallik laid her gently on the ground.

"With apologies and extreme regrets," J'merlia said quietly, his dark mandibles close to her ear. "But the way in is big enough for only one. It will be necessary to enter alone."

They were going to put her down and ask her to walk, just when the pain was becoming intolerable! Her burned foot would have to meet the floor. She began to plead with the aliens, to tell them that she could not bear it. It was already too late. She found herself balanced on one leg in front of the hatch.

"Hurry up," Max Perry urged from inside the ship.

She gave him a look of hatred. Then she saw his hands and forearms, blistered and split to the bone from contact with rough stones and pebbles during the ascent of the rock. He had to be feeling far worse than she was. Darya gritted her teeth, lifted her left foot clear of the ground, grabbed the sides of the doorframe, and hopped gingerly inside the ship. There was hardly room for the people already there. Somehow she managed to crawl across to the ship's side window and stood there on one leg.

What should she do? She could not stand there indefinitely, and she could not bear the thought of anything touching her foot.

Rebka's announcement that he would take them up to space at three gees answered that. His words filled her with dismay. She could hardly stand in a field of less than one gee. She would have to lie down, and then three gees of acceleration would press her ruined foot to the unforgiving floor.

Before she could say anything, Kallik's stubby body wriggled across toward her. The Hymenopt placed her soft abdomen next to Darya's injured foot and uttered a dozen soft whistles.

"No! Don't touch it!" Darya cried out in panic.

As she tried to move her leg away, the gleaming yellow sting emerged from the end of Kallik's body. It pierced inches deep into her lower calf. Darya screamed and fell over backward, banging her head as she went onto the supply chest behind the pilot's seat.

Liftoff began before she could move again.

Darya found she was flattened to the floor with her foot pressing onto metal. Her hurt foot! She had to scream. She opened her mouth and suddenly realized that the only parts of her body that were *not* in pain were that foot and calf. Kallik's sting had robbed them of all feeling.

She lay back and turned her head to rest its increased weight on her cheek and ear. A tangle of bodies covered the floor. She could see Kallik, right in front of her, cushioning Geni Carmel's head on her furry abdomen. Julius Graves lay just beyond, but all she could see was the top of his bald pate, lying next to J'merlia's shiny black cranium. Rebka, piloting the ship, and Max Perry, harnessed into the seat next to him, were hidden by the supply chest and the seat back.

Darya made a great effort and turned her head the other way. She could see out of the ship's side port, a foot away from her. Unbelievably—surely they had been rising for minutes—the ship was still below Quake's cloud layer. She caught a vivid lightning-lit view of the surface; it had shattered into crisscrossing fault lines, over which waves of orange-red molten lava were sweeping like ocean billows. The whole planet was on fire, a scene of ancient perdition. Then the ship lifted into black dust clouds so dense that the end of the vestigial control surfaces, just a few feet beyond the port, became invisible to her.

The turbulence and shear forces tripled. Darya rolled helplessly against Kallik, and both of them went sliding across the floor to collide with Julius Graves. Another moment, and all three were tumbling back, to crush Darya against the wall. She was still in that position, pinned by the weight of everyone except Rebka and Perry, when the *Summer Dreamboat* emerged unexpectedly from the clouds of Quake. The ship's port admitted one sunburst of intolerable golden radiation before the photoshielding came into operation.

Darya was lucky. She was facing away from the port, and she happened to have her head caught under Kallik's abdomen when that searing light-blast hit the ship. Everyone else in the rear compartment was blinded for a few seconds.

Rebka and Perry had been protected in the front seats, but they were facing forward and trying to coax a ship to orbit in circumstances for which it had never been designed.

So it was Darya alone, turning to look sideways and out behind the ascending ship, who saw everything that happened next.

The *Dreamboat* was soaring over the hemisphere of Quake that faced away from Opal. The disks of Mandel and Amaranth loomed low in the sky to her left. Reduced by the photoshielding to glowing, dark-limbed circles, the twin stars showed their bright disks pocked and speckled with sunspots. Their tidal forces were tearing at each other, just as they tore at Quake and Opal. Directly overhead, Gargantua shone pale and spectral, a giant whose reflected light was reduced by the photoshielding to a faint and insubstantial ghost world.

From a point very close to Gargantua's edge—Darya could not be sure quite where it lay, on the planet or off it—a glittering blue beam stabbed suddenly down toward Quake, bright with controlled energy.

Darya followed it with her eyes. It could not be a beam of ordinary light. That would be invisible in empty space, and she could see it all the way along its length. And where that pulsing ray from Gargantua struck the clouds, the dust-filled protective layer boiled instantly away. A circular area of Quake's surface, a hundred kilometers across, was suddenly exposed to Mandel and Amaranth's combined radiation. Already seething with molten lava, the surface started to deform and crater. A dark tunnel formed and became rapidly deeper and wider. Soon Darya could see the molten rocks of the planet's interior thrown back in waves to form a sputtering, sharp-sided edge to the hole.

The ship's motion was carrying Darya away from the tunnel, and her viewing angle was too steep to see the bottom of the pit. She leaned closer to the port, ignoring the pain in her bruised body and face. As the ship's altitude increased, Quake hung below her like a great, clouded bead, threaded onto that pencil of bright blue light. Where the ray struck, the dark hole through the bead was lit by a glowing rim of molten lava.

The next events came in such quick succession that Darya had trouble afterward in relating their exact sequence.

As Quake's rotation was taking first Mandel and then Amaranth below the horizon, a second blue beam came stabbing down from open space tō merge with the one from Gargantua. It did not come from any object that Darya could find in the sky, although her eye could follow it up and up, until it finally became a line too faint to see.

The new pencil of light skewered the tunnel in Quake's crust, and the hole widened—not steadily, but in one impossible jerk of displaced material. Narrow answering beams of red and cyan thrust back into space, following the exact center of the incident ones. And in the same moment, two silvery spheres crept forward from the depths of the tunnel.

They looked identical, each maybe a kilometer across. Rising slowly clear of Quake they hovered motionless, one just beneath the other, wobbling like two transparent balloons filled with quicksilver.

The blue beams changed color. The one from Gargantua became bright saffron, the other a glowing magenta. The pulses along their length changed in frequency. As they did so, the higher sphere began to accelerate, moving along the precise line of the magenta ray. Slow at first, then suddenly faster, it remained visible for only a split second and then was gone. Darya could not tell if it had been propelled out of sight—at huge acceleration—or had vanished through some other mechanism. As it disappeared, so did the magenta beam.

The second sphere still hovered motionless close to Quake. After a few moments it began to inch up along the saffron pencil of light. But its motion was leisurely, almost ponderous. Darya could follow it easily, a ball of silver climbing the saffron beam like a metal spider ascending its own thread. She tracked the shining globe as it crept upward.

And then her eyes were suddenly unable to focus. Around the bright ball the starfield had become twisted and distorted. The ball itself disappeared to become a black void, while around it scattered points of starlight converged and met in an annular rainbow cluster. The vanished sphere formed an ink-black center to that brilliant stellar ring. Still it ascended the yellow light beam.

While she was squinting at that hole in space, the *Dreamboat* performed a dizzying half roll and a surge at maximum thrust. She heard Hans Rebka, in the pilot's seat, cry out. A bright jet of violet, a starship's drive working at high intensity, flared across the starfield and moved across the bows of the *Dreamboat*.

Darya turned her head and saw the blunt lines of a Zardalu Communion vessel swooping in close to them. Concealed weapons ports sprang open on the ship's forward end.

The *Dreamboat* was the target—and at that range, there was no way the other ship could miss.

Darya watched in horror as all the weapons fired. She expected their ship to disintegrate around her. But impossibly, the attacking beams were veering away from their expected straight lines. They missed the *Dreamboat* completely and curved into space, drawn to meet the black sphere as it hung suspended on its golden thread of light.

The beams of the ship's weapons remained visible as glowing trajectories in space, coupling the Zardalu vessel with the dark ascending globe. The curved lines shortened. The other ship moved closer to the distorted dark region, as though the sphere were reeling in bright strands from the weapons.

But the Zardalu ship was not going willingly. Its drive flared to the brighter violet of maximum intensity, thrusting away from the sphere's dark singularity. Darya could sense the struggle of huge opposed forces.

And the starship was losing. Caught in the field's curvature, it moved along the twisting lines of force, drawn irresistibly toward the rising sphere. The sphere itself was moving upward, faster and faster. It seemed to Darya that the Zardalu vessel was sucked into that black void, one moment before the sphere itself flashed up the yellow thread and disappeared.

Then the *Summer Dreamboat* was moving on, around the curve of Quake. Gargantua sank below the horizon, and with it all sign of the pulsing beam of yellow.

"I don't know if anyone cares anymore." It was Rebka's laconic voice, startling Darya back to an awareness of where she was. "But I just checked the chronometer. Summertide Maximum took place a few seconds ago. And we're in orbit."

Darya turned to look down at Quake. There was nothing to see but dark, endless clouds and, beyond them, on the horizon, the blue-gray sphere of Opal.

Summertide. It was over. And it had been nothing like she had imagined. She glanced over at the others, still rubbing their eyes as they lay on the starship floor, and felt a terrible sense of letdown. To see everything—but to understand nothing! The whole visit to Quake at Summertide was an unsolved mystery, a waste of time and human lives.

"The good news is that we reached orbit." Rebka was speaking again, and Darya could hear the exhaustion in his voice. "The bad news is that the fancy flying we had to do a few moments ago took what little power we had left. We probably have Louis Nenda and Atvar H'sial to thank for that. I don't have any idea what was going on back there, or what happened to that other ship, and I really don't care. I hope Nenda and H'sial got their comeuppance, but right now I don't have time to bother with it. I'm worried about us. Without power, we can't make a planetary landing on Opal, or on Quake, or anywhere else. Commander Perry is working up a trajectory that may take us to Midway Station. If we get lucky we might be able to ride the Umbilical from there."

Working up a trajectory, Darya thought. How can he? Perry doesn't have hands, just burned bits of meat.

But he'll do it, hands or no hands. And if his foot were

burned like mine, he'd walk on it. He'd run on it, too, if he had to. Hans Rebka talks of luck, but they've not had much of that. They've had to make their own.

I'll never mock the Phemus Circle again. Their people are dirty and disgusting and poor and primitive, but Rebka and Perry and the rest of them have something that makes everyone in the Alliance seem half-dead. They have the will to live, no matter what happens.

And then, because she was becoming steadily more relaxed and sluggish in response to the anesthetic and mildly toxic fluid that Kallik had injected, and because Darya Lang could never stop thinking, even when she wanted to, her mind said to her: "Umbilical. We're going to the *Umbilical*."

The least of the Builder artifacts; she knew that, everyone knew that. An insignificant nothing of a structure, on the Builder scale of things. But it was to that very place, to that least of all artifacts, and to that very time, of Summertide Maximum, that all the other Builder artifacts had pointed.

Why? Why not point to one of the striking artifacts—to Paradox or Sentinel, to Elephant or Cocoon or Lens?

Now *there's* a worthwhile mystery, Darya thought: a puzzle that someone could usefully ponder. Let's forget the mess we're in and think about that for a while. I can't help Rebka and Perry, and anyway I don't need to. They'll take care of me. So let's think.

Let's wonder about the two spheres that came out from the deep interior of Quake. How long had they been there? *Why* were they there? Where did they go? Why did they choose this moment to emerge, and what made the black one take the Zardalu ship with it?

The questions went unanswered. As Kallik's narcotic venom spread steadily through her bloodstream, Darya was sinking toward unconsciousness. There was too little time left for thinking. Her concentration was gone, her energy was gone, and her brain drifted randomly from one subject to another. Drugged sleep was moments away.

But in the last moment, the single second before her mind vanished into vague emptiness, Darya caught the gleam of a new insight. She understood the significance of Quake and Summertide! She knew its function, and maybe their own role in it. She reached out for the thought, struggled to pull it to her, sought to fix it firmly in her memory.

It was too late. Darya, still fighting, floated irresistibly into sleep.

CHAPTER 23

REBKA WOKE LIKE a nervous animal, jerking upright and alert from a sound sleep. In that first moment his feelings were all panic.

He had made the fatal mistake of allowing his concentration to lapse. *Who was flying the ship?*

The only other person halfway competent was Max Perry, and he was too badly injured to take the controls. They could smash into Opal, fall back to the surface of Quake, or lose themselves forever in deep space.

Then, before his eyes opened, he knew things had to be all right.

No one was flying the ship. No one needed to. He was not on the *Summer Dreamboat*—he could not be. For he was not in freefall. And the forces on him were not the wild, turbulent ones of atmospheric reentry. Instead there was a steady downward pull, the fraction-of-a-gee acceleration that told of a capsule moving along the Umbilical.

He opened his eyes and remembered the final hours of their flight. They had meandered out to Midway Station like drunken sailors, the sorriest collection of humans and aliens that the Dobelle system had ever seen. He remembered biting his lips and fingertips until they bled, forcing himself to stay awake and his eyes to stay open. He had followed

Perry's half-incoherent navigational instructions as best he could, while they tacked for five long hours along the line of the Umbilical. With the help of the tiny attitude-control jets—the only power left on board the *Dreamboat*—he had brought them to a dazed docking at the station's biggest port.

He recalled the approach—a disgrace for any pilot. It had taken five times as long as it should. And as the last docking confirmation was received at the ship, he had leaned back in the pilot's chair and closed his eyes—for one moment's rest.

And then?

And then his memory failed. He looked around.

He must have fallen asleep at the very second of final contact. Someone had carried him into Midway Station and moved him to the service level of an Umbilical capsule. They had secured him in a harness and left him there.

He was not alone. Max Perry, his forearms caked and daubed with protective yellow gel, drifted on a light tether a few feet away. He was unconscious. Darya Lang hovered beyond him, her flowing brown hair tied back from her face. The clothing had been stripped from her left leg below the knee, and plastic flesh covered her burned foot and ankle. Her breathing was light. Every few seconds she muttered under her breath as though about to surface from sleep. With her face so relaxed and thought-free, she looked about twelve years old. Next to Darya floated Geni Carmel. From the look of her she was also heavily sedated, although she had no visible injuries.

Rebka checked his wristwatch: twenty-three hours past Summertide. All the fireworks in the Quake and Opal system should be safely in the past. And for seventeen hours, he had been out of things completely.

He rubbed at his eyes, noticing that his face was no longer covered with ash and grime. Someone had not only carried him to the capsule, but had washed him and changed his clothes before leaving him to sleep. Who had done that? And who had provided the medical care to Perry and Lang?

That brought him back to his first question: with the four of them unconscious, who was minding the store?

He had trouble getting his feet to the floor and then found that he could not loose the harness that secured him. Even after seventeen hours of rest, he was weary enough for his fingers to be clumsy and fumbling. If Darya Lang looked like a teenager, he felt like a battered centenarian.

Finally he freed himself and was able to leave the improvised hospital. He considered trying to wake Perry and Lang—she was still murmuring to herself in a protesting voice—and then decided against it. Almost certainly they had been anesthetized before their wounds were dressed and synthetic skin applied.

He slowly climbed the stairs that led to the observation-and-control deck of the capsule. The clear roof of the upper chamber showed Midway Station in the middle distance. Far above, confirming that the capsule was descending toward Opal, Rebka saw the distant prospect of Quake, dark-clouded and brooding.

The walls of the observation deck, ten meters high, were paneled with display units. Julius Graves, seated at the control console and flanked by J'merlia and Kallik, was watching in thoughtful silence. The succession of broadcast displays that Graves was receiving showed a planetary surface—but it was Opal, not Quake.

Rebka watched for a while before announcing his presence. With their attention on Quake, it had been easy to forget that Opal had also experienced the biggest Summertide in human history. Aerial and orbital radar shots, piercing the cloud layers of the planet, showed broad stretches of naked seabed laid bare by millennial tides. Muddy ocean floor was spotted with vast green backs: dead Dowsers, the size of mountains, lay stranded and crushed under their own weight.

Other videos showed the Slings of Opal disintegrating as

contrary waves, miles high and driven by the tidal forces, pulled at and twisted the ocean's surface.

An emotionless voice-over from Opal listed the casualties: half the planet's population known dead, most in the past twenty-four hours; another fifth still missing. But even before assessment was complete, reconstruction was beginning. Every human on Opal was on a continuous work schedule.

The broadcasts made clear to Rebka that the people of Opal had their hands more than full. If his group were to land there, they should not look for assistance.

He drifted forward and tapped Graves lightly on the shoulder. The councilor jerked at the touch, swiveled in his chair, and grinned up at him.

"Aha! Back from Dreamland! As you see, Captain—" He flourished a thin hand upward, and then to the display screens. "Our decision to spend Summertide on Quake rather than Opal was not so unwise after all."

"If we'd stayed on the surface of Quake for Summertide, Councilor, we'd have been ashes. We were lucky."

"We were luckier than you think. And long before Summertide." Graves gestured to Kallik, who was manipulating displays with one forelimb and entering numbers into a pocket computer with another. "According to our Hymenopt friend, Opal suffered *worse* than Quake. Kallik has been doing energy-balance calculations in every spare moment since we left the surface. She agrees with Commander Perry—the surface should have been far more active than it was during the Grand Conjunction. The full energy was never released while we were there. Some focused storage-and-release mechanism was at work for the tidal energies. Without it, the planet would have been uninhabitable for humans long before we left it. But with it, most of the energy went to some other purpose."

"Councilor, Quake was quite bad enough. Elena Carmel is dead. Atvar H'sial and Louis Nenda may be dead, too."

"They are."

"I'm glad to hear it. I don't know if you realize this, but they were in orbit around Quake at Summertide and they tried to blow us out of the sky. They deserved what they got. But why are you so sure they're dead?"

"Darya Lang saw Nenda's ship dragged off toward Gargantua with an acceleration too much for any human or Cecropian to survive. They had to be crushed flat inside it."

"Nenda's ship had a full star drive. No local field should have held it."

"If you wish to argue that point, Captain, you'll have to do it with Darya Lang. She saw what happened; I did not."

"She's asleep."

"Still? She became unconscious again when J'merlia started work on her foot, but I am surprised she is not waking." Graves turned in annoyance. "Now then, what do *you* want?"

J'merlia was hesitantly touching his sleeve, while by his side Kallik was hopping and whistling in excitement.

"With great respect, Councilor Graves." J'merlia moved to kneel before him. "But Kallik and I could not help hearing what you said to Captain Rebka—that Master Nenda and Atvar H'sial escaped from Quake, then they were hurtled off to Gargantua and crushed by the acceleration."

"*Toward* Gargantua, my Lo'tfian friend. Perhaps not *to* Gargantua itself. Professor Lang was quite insistent on the point."

"With apologies, I should have said *toward* Gargantua. Honored Councilor, would it be possible for Kallik and my humble self to be excused from duties for a few minutes?"

"Oh, go on. And don't grovel, you know I *hate* it." Graves waved them away. As the aliens headed for the capsule's lower level, he turned back to Rebka.

"Well, Captain, unless you want to collapse again into slumber, I propose that we go below ourselves and check on Commander Perry and Professor Lang. We have plenty of time. The Umbilical will not offer access to Opal for another few hours. And our official work in the Dobelle system is over."

"Yours may be. Mine is not."

"It will be, Captain, very soon." The grinning skeleton was as infuriatingly casual and self-assured as ever.

"You don't even know what my real work is."

"Ah, but I do. You were sent to find out what was wrong with Commander Perry, see what it was that kept him in a dead-end job in the Dobelle system—and cure him."

Rebka sank into a seat in front of the control console. "Now how the devil did you find that out?" His voice was puzzled rather than annoyed.

"From the obvious place—Commander Perry. He has his own friends and information sources, back in the headquarters of the Phemus Circle. He learned why you were sent here."

"Then he should also know that I never did find out. I told you, my job is unfinished."

"Not true. Your official job is almost over, and it will be done with very soon. You see, Captain, *I* know what happened to Max Perry seven years ago. I suspected it before we came to Quake, and I confirmed it when I queried the commander under sedation. All it took were the right questions. *And* I know what to do. Trust me, and listen."

Julius Graves hauled his long body over to a monitor, pulled a data unit the size of a sugar cube from his pocket, and inserted it into the machine. "This is sound only, of course. But you will recognize the voice, even though it appears much younger. I sent his memory back seven years. I will play only a fragment. No purpose is served by making private suffering into a public event."

. . . Amy was still acting goofy and playful, even in the heat. She was laughing as she ran on ahead of me, back toward the car that would take us to the Umbilical. It was only a few hundred meters away, but I was getting tired.

"Hey, slow down. I'm the one who has to carry the equipment."

She spun around, teasing me. "Oh, come on, Max. Learn to have some fun. You don't need any of that stuff. Leave it here—nobody will ever notice it's gone."

She made me smile, in spite of the growing noise around us and the sweat that covered my body. Quake was hot.

"I can't do that, Amy—it's official property. It all has to be accounted for. Wait for me."

But she just laughed. And danced on—on into that funny blurring of the surface, the fragile, shimmering ground of Summertide . . .

. . . before I could get near her, she was gone. Just like that, in a fraction of a second. Swallowed up by Quake. All that I could take back with me was the pain . . .

"There is more, but it adds nothing." Graves stopped the recording. "Nothing that you cannot guess, or should not hear. Amy died in molten lava, not in boiling mud. Max Parry saw that shimmering of heated air again, in the Pentacline Depression—but too late to save Elena Carmel."

Hans Rebka shrugged. "Even if you know what drove Max Perry into his shell, that's not the hardest part of my job. I'm supposed to *cure* him, and I don't know where to begin."

Rebka knew that his present sense of failure and incompetence should be only temporary, no more than a side effect of exhaustion following days of tension. But that did not make it any less real.

He stared at one of the wall displays, which showed a Sling floating upside down and shattered by the impact of mighty seas. All that could be seen was a wilderness of black, slippery mud from which jutted random tangles of roots. He wondered if anyone could possibly have survived when the Sling capsized.

"How?" he went on. "How do you pull someone out of a seven-year depression? I don't know that."

"Of course you don't. That's my area of expertise, not yours." Graves turned abruptly and headed for the stairway. "Come on," he said over his shoulder. "Time to see what's going on below decks. I think those pesky aliens are plotting a mutiny, but we'll ignore that for the moment. Right now we have to talk to Max Perry."

Was Graves going crazy again? Rebka sighed. Oh, for the good old days, when he was flying through Quake's clouds and wondering if they would survive another second of turbulence. He followed close behind the other man, down to the second level of the capsule.

J'merlia and Kallik were nowhere to be seen.

"I told you," Graves said. "They're down in the cargo hold. Those two are up to something, sure as taxes. Give me a hand here."

With Rebka's puzzled assistance, the councilor carried Max Perry and then Geni Carmel back to the upper level of the capsule. Darya Lang, still muttering to herself on the brink of consciousness, was left in her securing harness.

Graves placed Max Perry and Geni Carmel in seats at ninety degrees to each other and fixed them in position.

"Put extra bindings on those harnesses," he said to Rebka. "Make sure you don't touch Perry's injured arms—but remember I don't want either of them to be able to get loose. I'll be back in a minute."

Graves made one final trip to the lower level. When he reappeared he was carrying two spray hypodermics in his right hand.

"Darya Lang is waking up," he said, "but let's get this taken care of first. It won't take long." He injected Perry in the shoulder with one syringe and Geni Carmel with the other. "Now, we can begin." He began to count aloud.

The wake-up shot given to Max Perry was full strength. Before Graves had reached ten, Perry sighed, rolled his head from side to side, and slowly opened his eyes. He stared around the capsule's cabin with a dull and disinterested look, until his gaze found the still-unconscious Geni Carmel. Then he groaned and closed his eyes again.

"You are awake," Graves said in a reproving tone. "So

don't you go falling asleep again. I have a problem, and I need your help."

Perry shook his head, and his eyes remained shut.

"We'll be back on Opal in a few hours," Graves went on. "And life will start to return to normal. But I have the responsibility for the rehabilitation of Geni Carmel. Now, there must be formal hearings, back on Shasta and on Miranda, but that cannot be allowed to interfere with the rehab program. It has to begin at once. And the death of Elena makes the program very difficult. I feel it would be disastrous to let Geni go back to Shasta, with all its memories of her twin sister, until she is already on the road to recovery. On the other hand I myself *must* return to Shasta, and then go on to Miranda for the formal genocide hearing."

He paused. Perry still had not opened his eyes.

Graves leaned close and lowered his voice. "So that leaves me with two questions to answer. Where should the rehabilitation of Geni Carmel begin? And who should oversee the rehab process, if I will not be around?

"That is where I need your help, Commander. I have decided that Geni's rehab program should begin on Opal. And I propose to make you her guardian while it is proceeding."

At last Graves had broken through. Perry jerked bolt upright in the restraining harness. His bloodshot eyes opened wide. "What the hell are you talking about?"

"I thought I was clear enough." Graves was smiling. "But let me say it again. Geni will remain on Opal for at least four more months. You will be responsible for her welfare while she is there."

"You can't do that."

"I'm afraid you're wrong. Ask Captain Rebka if you doubt me. In matters like this, a Council member has full authority to proceed with prompt rehabilitation. And anyone can be pressed into service. That includes you."

Perry glared at Rebka, then back at Graves. "I won't do it. I have my own work—a full-time job. And she needs a specialist. I have no idea how to deal with her sort of problem."

"You can certainly learn." Graves nodded at the other chair, where Geni was slowly waking in response to her weaker injection. "She's starting to listen now. As a first move, you can tell her about Opal. Remember, Commander, she has never been there. It's going to be her home for a while, and you know as much about it as anyone."

"Wait a minute!" Perry was struggling at his harness and calling to Graves, who was already ushering Rebka out of the chamber. "We're tied in. You can't leave us like this! Look at her."

Geni Carmel was making no effort to escape from her harness, but tears were trickling down her pale cheeks, and she was staring in horror or fascination at Perry's mutilated hands and forearms.

"Sorry," Graves said over his shoulder as he and Rebka started down toward the lower level of the capsule. "We'll discuss this more later, but I can't do it now. Captain Rebka and I have something very urgent to take care of on the lower deck. We'll be back."

Rebka waited until they were out of earshot before he spoke again to Graves. "Are you serious about any of that?"

"I am serious about *all* of it."

"It won't work. Geni Carmel is just a child. With Elena dead, she doesn't even want to live. You know how close they were, so close they would die rather than be separated from each other. And Perry is a basket case himself—he's in no shape to look after her."

Julius Graves halted at the bottom of the stairway. He turned to look up at Hans Rebka, and for once his face was neither grinning nor grimacing. "Captain, when I need a man who can fly an overloaded, power-drained ship like the *Summer Dreamboat* off a planet that is falling apart underneath us, and take me into space, I'll come to you anytime. You are very good at your job—your *real* job. Can't you do me the favor of admitting that the same could be true of me? Isn't it conceivable that I might do my job well?"

"But that isn't your job."

"Which only shows, Captain, how little you know of the duties of a Council member. Believe me, what I am doing will work. Or would you prefer a wager? I say that Max Perry and Geni Carmel have more chance of curing *each other* than you or I have of doing anything useful for *either* of them. As you said, she is just a child who needs help—but Perry is a man who desperately needs to *give* help. He's been doing penance for seven years for his sin in allowing Amy to go with him to Quake during Summertide. Don't you realize that burning his arms like that will *help* his mental condition? Now he has a chance to obtain total absolution. And your job on Opal is finished. You could leave today, and Perry would be fine." Graves snapped his fingers and held out his hand to Rebka. "Would you like to bet on that? Name the amount."

Rebka was saved from a reply by an angry voice ahead of them.

"I don't know who to thank for this, and I'm not about to ask. But will someone *get me the hell out of here*! I have work to do."

It was Darya Lang, fully conscious and struggling to free herself from the harness. She sounded nothing like the shy theoretical scientist who had first arrived on Opal, but her practical skills were still lacking. In her efforts to free herself she had managed to tangle the bindings, so that she was hanging upside down and could hardly move her arms.

"She's all yours, Captain," Graves said unexpectedly. "I'm going to find J'merlia and Kallik." He popped down the hatchway at the side of the chamber and vanished from sight.

Rebka went across to Lang and studied the way the harness had been knotted. Less and less, he understood what was going on. With their escape from Quake, everyone except him should have been able to relax; instead, they all seemed to have new agendas of their own. Darya Lang sounded urgent and furious.

He reached out, tugged gently at one point of the harness and hard at another one. The result was gratifying. The bindings released completely to deposit Darya Lang lightly onto the chamber floor. He helped her to her feet and was rewarded with a surprising and embarrassed smile.

"Now why couldn't I have done that?" She put pressure tentatively on her injured foot, shrugged, and pressed harder. "Last thing I remember, we'd just reached the Umbilical, and Graves and Kallik were fixing me up from the med kits. How long have I been asleep—and when do we reach Opal?"

"I don't know how long you've been asleep, but it's twenty-three hours since Summertide." Rebka consulted his watch. "Make that closer to twenty-four. And we ought to touch down on Opal in a couple of hours. *If* we can touch down. They took a real beating there. There's no rush, though. We have plenty of food and water on board. We can live in this capsule for weeks—even go back up the Umbilical to Midway Station if we have to, and stay there indefinitely."

"No way." Darya was shaking her head. "I can't afford to wait. I've only been conscious for a few minutes, but I spent all of them cursing the man who filled me with drugs. We have to get down to the surface of Opal, and you have to get me a ship."

"To go home? What's the rush? Does anyone on Sentinel Gate know when you'll be going back?"

"No one does." She took Hans Rebka by the arm, leaning on him as they walked over to the capsule's miniature galley. She sat down, taking her time as she poured herself a hot drink. Finally she turned to him. "But you have it wrong, Hans. I'm not going to Sentinel Gate. I'm going to Gargantua. And I'll need help to get there."

"I hope you're not expecting it from me." Rebka looked away, very conscious of her fingers on his biceps. "Look,

I know that Nenda's ship was dragged off there, and they were killed. But you don't want to be killed, too. Gargantua is a gas-giant, a frozen world—we can't live there; neither can the Cecropians."

"I didn't say that the ship and the sphere went right to Gargantua. I don't think that. I believe the place I need to go is probably one of Gargantua's moons. But I won't know that until I get there."

"Get there and do what? Recover a couple of corpses. Who cares what happens to their bodies? Atvar H'sial left you to die, and she and Nenda abandoned J'merlia and Kallik. Even if they were alive—and you say they're not—they don't deserve help."

"I agree. And that's not why I have to follow them." Darya handed Rebka a cup. "Calm down, Hans. Drink that, and listen to me for a minute. I know that people from the Phemus Circle think everyone from the Alliance is a dreamy incompetent, just the way we think you're all barbarian peasants who don't bother to wash—"

"Huh!"

"But you and I have been around each other for a while now—long enough to know that those ideas are nonsense. You acknowledge that I'm at least a decent observer. I don't make things up. So let me tell you what I *saw*, not what I think. Everyone else here may miss the point of this, but I trust you to draw the right conclusions.

"Remember now—listen first, then *think*, then react— not the other way round." She moved closer to Rebka, positioning herself so that it was difficult for him to do anything other than listen to her.

"When we came up out of the clouds on Quake, you were too busy piloting the ship to look behind, and everyone else in the rear compartment was blinded by Mandel and Amaranth. So no one else saw what I saw: Quake opening, deep into the interior. And two objects coming out. One of them flew away, out of the plane of the galaxy. I lost sight of it in less than a second. You saw the other one. It took off toward Gargantua, and Louis Nenda's ship was carried with it. That was significant, but it isn't the important point! Everyone said that Quake was far too quiet for so close to Summertide. Sure, I know we *thought* it was violent, when we were down there. But it wasn't. Max Perry kept saying it: where's all the energy going?

"Well, we know the answer to that now. It was being transformed and stored, so that when the right time came the whole interior of Quake could open up and eject those two bodies—spaceships, if you think they were that.

"I saw it happen, and I caught the sniff of an answer to something that had kept me baffled for months, long before I left Sentinel Gate:

"*Why Dobelle?*

"Why such a nothing place, I mean, for such an important event?

"The idea of visiting Dobelle occurred to me when I calculated the convergence time and place for influences spreading out from all the artifacts. There was a unique solution: Quake at Summertide. But when I proposed that, the Builder specialists in the Alliance laughed at me. They said, look, Darya, we accept that there is an artifact in the Dobelle system—the Umbilical. But it's a *minor* piece of Builder technology. Something we understand; something that isn't mysterious or big or complex. It makes no sense for the focus of all the Builder activities to be at such a second-class structure, in such a worthless and unimportant part of the Galaxy—I'm sorry, Hans, but I'm quoting, and that's the way people in the Alliance regard the worlds of the Phemus Circle."

Rebka shrugged. "Don't apologize," he said gruffly. "That's the way a lot of us think about the Circle worlds, and we *live* here. Try a weekend on Teufel, sometime—if you can stand it."

"Well, whatever they said about the Phemus Circle and the Umbilical, they couldn't argue with the statistical analysis. In fact, they repeated it for themselves and found that everything did point to Dobelle, and to Quake at Summertide. They had to agree with me. The trouble was, I was forced to agree with *them*. Dobelle made no sense as a place for important action. I mean, I was the one who had *written* the Catalog description of the Umbilical—'one of the simplest and most comprehensible of all Builder artifacts'! People were parroting back my own words.

"So I was baffled when I arrived here. I was still baffled when you flew us up through the clouds, trying to get off Quake in one piece. I couldn't make sense of Dobelle as the convergence point.

"But then I saw that pulsing light beam shine down from Gargantua and watched the whole of Quake opening up in front of me. And just before I passed out I realized that we had all been missing something obvious.

"All the references on the structure of the galaxy make the same comment, the Dobelle system is 'one of the natural wonders of the local spiral arm.' Isn't it wonderful, the books say, how the interplay of the gravitational fields of Amaranth and Mandel and Gargantua has thrown Dobelle into such a finely balanced orbit—an orbit so placed that once every three hundred and fifty thousand years, all the players line up *exactly* for Summertide and the Grand Conjunction. Isn't that just amazing?

"Well, it is amazing—if you believe it. But there's another way to look at things. The Dobelle system doesn't just *contain* an artifact, the Umbilical. The Dobelle system *is* an artifact! The whole thing." She grabbed at Rebka's arm again, caught up in her own vision. "Its whole orbit and geometry were created by the Builders, designed so that once every three hundred and fifty thousand years Mandel and Amaranth and Gargantua are so close to Quake that a special interaction can take place between them. Something inside Quake captures and uses those tidal energies.

"Before I came to Quake, I thought that the Builders themselves might be here—maybe even appear at this particular Summertide. But that's wrong. The Grand Conjunction serves as a *trigger* for the departure of those spheres—ships, or whatever they are—from Dobelle. I don't know where the first one went—out of the galaxy, from the look of it. But we have enough information to track the other one, the one that went toward Gargantua. And if we want to know more about the Builders, that's where we have to go.

"And soon! Before whatever it is that happens out near Gargantua is over and done with, and we have to wait *another* three hundred and fifty thousand years for a second chance."

Finally able to get a word in edgewise, Hans Rebka asked a question of his own. "Are you suggesting that Quake splits open, and something comes out of it at *every* Grand Conjunction?"

"I certainly am. That's the *purpose* of the Grand Conjunction—it provides the timing trigger and the tidal energy needed to open up the interior of Quake. So when Quake opened—"

But it was Rebka's turn to talk. "Darya, I'm no theorist. But you're wrong. If you want proof of that, go and talk to Max Perry."

"He wasn't watching what happened when we left Quake."

"Nor was I, particularly. Max and I had other things on our minds. But when I first arrived on Opal, I asked about the history of the doublet. The history of Opal was hard to determine, because it has no permanent land surface. But Perry showed me an analysis of the fossil record of Quake. People had studied it in the early years of colonizing Dobelle, because they needed to know if the surface of Quake was stable enough to live on through Summertide.

"It isn't, for humans—we proved that pretty well for ourselves. But there has been native life on Quake for hundreds of millions of years, since long before the planet went into its present orbit. And any recent opening of the deep interior of Quake—like the one that you saw—would show clearly as an anomaly in the fossil record."

He reached out for the display control and set it to show an image of the space above the capsule. Mandel and Amaranth were visible, still huge in the sky, but they were less bright. The knowledge that they were on the wane for another year was comforting. As the stellar partners dimmed, Gargantua shone brighter in the sky over to their right. But the giant planet was well past its own periastron, and the orange-brown disk was already smaller. No blinding beam of light shone forth from Gargantua, or from one of its satellites. Quake hung above the capsule, its surface dark and peaceful.

"You see, Darya, there's no evidence in the whole fossil record of a deep disturbance of Quake, comparable with what you saw. Not three years ago, or three hundred, or three hundred and fifty thousand. The deep interior of Quake has been hidden from view, as far back as people can trace the history of its surface. And that's at least five million years."

He expected Darya to be crushed by his comments. She came back stronger than ever. "So this Grand Conjunction was special. That makes it *more* important to find out why. Hans, let me give you the bottom line. You can go back to your work on the Phemus Circle tomorrow. But I can't go back to Sentinel Gate. Not yet. I *have* to go on and take a look at Gargantua. I didn't spend my whole adult life studying the Builders and then come all this way just to stop when the trail gets hot. Maybe the Builders aren't out near Gargantua—"

"I'm sure they're not. People would have found them when they first explored the Mandel system."

"But *something* is out there. The sphere that took Nenda's ship wasn't just leaving Quake. It was *going* somewhere. I have to find a ship of my own and hustle out there fast. Otherwise I may lose the trail completely."

She was still gripping his arm, hard enough to hurt.

"Darya, you can't dash off to Gargantua like that. Not on your own, or you'll kill yourself for sure. The outer part of the Mandel system is cold and hostile. It isn't an easy place, even for experienced explorers. As for you, coming from a nice, civilized world like Sentinel Gate . . ."

Hans Rebka paused. First she booby-trapped him and knocked him unconscious by accident. Then she took him to the waterfall cave, fussing over him and *caring* about him, in a way that no one had ever cared. And now she was booby-trapping him again. He had to be careful and not commit himself to anything.

"I don't know how to find a ship," he said. "It's too much to ask the people on Opal—they have no resources to spare after Summertide. But I'll scratch around and see what I can do."

Darya Lang released his arm, but only because she had other things in mind. Her bear hug was interrupted by a cough from the stairway. Julius Graves had reappeared in the chamber. Close behind him came J'merlia and Kallik.

Graves gestured J'merlia forward. "Go on. Say it for yourself—it's your speech." He turned to Hans Rebka. "I told you they had trouble in mind. And I told *them* that this sort of thing was not my decision, though I do have an opinion."

J'merlia hesitated, until he was given a hard nudge from one of Kallik's spiky elbows, accompanied by a hiss that sounded like "S-s-s-spee-k."

"Indeed I will. Honored Captain." J'merlia was moving to debase himself before Rebka, until a warning growl from Graves stopped him. "Distinguished humans, the Hymenopt Kallik and I face a grave problem. We beg your help, even though we have done nothing to deserve it. We would not do so, if we could see any way to proceed without asking your assistance. Already we have been a burden to you. In fact, by our stupid actions on the planet Quake, we endangered the lives of every—"

This time both the growl and the nudge came from Julius Graves. "Get on with it!"

"Yes indeed, honored Councilor." J'merlia shrugged at Rebka with a near-human gesture of apology. "The point, distinguished Captain, is that the Hymenopt Kallik and my humble self believed when we left Quake that Louis Nenda and Atvar H'sial had surely been killed, or had decided—as is their perfect right—that they did not choose to make use of our services anymore. Both possibilities were deeply disturbing to us, but we saw no alternative to accepting them. We would then be obliged to return to our home-worlds, and to seek new masters for our services. However, a few minutes ago, we heard that Masters Nenda and Atvar H'sial escaped from the surface of Quake."

"True enough." Rebka looked at Darya. "But Professor Lang saw what happened, and Nenda and Atvar H'sial were killed."

"I know you think that. But Kallik points out that this may not be the case. She notes that if the ship were *gravitationally* accelerated in its departure, the beings inside would feel no forces on them—it would be exactly as though they remained in free-fall. Then they would have been carried away *alive* toward Gargantua, against their wishes, and may now be in need of assistance. And if this is the case, it is the clear duty of the Hymenopt Kallik and my humble self to pursue them. They are our owners. At the very least, we cannot leave the Mandel system until we are assured that they either do not want, or cannot make use of, our services. We therefore ask you, bearing all these facts in mind, and with due consideration of the possibility that—oof!"

J'merlia had received another nudge from Kallik, and the yellow tip of the Hymenopt's poison sting appeared and touched one of J'merlia's hind limbs. He flinched and hopped forward a step.

"Did you know, J'merlia," Julius Graves said in a pleasant conversational tone, "that Professor Lang was for a time convinced that you were incapable of independent speech? Now she is probably regretting that she was wrong."

"I am sorry, Councilor. I am accustomed to the translation of thoughts, not their creation. But in summary, the Hymenopt Kallik and I request that we be allowed to borrow a ship; and we request that we be allowed to follow Masters Nenda and Atvar H'sial to Gargantua, or to wherever their trail may lead."

"No." Rebka answered at once. "Definitely not. I reject your request. Opal is too busy digging out from Summertide to waste time looking around for starships."

Kallik clucked and chirped urgently.

"But that will not be necessary," J'merlia said. "As the Hymenopt Kallik points out, we do not need to descend to Opal. A starship is available—the *Summer Dreamboat*. It is at Midway Station, and it will be easy to return there and restore it to full power. We will find ample provisions on the station, and Kallik and I are sure we can fly the ship."

"With one extra passenger," Darya Lang said. "I'm going along, too."

Rebka glared at her. "You're injured. You're too sick to travel."

"I'm well enough. I'll convalesce on the way to Gargantua. Are you telling me a burned foot would stop *you* from doing your job, if you were in my position?"

"But the *Summer Dreamboat* isn't the property of the Dobelle system." Hans Rebka avoided answering her question and tried another approach. "It's not in my authority, or Max Perry's, to grant you the use of that ship."

"We agree." J'merlia was nodding politely. "Permission would of course have to come from Geni Carmel, who is the owner."

"And what makes you think she would grant it?"

Julius Graves coughed softly. "Well, as a matter of fact, Captain Rebka, I have already discussed that matter with poor Geni. She says she never wants to see or hear about that ship again. It is yours, for as long as you like to use it."

Rebka stared at the other man. Why did everyone seem to assume that he would be going along?

"It's still no, Councilor. So we can get a ship. That makes no difference."

J'merlia bowed his head and groveled lower, while Kallik whistled in disappointment. It was Julius Graves who nodded and said quietly, "That is certainly your decision to make, Captain. But would you be willing to share with me the logic of your thinking?"

"Sure I will. Let me start with a question. You know Louis Nenda and Atvar H'sial. Would *you* go to Gargantua to look for their bodies?"

Rebka's own position was quite clear in his mind. The idea that you should try to find people who had tried to destroy you was all wrong—unless you were proposing to kill them yourself.

"Me, go to Gargantua?" Graves raised his eyebrows. "Certainly not. In the first place, it is imperative that I return to Miranda. My task here is complete. In addition, I regard Atvar H'sial and Louis Nenda as dangerous criminals. If I went to Gargantua—which I do not propose to do, since I believe that they are dead—it would be only to arrest them."

"Very good. I feel the same way. Now, Councilor." Rebka pointed at Kallik. "Do you know how Louis Nenda controlled her? I'll tell you. He used a whip and a leash. He said Kallik was his pet, but nobody should treat a pet like that. She wasn't an equal to him, and she wasn't a pet. She was a downtrodden and disposable slave. He was quite willing to leave her behind to die on Quake. Before Kallik came to Opal she understood very little of human speech, but only because he had deprived her of the opportunity to learn. And yet it was *Kallik* who performed all the calculations showing that something unique would occur at Summertide. She did that, you know, not Nenda. She's a whole lot smarter than he is. Isn't that true?"

"It is quite true." Julius Graves had a little smile on his face. "Please continue."

"And J'merlia was no better off. The way that he was treated when they arrived on Dobelle was an absolute disgrace. You're the specialist in ethics, and I'm surprised that you didn't notice it before anyone else. Atvar H'sial made J'merlia into a nonentity. Now he speaks freely—"

"That is one way to put it."

"But when the Cecropian was around, J'merlia was afraid to say one word. He was totally passive. All he did was interpret her thoughts to us. He has a mind, but he was never allowed to use it. Let me ask you, Councilor, do you think that Louis Nenda and Atvar H'sial did anything to *deserve* loyalty?"

"They did not."

"And isn't it totally wrong for rational, reasonable beings like J'merlia and Kallik to be treated in that way, with all their actions controlled by others?"

"It is more than wrong, Captain, it is intolerable. And I am delighted to see that you and I hold identical views." Julius Graves turned to the waiting aliens. "Captain Rebka agrees. You are mature, rational beings, and the captain says that it would be totally wrong for you to be controlled by other people. So we cannot dictate your actions. If you wish to take a ship, and seek Louis Nenda and Atvar H'sial, then that is your perfect right."

"Now wait a minute." Rebka saw the grin on the face of Julius Graves and heard a whistle of triumph from Kallik. "I didn't say that!"

"You did, Hans." Darya Lang was laughing at him, too. "I heard you, and so did Councilor Graves. He's right. If it was wrong for Nenda and Atvar H'sial to control Kallik and J'merlia, it would be just as wrong for us to do it. In fact, it would be worse, because we would be doing it more consciously."

Rebka looked around the group, from the mad and misty blue eyes of Julius Graves, to J'merlia and Kallik's inscrutable faces, and finally to the knowing smile of Darya Lang.

He had argued and lost, on all fronts. And curiously, he did not mind. He was beginning to tingle with the curiosity he had felt when they were planning a descent into Paradox. There were sure to be problems ahead; but they would call for action, not the psychological manipulations that Graves found so easy and natural.

And what might they find at Gargantua? That was an open question. Atvar H'sial and Louis Nenda, dead or alive? The Builders themselves? Or mysteries beyond anything on Opal and Quake?

Hans Rebka sighed as the first whistle of atmosphere began along the smooth sides of the capsule. Touchdown was only a few minutes away. "All right, Councilor. We'll drop you, Max, and Geni off on Opal. The rest of us will head back up the Umbilical to Midway Station and the *Dreamboat*. But what's out there at Gargantua . . ."

"Is anybody's guess," Darya said. "Cheer up, Hans. It's like Summertide, and a bit like life. If you knew just what was going to happen, it wouldn't be worth taking the trip."

About the Author

Charles Sheffield is Chief Scientist of Earth Satellite Corporation. He is a past-president of the Science Fiction Writers of America and of the American Astronautical Society, a Distinguished Lecturer of the American Institute of Aeronautics and Astronautics, and a Board Member of the National Space Society. Born and educated in England, he holds bachelor's and master's degrees in mathematics and a doctorate in theoretical physics (general relativity and gravitation). He now lives in Bethesda, Maryland.